Starting Over
at
Acorn Cottage

ALSO BY KATE FORSTER

The Sisters
Finding Love at Mermaid Terrace

Starting Over at Acorn Cottage

Kate Forster

An Aria Book

First published in the United Kingdom in 2020 by Aria,
an imprint of Head of Zeus Ltd
This edition first published by Aria in 2021

9 7 5 3 1 2 4 6 8

A CIP catalogue record for this book is available from
the British Library.

ISBN (PB): 9781800247352
ISBN (E): 9781788544382

Typeset by Siliconchips Services Ltd UK

Printed and bound by CPI Group (UK) Ltd, Croydon, CR0 4YY

MIX
Paper from
responsible sources
FSC® C020471

Aria
c/o Head of Zeus
First Floor East
5–8 Hardwick Street
London EC1R 4RG
www.ariafiction.com

For my grandmothers.

*Thank you to Marjorie for seeing something
in me that others did not.*

*Thank you to Jean for the last conversation we had
where everything finally made sense.*

Spring

I

Clara Maxwell's love life was in the bin. The whole thing. Every card, letter, note and photo of her and Giles was now in the rubbish. Mostly it was she who had penned the notes and cards and held the phone out for the selfies but she had excused Giles for his lack of romantic gestures as he was so reliable in other ways, like putting the toilet seat down or putting the bins out – which is where the last vestiges of their relationship now lived.

As Clara tripped over a box in the living room, she wondered why she thought him doing the most basic of tasks in their relationship was a romantic gesture. Why had she thought him doing the basics in life was something to celebrate? She would give credit where credit was due, but she wasn't about to applaud a dog for barking.

Clara's mum had once said to her that women settled for average men because very few were spectacular. But when they had a taste of the spectacular, they realised they could never go back. The best in life was often troublesome because it made you yearn for more and women who yearned for more were considered nags or troublesome, or – the worst insult – high-maintenance.

Once Clara had been upgraded on a flight from Berlin

back to London whilst on a work trip. Everything about the flight was so wonderful, from the blankets to the way the airline hostess had offered a selection of international magazines to the perfect chicken salad and chilled Chablis that she was served, that Clara had never wanted to turn right in a plane again.

Perhaps that's what Giles had felt when he had sex with her best friend. That Judy was first-class and Clara was a stale muffin and a can of Sprite up the back near the toilets.

Now as she ripped the photos from their fridge and shoved them in the rubbish, she wondered why he had stayed if he was so unhappy with her. Why did he stay and pretend to be with her when he was skulking around with Judy? Clara could never understand why anyone would stay anywhere they weren't happy. She had seen what lingering in an unhappy relationship could do to a person.

Clara threw her collection of *Learn to Craft* magazines into the garbage bag and swallowed back her tears. Two years of a relationship down the drain. Two years of investing in something with no return. Their relationship was a bad loan and Giles was a dud product.

Picking up the last of her paperback novels and cookery books, Clara shoved them into the large rubbish bag. She looked around the apartment they had shared for the past eleven months. Most of her things had been packed and were already in the van, and she had taken great pleasure in leaving Giles with the bare essentials.

One knife.

One spoon.

One fork.

One plate.

One cup.

One glass.

One towel.

One roll of loo paper.

She knew it was petty but sometimes petty was the only answer a person had in the face of extreme humiliation, and that was what she felt. A red-hot shame flushed from her toes to her scalp when she thought about the duplicitous behaviour of the two people who were supposed to love her.

Clara picked up the file that had all their shared paperwork in it for the flat and their savings account. She had loved this little flat they had rented while they supposedly saved for their dream house, but she seemed to be the only one who contributed to the savings account. Giles always had an emergency expense such as a golf club membership or a work function ticket or something last-minute that meant he couldn't put money into the account each month.

Clara had supplied everything in the flat they shared and had decorated it, so it was cosy, thanks to her touches of soft throw rugs and houseplants. She had tried to create a home for them and instead Giles had created an affair, with her best friend, Judy.

Judy, who had always been the more interesting friend while Clara was the sensible one. Judy, who was a feminist pole dancer and who made her own scented candles and owned cats named Dali and Gala. Judy, who was tall and lithe and blonde (thanks to a bottle of Nordic Mystery peroxide) and had tattoos of climbing roses on her chest. Judy, who was the exact opposite of Clara.

Clara was what her grandmother used to call old-fashioned pretty. Dark bobbed hair, big eyes and bow-shaped lips, but short at just over five foot and with a tiny waist but curvy elsewhere. People told her she was cute, which made her feel angry, as though she was a kewpie doll, so she strived to annul this assumption by being business-like in her life. She had a finance degree. One of the youngest and few female bank managers at her bank, and very good with money, Clara never did anything that was a real risk. She always bought tickets early to events, she had insurance for everything – including a very good life insurance policy that Giles would have benefitted from if she popped her clogs early – and she kept receipts for everything she ever bought, just in case she had to return anything. She wished she could return Giles and Judy.

More like Piles and Judas, she thought, as she put her *Learn to Knit* books into the bin bag and tied it off at the top and threw her *River Cottage Cookbook* that Giles had given her into the actual bin.

How could her best friend and boyfriend have betrayed her? She wiped away the tears that hadn't seemed to stop falling since the dinner four weeks ago. Why hadn't she seen the signs? No real intimacy. No real connection. No real love. But then again, Giles had not been into sex even before they moved in with each other, and Clara was tired from her job at the bank, so they were like housemates: polite and respectful, but with no passion. But Giles was stable, a sensible accountant; he would be reliable for life. And with her best friend, who was now dancing on his pole. God, Clara hated her.

Clara had always tried to be what she thought was a responsible, sensible adult. The business degree, the savings account, the accountant boyfriend who didn't drink or swear, the most sensible man she had ever met, so far removed from her own father – she was so sure she had chosen well.

Judy was her best friend because Judy had said so – and Clara agreed because she didn't have time for friends. Judy had sort of pushed her way into Clara's life a few years ago when she came for a loan at the bank for a mobile pole dancing service. Clara declined the opportunity for the bank to invest in Judy's Pole Dancer on the Move bus, but Judy still pursued the friendship.

Giles had always said Judy was a flake and she was pretentious. He'd also said she was a slut, and Clara had told him off for that because having sex didn't make you a slut. He'd always made fun of Judy's pole dancing career and told Clara off when she loaned Judy money as a friend, not as a bank manager. Not that it was ever paid back, as Judy was always in some sort of financial and emotional crisis. It seemed to be her default position. But mostly Clara had felt sorry for Judy. She was always wanting something that other people had. A dress, a necklace, a handbag, a boyfriend.

For three months Judy had been telling Clara to leave Giles after she confided that she would have liked more connection, more conversation and now she knew why. Judas was getting Giles's love and Clara had the privilege of cooking him dinner.

And that was ultimately how she found out.

She'd found her Tupperware container – the one she had filled with cottage pie and given Giles for his 'weekend away with the lads' – at Judy's house. It wasn't any old Tupperware container. It had her name underneath it, written in marker, with the orange lid and a tiny burn mark on the corner of it from once being too close to the hotplate. Judy had never cooked a cottage pie in her life; her hapless on and off boyfriend, Petey, did everything for her.

Clara had found the evidence in Judy's kitchen while looking for a bowl for nuts, and she had wanted to put Giles's nuts in the container there and then.

'Why is this here?' she'd asked Giles and Judy and Petey at their monthly Food of the World Dinner. The dinners had started as a joke when Clara had received a sushi making kit from Giles and she made so much sushi that she had to invite Judy and whatever boyfriend she had at the time to eat it. The dinner turned into a thing and now they were eating their way around the world. Except that night was Italian, which Judy always resorted to when she was lazy or pressed for time, which was often. Clara knew the lasagne was a store-bought one, shoved into a glass lasagne dish that she knew was hers and Judy hadn't yet returned. Judy seemed to have a habit of doing that. Clara had waved the Tupperware container at the audience eating their soggy dinner.

'You said you took this to Cornwall,' Clara had said to Giles.

'I did,' Giles had answered but she saw the red flush rise up his neck that was his tell when they played Scrabble and he had a good word.

'But you didn't because it's here,' she'd said calmly. 'You were on the lads' weekend last month, and Petey, where were you on the weekend of the 5th?' She was starting to feel like Hercule Poirot but in a less smug way and more of a 'my boyfriend is cheating' way.

Petey had looked worried. 'I was at a conference in Guilford.' He had turned to Judy. 'You said you couldn't come because you had to help Clara with cleaning out her mum's house. You told me how messy the house was when I came back, and that Clara's mum must have been off her rocker from the medication.'

Clara had gasped at this comment because while Lillian, her mother, was off her rocker from the morphine for the cancer, only Clara could say so and she was furious that Judy had used her in her lies.

Sure, maybe her mother was a little strange with her organic composting and worm farm and the papier mâché seed pod coffin she was making for her own funeral but only Clara had the right to say that. Now her mother was gone, so the betrayal of Giles and Judy was even more painful.

'You used my dead mother in your lies?' she had asked Judy. This was worse than the betrayal of cheating with her boyfriend. Judy knew what her mum had meant to her, and while her best friend didn't know everything about her mum she knew more than most, even more than Giles.

Giles hadn't said a word, and then Petey had taken on the role of Poirot.

'So, you didn't help Clara then, Judy? What did you do?' Petey's mouth had opened and shut like a fish gasping for water.

Clara had lost her temper then.

'Oh, do catch up, Petey, she and Giles are having an affair, and eating my cottage pie, and lying to us both,' she had yelled.

And she had seen Giles's hand reach across the table to Judy's, who had smiled at him in a sickening manner.

'We're in love,' he had said to Clara as though she was missing out on something wonderful, and that was when she had thrown the breadstick from the table at him, knocking over the wine, knocking over the candle, which set fire to the whole evening. She left with her Tupperware and what little of her dignity was in the bottom of the container.

And now she had thrown her whole life into the bin including her job. She had cashed in her life savings and bought a cottage in some tiny village called Merryknowe, which consisted of a post office, some depressing-looking tearooms with a little bakery attached, and a pub and a few other ragtag shops. She had bought the cottage on a whim, fulfilling her retirement dream about fifty years early.

Clara had always dreamed of living a simple life. Jam-making, knitting, having a garden and pottering about while she was waiting for the bread to rise.

It was what she and Giles had talked about. They would look at photos online of houses for sale and discuss their plans, both working hard saving money for the dream.

Now she was the owner of a small thatched cottage, almost untouched except for a kitchen and bathroom that looked like they were last updated in the 1950s.

It had a sagging gate, but it also had garden beds and enough land for her to fulfil her vision of her own quiet life. Except it was supposed to be with Mother, and then she died. So, it was supposed to be with Giles. Where their grandchildren would come and visit them, and she would have taken up a craft and would finally learn how to bake and Giles would maybe chop wood and tie the tomatoes up on perfect tee-pee stakes.

'Too many episodes of *Escape to the Country* while

drinking wine,' her work friends had told her after she shared the news that she was the new owner of Acorn Cottage.

Clara couldn't disagree with the dig about either the wine or the TV show. She loved to change into her stretchy clothes, pour a glass of wine and watch the show, deciding which perfect cottage she and Giles would have chosen if they were on the show. It was a habit she had enjoyed with her mum before she died and then shared with Giles. Except they never bought a house on the show but the news from Piles and Judas, and the added information that Petey had moved out and Piles would stay there until Clara had left, stirred her into action to buy – especially after a bottle of plonk from the shop on the corner. She found the cottage online, emailed the agent matching the offer and it was accepted within an hour.

She didn't ask to see it and she didn't tell Piles about it either. She wanted to be away from him, Judas and everyone else who knew and looked at her like she was a complete idiot.

God, she was furious, she thought as she pulled the last of her underwear out of the drawer in the bedroom. She found the black lace teddy she had bought but never worn, the pink satin knickers with bows on the sides for easy removal, and the gorgeous coffee-coloured bra, which looked beautiful on, but she had been saving to wear. Saving for what? For who? She hadn't even put them on for Giles.

Instead, she had worn the old knickers and bras, the ones that forwent style for comfort. Giles hadn't looked at her anymore and she hadn't tried to seduce him. Perhaps she hadn't wanted him any more than he had wanted her.

She stood holding the lingerie with the tags still on them, and then shoved them into her overstuffed handbag.

She was starting her new life as soon as she had packed everything she owned and would soon be driving to the village of Merryknowe.

The letter of resignation had been accepted by the bank and, after cashing in her investments and taking the money her mother had left her, she had enough to renovate the cottage and to keep her going for a while until she found what she wanted to do.

She was a good bank manager but she worried about some of the people whose loans were approved by Head Office. When she brought up the ethical problem she was told, 'Don't worry about it.' The powers that be said to her, 'Let a different department look after it.'

But Clara had worried about the people who had taken the loans for things they couldn't afford and then rang her office asking for help in repaying the money.

She hated the bank and she hated Piles and she hated her life in London, which was why, after two months of tying up all the loose ends in her life, she could now slam the door of the flat behind her and say goodbye to the old Clara life and look forward to the new Clara life. But only after tipping the kitchen bin contents replete with potato peelings and coffee grounds onto his bed and feeling no regrets at all.

Summer

2

Henry Garnett was a rare man in modern times. He could fix anything. It didn't matter if it was run by electricity, water, steam or by hand, he could fix it. The only thing he couldn't seem to mend was his heart.

Naomi was fine and then she wasn't. She died within weeks of the diagnosis of the tumour. She had wanted to die in the van, but no one was having it, not even Henry. He didn't want Pansy's last memories of her mother to be in a cramped van with a drip hanging from the brass hook above her head and God knows what else going on as she died.

In the end, it didn't matter where Naomi was when she passed because the tumour had taken over most of her brain and her last words to Henry were garbled, nonsensical. He had spent so much time running over her words, trying to find meaning in them.

'Say yes,' she'd said, opening her eyes for the first time in days.

'To what, my darling?' he'd asked. She hadn't eaten in a week. She had stopped drinking last night. He knew it was close to the end.

But Naomi had shaken her head and said it again. 'Say yes.'

He'd tried to get her to open her eyes again. She always had the right advice, the right way to do things, to say things. Naomi was everything and then she was nothing.

The nurse had put up the drip as Naomi was clutching the sheets in her tiny hands. Those hands could make anything. They could turn roadside flowers into a display worthy of a royal wedding. They could plait pastry and spin wool and tame Pansy's curls into bunches with ribbons intertwined.

But the hands were soon still, and Henry had to say goodbye to his Naomi and send her body to be turned into ashes.

'Bury me in the vegetable garden when you find the right house for you and Pansy. I promise to help your crops grow. You can call it Naomi's Veggie Patch,' she had laughed.

Henry hadn't laughed because he didn't want her to be in the garden, with the worms and the cold damp soil. Three years later and he still hadn't bought a house and Naomi's ashes were still in the cupboard next to the potatoes and onions.

Instead he and Pansy had been on the road for those three years. He had the tiny house on wheels painted by Naomi, with intricate scrolls, vines and flowers around the front to look like a real garden. There were yellow shutters on the real glass windows, and a blue door and a little thatched roof to advertise that he did thatching for a living, but he did anything he could to pay the bills and keep busy. Repairs, painting, gardening and some labouring.

Pansy was now six and probably more self-sufficient than she should be for a child of her age. She was happy to keep him company with her drawing and colouring books, but he knew she needed to be in school – that would mean settling down and finding a vegetable patch. Not yet, he told himself.

Naomi and Henry had met in art school when Henry was studying to be a sculptor, and Naomi was studying painting. He swapped to fine art to be near her. She won the art prize at college and he won her heart. They graduated happy, in love and ready to share their creativity with the world. The first work of art they brought into the world was born just after midnight during a balsamic moon. They named her Pansy Jean Garnett and she was everything they had hoped for and more.

With their van and Henry doing odd jobs and Naomi painting, it was an idyllic life, with hopes to save enough money to buy a little cottage one day for them to settle down in as a family.

It was funny how life knew exactly where to place the cuts to make you bleed and hurt the most, thought Henry as he drove towards a small village called Merryknowe. He was to give a quote on a thatched cottage for a woman who had emailed him saying there was a hole in the roof.

Probably a weekender. He glanced at Pansy asleep in the seat behind him, her copper curls falling over her face, the curls he hadn't been able to tame as Naomi had.

Henry drove into the dull little village and found a parking spot big enough for the van and checked the time. He had to quote a job tomorrow morning at a nearby house so he thought he would stay in the area for the night.

He looked up and down the grey street. A few shops but nothing thrilling and certainly nothing that would make you want to stay. Some villages were so picturesque they looked like something from the front of a chocolate box, and others were a mix of function and frill, but Henry wasn't sure if Merryknowe had ever had any frill because it certainly didn't have any function.

A pub. A post office. A tearoom and a bakery and a few other little shops dotted the street. A small creek ran alongside the main road, with a green grassy bank and a stone bridge barely big enough for his trailer to cross.

'Let's get something nice for lunch,' he said to Pansy, who was waking up.

'Can I have cake?' she asked sleepily.

'Yes, my little Marie Antoinette, you may have cake but after something that isn't cake, okay?'

After gently unstrapping her from her seat he carried her out of the car and looked around.

Pansy grumbled something into his neck and then pushed herself out of his arms and jumped down onto the pavement.

He missed the days when she was little enough for him to carry her in the backpack. Now she was independent, he worried she would wander off on a job, or onto the street and be hurt by a car.

Although he had to admit, this street didn't seem to offer any cause for concern. He hadn't seen a car pass yet, and when he peered inside the window of the tearoom, it looked sad and lonely.

The bakery had a little more promise, with some delicious-looking apricot tarts in the window and the scents coming from the slightly opened door were enticing.

'In here, Pans,' he said and pushed the door open.

Yes, he'd made the right decision. The bakery was warm

and smelled good, exceedingly good, he thought as his stomach rumbled.

There wasn't much on display but what was looked wonderful. Rabbit pies and sausage rolls and plain scones and cheese scones and some nice-looking jam tarts and little butterfly cakes.

'Can I help you?' A young woman in a pink apron was at the counter. She had a drawn face with dark circles under her eyes, and a nasty bruise on her cheekbone.

Henry got a shock at the sight of the bruise and paused, so as not to not show his response. 'Hello, yes please, everything looks lovely.'

Pansy was looking at the cakes in the counter display.

'I want one of those,' she said, pointing to the butterfly cakes that were beautifully arranged with whipped cream and a dusting of icing sugar.

'And a sausage roll please, and a rabbit pie,' he added. The woman put the items into bags as Pansy stood up and looked at the woman.

'Why do you have a blue mark on your cheek?' She asked the question Henry had wanted to ask but didn't wish to be rude. 'Were you painting and leaned on your hand? I did that once but with green, so I looked like a monster,' said Pansy with deep concern on her little face.

'I hit my cheek on a cupboard door,' said the woman, handing the bags to Henry in exchange for the money.

'That's a silly cupboard door to do that to you,' said Pansy, looking cross on behalf of the woman's cheekbone.

'Yes,' said the young woman handing the change back to Henry but not looking him in the eye.

He took the packages from her and took Pansy's hand.

'Let's go, poppet,' he said. He looked at the woman, who was looking at Pansy – dare he say it – almost wistfully.

'Take care,' he said to her, wishing he could say more to help. But what could he say? He was making an assumption that it wasn't the cupboard door but a man who caused the injury. Naomi would have known what to say to her, probably would have got the story out of her and found a solution for the whole mess and that would be that.

He sighed as he pushed open the door of the shop and held Pansy's hand on the way back to the van to eat their lunch.

The woman had something happening in her life and it wasn't his business, he told himself. But as he sat in the van, eating the best rabbit pie he had ever tasted, he couldn't stop thinking about the bruise on her face and wondering how it came to be there.

He looked at Pansy and hoped to God Naomi would protect her from any pain and heartbreak. He decided he would teach Pansy how to throw a punch, just in case any boy ever tried to hurt her. He knew Naomi would be furious with his thoughts but sometimes he didn't have all the answers and if anyone hurt his girl, he hoped to God she would have enough strength to walk the hell away – but only after hitting him square on the nose.

He glanced out the window of the van and saw a curtain twitch in the house they were parked out the front of. He laughed to himself. There were always old women who were busybodies, ready to push him and the van out of the village. The number of times old biddies had told him to move on was more than he could count on his fingers and toes.

He flicked the shutter closed so whoever the old dear was, she couldn't see in as they ate. The sooner he quoted this cottage, the sooner he could be on the road again with Pansy and Naomi.

3

Merryknowe Bakery and Tearooms was the most visited shop in the tiny village, which wasn't a point of pride – not when the village was dying a slow death from lack of visitors and actual inhabitants.

It wasn't the prettiest village in Wiltshire and Rachel Brown tried to bring some elegance to the window of the bakery with her baked goods.

Sometimes she made cupcakes with pink iced roses or chocolate eclairs with satiny icing but today she had cream-filled butterfly cakes on the silver tray.

She watched the man and his child walk away from the shop until they were out of sight and she felt herself turn red when she remembered the way he'd looked at the bruise on her cheek. *It's not what you think*, she had wanted to say to him.

She knew people thought it was a man who did this to her, but it wasn't a man. Rachel had never been close enough to have a man touch her in passion or anger. There was no way she could even meet a man, not with what she had to do every day. She was a slave to her existence. Her routine was exactly the same day in or out.

Wake at four in the morning. Do the baking. Help

upstairs. Wash and dress. Serve in the shop. Clean up the shop. Make dinner and clean up upstairs. Go to bed at nine and then do it all again the next day.

She had one day off a week where she had to do all the week's washing and do the hoovering and order for the shop. She had to mop the floors downstairs with bleach and soap flakes and then she had to go through the accounts and make sure everything added up.

Maths was never her strength as a child and still now, numbers made her head fuzzy unless it was in direct relation to a recipe. But she had to get the accounts right, or she would be punished and the bruise on her cheekbone was testament to this fact.

Rachel pushed that memory out of her head and thought about the little girl who had come into her shop with her dad. She was so sweet, and Rachel wondered where her mother was, but she looked happy and well with her russet-coloured curls, sweet denim pinafore and green shoes. Rachel wished she could have shoes as pretty as the little girl's.

At twenty-five years of age, she knew she looked older than other girls she had gone to school with. She hated the drab clothes she was told to wear, and the way her hair was lank and thin and pulled into a tight bun because it was how she was told to wear it, even though her scalp ached at the end of the day.

She hated the shoes she wore. Mother ordered them for her from the pharmacy because she had flat feet and was susceptible to heel spurs. They were rubber-soled and they sometimes made a squeaking sound when she walked and then she was yelled at for being too loud.

She hated the bakery and the tearooms, which no one ever really visited. They could be so much more, but no one ever listened to her ideas. It was plain and dull now but, in her mind, it could be charming and fun and somewhere people wanted to visit.

Rachel baked because that was her job, but she didn't like the things she was told to make. Sometimes she went off-plan, like today when she had made the rabbit pie after getting the fresh rabbit meat from the butcher. She had used cider and fennel seeds and French wholegrain mustard and double cream. It was a triumph but only possible because she was alone and there was no one to question the scent coming from the kitchen.

The man and his daughter had bought the last pie, with Joe the butcher buying two, and promising not to tell Mother. Mr Toby, the bus driver, had also made the same promise after buying one. People were happy to make that promise because Mother was so nasty. Rachel had saved a pie for herself because she wanted to taste her success and also because she needed to rid the bakery of the evidence.

She touched her cheek; her fingers were cool on her skin. The bruise was older, and it looked worse than when it was still waiting to erupt into the green and blue that it was today.

Rachel knew the stages of the rainbow from a bruise and this was day five. It would turn an unfortunate shade of yellow, and then it would be gone, and it wouldn't be mentioned again until the next one started to show.

Arnica cream helped bring out the bruising quicker but lately, she had stopped putting on the cream. Why should she try and make the bruises disappear faster? It wasn't as though she put them there herself. Or did she want someone to ask more questions?

At night, in her single bed with the small bedside table, holding a copy of *The Joy of Cooking*, she would wonder if anyone thought about her. If anyone ever thought about how they could help her. If anyone out in the world worried how long she could go on like this for, or if anyone knew what her life was like.

But Joe the butcher didn't seem to talk to her unless it was about the gravy beef or fresh rabbit he had caught and minced. And Mrs Crawford told her she was clumsy, had always been clumsy, even as a child in the village. She told her she was clumsy as though it was an accusation, as though Rachel deserved the rainbow of bruises because of her heavy step and careless movements. She was sure Mrs Crawford from the post office knew what was happening to her but didn't help, which had made her not want to give her a vanilla custard tart, but she knew then, she would have been told on to her mother.

Then other times Rachel would lie in her bed reading the recipes in the book and imagine turning the tea shop into the restaurant she had seen in the magazines at the library in Chippenham. Wooden tables and comfortable chairs where people could sit and chat and hold hands and smile and laugh and eat delicious food. She would have gorgeous painted walls in either peacock blue or Indian pink – she couldn't decide – and she would have lamps and bookshelves filled with the books she loved, the books that had kept her company through her young life. All the characters in the books who were her friends and enemies and who taught her that she was worth more than what she had been told so far in her existence.

A tourist bus arrived, and Rachel waited for them to come to the tearooms. They would be disappointed. Everyone was. The tearooms were cold and so was the tea as it took a while for her to serve all the customers by herself.

A plate of pinwheel sandwiches and a plate of iced fancies were included in the deal with the tour company. Rachel sighed and started to make the tea as the tourists shuffled into the tearoom.

She had three hours of freedom left and she was spending them serving disappointed people a disappointing afternoon tea with disappointment all over her face.

When the final tourist had left, and Rachel had cleaned up the tearooms and the bakery and put whatever hadn't sold in the fridge, she went upstairs and took off her ugly shoes and put on her slippers, her toes curling with relief.

'Are you finished downstairs?'

The voice made her eyes shut, and she squeezed them tight, as though summoning up courage or a spirit to take her far away from where she was now.

'Nearly, a few things to sell still,' she answered.

'Did you put everything away?'

'Yes.'

'Did the tour come in?'

'Yes.'

'Did you buy a rabbit from Joe and make pies?'

She paused.

'I sold them all. More than the usual beef pies.'

'Are you saying my beef pie recipe isn't as good as your fancy French rabbit pie recipe?'

Rachel sighed. 'No, I am not saying that. Joe said the rabbit was good and it was cheaper than the beef.'

There was silence. Money was always good to use in these sorts of negotiations. The tearooms and bakery weren't exactly thriving and even the tours were slowing down in recent months. There were other villages with more active communities or money or tourist attractions. Merryknowe wasn't much of a drawcard, despite the flowing creek and bridge, and cottages lining the streets.

'You should have told me about the rabbit.'

'I was planning to,' Rachel lied.

'Come and run me a bath and help me get into it. I'm tired from seeing the hairdresser today.'

Rachel blinked back tears. She was so tired and there was still work to be done.

'Hurry up.' There was a tone, a warning, one that Rachel knew too well.

'Yes, Mother,' she answered, and set to her task before the other cheek started to change into the colours of the rainbow.

4

To start your day properly, you had to pour yourself good China tea into a fine bone china teacup.

Tassie McIver drank hers from a Wedgwood cup and saucer with a faded pattern of green trailing ivy that had belonged to her great-grandmother. It was a peony-shaped cup that allowed the right amount of depth and width for the leaves that she read every morning.

While the tea was important, it was the tea leaves that set the tone for the day.

The tea must be drunk with the left hand as that was closest to the heart, which suited Tassie as she read the paper, first checking for her own death notice, because, as her own mother said, if her name wasn't in the paper, she was still free to live another day. She then moved to the crossword before moving to the weather forecast.

Leaving half a teaspoon of tea in the cup, she turned the cup three times on the saucer, from left to right. Tassie moved the cup swiftly and then she slowly turned it over onto the saucer, with its bottom in the air, letting the tea drain away and the tea leaves settle with the news of the day.

Tassie checked on the weather for the day as she waited

for the tea leaves to settle. She saw no difference between the forecast for the weather and the forecast for her day from a teacup. The weather people were more often wrong about the rain and sunshine than she was about what was coming and going in the village and her life.

Turning the cup over, Tassie peered inside.

The handle was pointing to her. Interesting, she thought. Something was coming that would involve her. This was already unusual. All the leaves were near the rim. The events would happen soon, she noted. A ladybird symbol showed itself inside the cup. Betoken visitors, Tassie thought. A visitor for her.

The sound of knocking on the front door made her jump.

'Mrs McIver, it's the nurse,' called the woman from outside the small house.

Tassie McIver sighed. The cup was playing with her, she thought, as the district nurse was not a wanted or welcome visitor. It took her some time to stand up, and sometimes the new nurses left before she managed to shuffle to the front door, but this nurse had too much bonhomie in her voice to be going anywhere soon.

Today the air felt warm, and Tassie's arthritis was behaving but even so, she felt every step in every bone, as she managed to get to the door.

She opened it to find a cheerful nurse whose condescending smile put Tassie immediately into a bad mood.

What did she have to be so cheery about? Sponge-bathing old men and changing dressings on ancient skin like Tassie's was not living her best life.

Tassie had watched *The Oprah Winfrey Show* in the hospital and learned about living her best life, and she wondered if she had, at eighty-nine years old, lived her best life.

Eighty-nine years living in one place – Merryknowe village. Nothing happened in Merryknowe without Tassie knowing, even if the villagers didn't know she knew – she knew all but she kept it quiet.

It wasn't that Tassie was a witch, or even vaguely religious, but she understood the rhythms and cycles of life, and believed that at the bottom of the deepest rut lay jewels if you were prepared to be patient and dig down inside yourself a little further to draw them out.

'Morning, Mrs McIver, how are you today?' asked the overly cheerful nurse.

'Not as good as you,' she said to the nurse, but it was not meant to be mean. It was a statement of fact. She doubted that anyone in the world was as cheerful as this nurse was about her life.

'I had a wonderful night's sleep,' said the nurse, but Tassie looked at her and hid a little knowing smile. That nurse was not sleeping alone, but Tassie couldn't see a wedding ring – not that it mattered anymore.

Tassie was never one to live by convention anyway. How could you live your best life if you were so busy being what other people wanted, that you forgot what you really wanted?

The nurse changed the dressing on her shin, where she had torn it on a branch that fell in the garden.

Her skin had once been supple and brown in summer, now it was the shade and texture of the bark from a birch tree and had the healing capability of a corpse.

Sometimes that's how she felt on her worst days.

A walking corpse with no family, no friends left, and her days spent in front of the television or listening to the radio.

'See you in a few days,' said the nurse when she left.

'I might be dead by then,' called out Tassie.

'Oh, Mrs McIver, you make me laugh.'

The nurse drove away in her car. Did the idea of Tassie's death amuse the nurse? She wouldn't be amused if she came to the house and opened the door and found Tassie dead in her chair. In this heat, Tassie would be well and truly ripe by the time the nurse came, like a pear about to split its old, wrinkled skin.

Tassie looked out the window of her living room and saw Rachel Brown turning over the sign on the door of the bakery and tearooms to tell everyone it was now open for business.

Poor Rachel Brown. If Tassie was younger, she would have tried to help the girl but at eighty-nine, she didn't think there was much she could do other than speak kindly to her when she managed to cross the road for a tea and a butterfly cake.

Tassie went into her little kitchen and turned on the kettle. She took her breakfast of stewed apples and yoghurt out of the fridge and sighed. She wanted eggs and sausages but those days were long behind her. Dinner consisted of a meals on wheels affair that came from the next village, one she heated up in the oven. Stringy beef stew with Yorkshire pudding and carrots and peas – it sounded far better than it tasted.

And then there was fish, chips and mushy peas, which almost had her signing up for the death clinic in Switzerland that she had read about in a large-print book from the mobile library. Getting old was depressing, she had decided nine years ago, and now she was truly dispirited about still being here. She sat at her pine table eating her apple and yoghurt and cheated by dripping honey on top that Nahla the cleaner from the council had given her from her husband's hives on his allotment.

The nurse said she shouldn't have honey or cream cakes or sugar in her tea but Tassie really didn't care anymore. If she died in a diabetic coma it was better than trying to swallow the mushy peas and fish combination, which was its own sort of special hell.

The morning passed slowly, and more than thrice Tassie checked the traffic at the bakery. She worried for the business. Tourists didn't come to Merryknowe very often, mostly because there wasn't anywhere decent to eat and the Merryknowe Tearooms were not a drawcard with their ugly plastic tablecloths and that horrid Mrs Brown, the mother, hovering about.

Just as she was looking at the bakery, she saw a small truck with a van attached to the back of it shaped like a cottage. It had a thatched roof and was painted sunflower yellow, with painted flowers like a traveller's van, and curtains on the windows.

Tassie had never seen anything like it in her eighty-nine years. When it stopped and a tall man stepped out and then took a sleepy child from the truck, she felt a shiver of something she hadn't felt in a long time run up her head and over her scalp.

Something new in the village – more than new, it was something spectacular, and she watched him walk into the bakery with the little girl who had jumped down from his arms.

She looked at the van for the longest time, willing it to stay. For years she had known Merryknowe would die when she did. She was the last surviving long-term resident. She knew the tearooms' failing would be the final nail in Merryknowe's coffin and yet there was nothing she could do, until the man in the van walked into the shop across the road from where she lived.

This was what she had been planning in her mind. New energy and new love. But the man wasn't for Rachel Brown, no, he was meant for someone else, but they hadn't arrived yet, and Tassie McIver hoped to hell whoever it was, would come soon.

5

Clara turned off the main road, checked the map on her phone and enlarged the image, peering at it closely.

There didn't seem to be anything on the image that looked like a cottage. Just a huge number of trees and what looked to be an unmade road.

The cottage's formal address was Acorn Cottage on Shears Lane but there was no sign for the lane, so she took a punt and drove to where she thought the lane should be.

It must be close, she thought as she put the car into drive and went further down the bumpy road, which was lined with trees.

They cast a beautiful green light over her as she drove slowly, and her stomach flipped with anticipation. This was her dream about to come true. Everything she had wished for as a child was about to become a reality because she had worked hard and she had taken a chance. Sure, she was drunk when she did it – Clara rarely drank and was a lightweight so the bottle of wine really pushed her over the edge – but here she was. She turned into a clearing, the green light disappearing, and the cottage was before her, waiting.

Clara stopped the car and burst into tears.

'Oh shit,' she said aloud. 'Oh my God.' Her eyes tried to take in everything at once.

It was a dump. Whatever filter the agent had used on the photographs should be called, Lies and More Lies, she thought. The cottage looked like it was drunk. It looked like a cottage bought when drunk and was the living embodiment of her bad decision.

Clara wasn't used to making bad decisions. She had only ever made one significantly bad decision before the cottage but she didn't like to think about that. And choosing Giles could arguably have been a bad decision but this cottage was the worst decision she could have made.

This is what happens when you drink and buy property, she told herself as she stepped out of the car and walked towards the cottage. Why did she do something so rash? She was like the customers at the bank she had tried to protect. She had made a rash decision and it was giving her an anxiety rash, she thought as she scratched at her neck. She had spent her savings on this sad, lonely cottage that looked slightly lopsided.

There was a wooden gate, the paint long washed away, with a sign reading *Acorn Cottage*. She pushed open the gate and it promptly fell onto the overgrown path.

It had been two months since she had bought the property. For two months she had spent every weekend crying in the flat, knowing Piles was over with Judas, probably laughing about her and her sad life.

And Petey... she wondered what had happened to him. He had moved out, according to Piles, but Clara didn't ask for more details. It was just all so awful and tawdry. Clara had tried to live a life with no surprises and now she had been sucker-punched again by this cottage.

She had lost her mother and her relationship in the space of a year and now she had a derelict house to live in.

The agent told her the roof needed work, and he had given her the number of a man who was a thatcher. She had emailed the thatcher to come and look at it today, and wondered how bad it could be. Now she wondered if she wanted to know how bad it actually was.

The cottage was dated back to the 1800s according to the title. The last owner had died in the 1990s and since then it had gone to seed, as it were. The garden was wild, with climbing roses reaching out with long thorny stems grabbing at her top as she passed them.

Clara slapped them away as she tried to make sense of the images she'd seen online and what she was looking at now.

The grass was long like a meadow, filled with dandelions. The lavender bushes were stringy and leggy, with a few bees hanging around the flowers in hope.

Weeds were everywhere through the garden beds; thistles and other grasses and huge trees surrounded the cottage, which was more spooky than charming. It was a mess. A huge mess of huge proportions with a huge task to make it liveable.

This wasn't what Clara had hoped for. The agent had told her to come and see it but she'd said she was too busy – which she was as she finished her role at the bank and her relationship with Giles. Perhaps she didn't want to admit she had a gnawing feeling she had made a huge mistake, so she had avoided her decision and this was the outcome.

It had seemed like such a good idea when she was trying to prove to Giles that she would live her life without him, but now she felt like an idiot. She hadn't done the due diligence on the investment, and here was her reward.

There was a stand of oak trees circling the front of the property and an outlook over green land with a white fence that belonged to the farm a long way down the lane.

The grass was overgrown on her property, with dandelions waving obnoxiously as though laughing at her poor decision-making.

What had the estate agents thought when they listed this property?

She'd had no time to come and see it before, not with moving out and leaving the bank and finalising her mother's estate. The agent had promised it was liveable. He had used the word charming. More like disarming.

The sound of a car on the unmade road made her turn from the rural nightmare.

But it wasn't a car, it was a van of some sort, with a little mini cottage on top, complete with a thatched roof. Oh God, it was a mobile *Snow White and the Seven Dwarves* roadshow, she thought in horror.

'God help me,' she muttered to herself as the van stopped and a man stepped out of it, smiling at her.

'Oh shit,' she whispered. He was as handsome as anyone she had ever seen in her life, even with the beard, which to his credit looked well-tended – unlike when Piles had tried to grow a beard and she'd asked him if he had dirt on his upper lip, and he hadn't spoken to her for a week.

'Clara?' the handsome bearded man asked.

'Hi.' She tried to wave back like she had seen Carrie

Bradshaw do on TV, casual, cute, sexy, but then decided at the last minute she would do a casual nod and stick her hand up like she was on roll call at camp, but it ended up being a combo she was sure looked like she was pretending to yank a chain on a toilet or the emergency brake on a train.

He was getting something out of the van, so hopefully he hadn't seen her weird callisthenics move. She put her hands into the pockets of her jeans and found a G-string she had shoved in there last-minute when she had left Piles's flat.

'Henry Garnett,' he said as he walked towards her, carrying what looked to be a large sack of clothing until the sack lifted its head and peered at Clara.

'It's a child,' she said.

'Yes, this is Pansy, my daughter.'

It made sense a man like this had a child. Mrs Garnett was probably inside the van spinning wool and then dyeing it pink from avocado skins or nettle blue or something.

'Hi, Pansy, how are you?' she said.

Pansy looked unimpressed with Clara and the cottage and snuggled her head back into Henry's shoulder.

'So this is the little doer-upper?' Henry said, as Pansy suddenly pushed herself down from his arms and stood staring at the house, her hands on her hips.

'It's a shithole,' the child said emphatically.

'Pansy!' Henry looked horrified. 'Where did you hear that word?'

'The plasterers on the Moorcroft house. They said it was a shithole and that Mr Moorcroft was an absolute bast—'

Henry put his hand over his daughter's mouth, his face bright red.

'God, I am sorry, she comes on jobs with me and some-times there is less than desirable language flying around the place. Oww!' he cried.

Henry held his hand and then started to shake it. 'You bit me.'

'I did. Your hand smells like onions,' said Pansy calmly and she walked into the garden.

Clara started to laugh. This child was incredible, she thought. She had never liked children but this one, she liked.

'She's incredible,' she said to Henry.

'She's a changeling and any day the Goblin King is coming to take her back.' He was still rubbing his hand.

'Why does she come on the jobs? Where's Mum?' she asked casually, trying to sound non-judgemental.

'Inside, next to the onions and the potatoes.'

'Peeling them for dinner?' asked Clara.

'No, she's dead. Her ashes are in the van.' Henry shrugged. 'She died three years ago. Pansy and I live in the van and go from job to job.'

Clara was taken aback. Now the Piles and Judas betrayal didn't seem so terrible compared to him raising a child in a van, alone.

'Tell me about the cottage,' he said, his tone clearly a sign that he was changing the subject.

'It was built in the 1800s and it is, as your changeling stated, a shithole and I have mad regrets about buying it.'

Henry started to laugh now. 'I have seen worse.'

'Where? In war-torn countries? I haven't even been inside. I'm scared of what I will find.'

'Let's do the tour together,' he said. 'Pans, we are going inside.'

Pansy was picking dandelions from the long grass. 'Good luck,' she said, not looking up.

'How old is she?' Clara asked.

'Six going on sixty,' he sighed.

'She's not in school yet?'

'Not yet.'

She heard his tone change again and she left it. It wasn't any of her business, she reminded herself.

But she thought about her mother, Lillian, and her insistence on education for Clara, her only child. There were only the two of them, and Lillian had worked hard for Clara to have as much as she could afford, even though she worked in a nursing home as a carer. She never missed a concert or an awards assembly and even managed to buy a little flat for them both.

Thinking of her mother made her eyes sting, and she focused on the cottage.

'Have you got a key? We can do this together if it's easier.'

Clara thought about Piles and this being their dream and her eyes stung again.

Pulling the large old-fashioned key out of her handbag, she went to the front door and tried to turn it in the lock, but it wouldn't move.

'It's stuck,' she said to Henry.

'Wait on,' he said and he half-walked, half-jogged to the van.

'Let me put some of this in your keyhole,' he said, pumping something from a can into the door lock.

'Steady on, ask me for a drink first.' Then she realised she had said it aloud.

Henry looked at her in a slightly panicked fashion.

'Jokes,' she said, feeling like a predator, as she reinserted the key and turned it. 'Sorry, inappropriate jokes. The key works,' she said, opening the door.

A pigeon flew out above them.

Clara looked up at where the roof was supposed to be and saw clear blue skies.

'It's a hole,' she said slowly. 'A big, gaping hole.'

'A complete shithole,' said Henry, looking around him. With that, Clara burst into loud sobs, not even soothed by Henry's hugs and her face fitting perfectly into the curve of his neck.

6

There was no doubt the cottage was a disaster. The lack of furniture was one issue, as the images in the photos had clearly been styled to resemble a scene out of a Beatrix Potter drawing with a fire in the grate and pretty rugs and curtains, which were nowhere in sight now.

'I should sue them for not disclosing the true condition,' Clara said after she had wiped her face with her sleeve.

'Did you look at it before you bought it?' Henry asked.

Clara paused. 'No, I bought it on a whim. A sad, wine-induced whim.'

Henry raised his eyebrows. 'Do you want to talk about it?'

'Not particularly.'

'Fair enough.' He shrugged and she respected that he didn't want to know the ins and outs of her sad life choices and that he wanted to keep proper boundaries between them, even after she had snotted on his shoulder.

The hole in the thatching was large and there was mud on the floor, and some sort of animal droppings.

'Fox, most likely,' said Henry as he kicked it.

'They said it was furnished,' Clara stated as she looked

at the large dust sheets creating unattractive shapes in the living room.

She pulled one back to reveal a wooden chair with a high back.

'God, sitting in that for too long would be a punishment,' she said.

Henry laughed as she walked into the tiny kitchen.

'I think the hole in the roof isn't that old, and the kitchen is okay,' Henry said.

But all Clara saw was dust as thick as icing on the table, and some odd and unmatched coloured wooden chairs stacked against the wall.

There was an old refrigerator and an Aga.

'I always wanted one of those stoves,' she said, trying to rustle some cheer about it all.

Henry had opened the back door and was looking outside. 'Wow,' he said.

'Do I want to know?' Clara asked. 'I don't think I can bear any more disappointment.'

'No, it's good.' Henry turned and smiled at her and her heart skipped a beat.

Gosh, he was handsome.

She walked to his side, looked outside and gasped.

Clara had never noticed trees before but the tree at the back of the cottage was spectacular. Tall, with a wide trunk and thick glossy leaves, it spread across the back of the property with perfect branches to climb on, some dipping along the ground and up again.

'Oh, now that almost makes it worth it,' said Clara staring in awe at the grand tree.

'That is the most perfect tree I have ever seen,' said Henry. 'A solid ten out of ten.'

'Do you usually rate trees?' Clara asked.

'No but this one requires a score, don't you think?'

Pansy walked around the side of the house, carrying a bunch of dandelions.

'It's perfect for climbing,' said Henry and Clara glanced at him.

His jawline under his beard was strong and she couldn't help comparing it to Piles and his lack of chin.

'How long have you had your beard for?' she heard herself asking. *Oh shit, Clara, use your mental filter.* That was a boundary-crossing question and also it was weird. It was the sort of question you asked someone while you lay in their arms after passionate sex, not standing in your derelict cottage rating trees.

'Since I was twenty-five, so ten years,' he said, not seemingly bothered by her question.

'I'd like to grow a beard,' she said. *Oh my God, Clara. Stop speaking, never speak again.*

'Really?' Henry was looking at her as though she was an alien.

'I mean, if I could... They look fun.'

STOP. TALKING.

Thankfully Pansy was coming towards them.

'So, what's the dealio?' she asked them.

'Pardon?' asked Clara. This little girl wasn't what she thought a six-year-old should be.

'The house, are we working on it, Dad, or going to look at the Dale house?' Pansy had her hands on her hips again and was looking at them to make a decision.

Henry looked at Clara. 'I should get you a price for the roof then.'

Clara walked back into the kitchen. 'I need more than the roof; I need it all done. And I have no idea what I'm doing or what tradesmen to get and honestly, this is all a bit of a disaster.'

Henry put his hands in his pockets and rocked back and forth in his work boots.

'I can do it all but it would be expensive.'

'I have money,' said Clara quickly. She didn't know why she trusted him but she did, even if his kid was like a mafia boss.

'I can make it liveable to start with and then you can decide what needs doing in what order,' he said.

Clara thought for a moment. She didn't have another choice or anywhere else to go. She had made a decision and she had to deal with it.

'Okay, let's start with the roof and go from there.'

Pansy was looking at each of them as they spoke.

'You'd better let Don Dale know we won't be coming,' she said to her father.

'Yes, I am aware of the procedure, Forewoman Pansy.'

Clara tried not to laugh at the disdain on the girl's face.

Henry cleared his throat and Clara looked at him.

'When Pansy and I do a job, I usually stay on the land or as close as possible. That way it's easy for me to take the van off the car and we can settle here for however long it takes. We don't get in the way; we're self-sufficient.'

'Oh wow, you really do live in it. Well, that's fine. Park wherever you want. I might need to come and borrow a cup of sugar, so it would be wonderful to have neighbours.'

She knew she was talking too much again. Her mother used to say it was because she was nervous and needed to fill the space. Piles had said it was overcompensating for not thinking she was interesting enough. She wondered now if he had thought she was uninteresting. Perhaps he had said it as a way to try and get her to look at herself and what she talked about. Was she boring? Most people thought they were interesting and funny, but not everyone was. Piles was the perfect example of this.

'I will get you a quote to be sure you want to move ahead though,' said Henry. 'I think you need to have the entire roof replaced.'

Clara sighed. 'I guess I'd better look at the rest of the place. Will you do the tour with me? In case I decide to throw it all in and set fire to the lot?'

Henry laughed. 'Don't you dare. This place is going to be gorgeous. You can come up from London and spend weekends here and get a dog and live happily ever after.'

Clara looked around the kitchen.

'It's my forever home. I threw it all in, back in London, and dumped the boyfriend,' she said, refusing to let Piles win that one. 'I guess I have to make it work because I don't have anything or anyone else.'

'You have us,' said Pansy. Clara looked down at the child who pulled a dandelion from behind her back and handed it to Clara. 'Blow on it and make a wish.'

So Clara closed her eyes and blew on the dandelion and made her wish.

7

That afternoon the moving van rolled up outside the cottage and two men jumped down.

'This it, love?' one of the men with a single tooth asked Clara.

'Oh God, my stuff is here,' she said to Henry.

'Tell them to put it all in the living room and I'll push the furniture back and you can unpack as you need. Did you label the boxes?' he asked Clara, who frowned.

'No, I was in a rush,' she tried to explain. Why hadn't she labelled the boxes? She knew the answer. Because she was furious when she packed, tipping entire kitchen drawers into boxes with entire drawers of underwear.

She had books mixed with bathroom products, which had probably leaked knowing her luck, and she had artwork wrapped in floor rugs and tea towels.

It was Clara Maxwell at her worst and she knew it but how could she explain to Henry and these moving men that she had cried as she packed every box? Cried for her friendship with Judy and the loss of Giles and their dreams. Most of all she had cried with the shame of being the one they probably laughed at when they were in bed together rubbing feet.

Clara the loser, who sent her boyfriend on a golf trip with a container of cottage pie. God, she was so stupid, she thought now as she watched the men try and get her bed frame upstairs.

They contorted themselves like they were in *Cirque du Soleil* but they simply couldn't get the sleigh bed up the tiny staircase.

'Leave it outside,' said Clara, aware this was costing her by the hour. 'It won't fit in the living room.'

She loved that bed so much. She had bought it at an antique auction, and the intricate wood embellishment made her happy, even though Giles said it was cumbersome.

His use of the word had made her angry. He was cumbersome, she thought unkindly, with his portly stomach and ladylike hips, which she knew he hated. She had never mentioned his womanly shape but now, filled with bitter thoughts, she wished she had said something to him.

The men took the mattress upstairs. Clara followed them and saw them throw it onto the floor and dust rose up like a fog descending.

'The fog of doom,' she said to herself.

'All okay?' asked Henry from behind her.

'Besides me sleeping in a room that looks like a workhouse in a Charles Dickens novel, it's peachy,' she said, trying to keep the quiver from her voice.

Since the discovery of the betrayal she had felt as though the world was off centre. Now she felt as though it was spinning into an abyss and she would soon meet her certain death.

'I think I'm going to faint,' she said but then she realised she had never fainted before, so she wasn't sure if this was what it felt like but whatever it was, it made the room spin.

She was suddenly in Henry's arms and he laid her down on the mattress.

'It's okay, you're okay,' he said.

'Did I faint?' she asked.

'I think you had an NFE,' he said with a smile, kneeling on the floor next to her.

'Oh my God, what is that?' Was she sick?

'A near-fainting experience,' said Henry.

Clara closed her eyes. 'I am a pathetic woman. I'm Miss Havisham, living in my decrepit home, with dust and cobwebs as my aesthetic.'

Henry laughed. 'No, you're tired, you probably haven't eaten and you need some breathing space, preferably without the dust.'

Clara sat up on the mattress, aware she was being comforted by a virtual stranger on his knees at her bedside. Her life was ridiculous.

Henry looked at her closely as he spoke, as though instructing a child. 'Go into the village. There's a nice little bakery there. Get some food and take a moment and I will sort the movers, okay?'

She nodded, grateful for someone else to have taken charge for a moment.

'Okay, I will. If you don't mind?'

Henry shook his head. 'It's fine, I promise.'

Clara drove into town to buy some supplies and try and take stock of her situation. Thankfully there was power and water at the cottage but that was it and she needed to clean the place. Henry was at the cottage with Pansy, working out his quote for the roof, and she had asked him to write a list of what else he thought needed to be done if the place was his.

She knew she should be excited but she felt sick at the thought of what was to come.

There was a small shop with overpriced cleaning items, which she begrudgingly bought as she heard her stomach rumble. She needed something to eat and she saw the drab bakery sign above a shop across the road.

She put the cleaning supplies into the car and walked up to the bakery.

A bell over the door rang, signalling her arrival, and an older woman came to the counter and smiled. 'Hello, dear, welcome to the Merryknowe Bakery and Tearooms. How can I help you? Would you like a cup of tea and something to eat?'

Clara looked around at the tearoom, which was empty except for an old woman who was looking at her like she had done something terrible and was about to be found out.

She *had* done something terrible. She'd bought that stupid cottage. Perhaps she would sit down and eat, as she felt like she could murder a cup of tea.

'That would be lovely, thank you,' she said, matching the woman's formality. The woman had on a lot of makeup and had her blonde hair carefully set as though she had just been at the hairdresser. Her skin was brown – fake-tan brown – and she had rings on nearly every finger, and a white and silver knitted top with ropes of gold chains around her neck.

'Rachel, come and see to this young lady and give her the best table,' the woman called out into a doorway, presumably where the kitchen was.

'That's fine, I'll take any table,' said Clara.

A mousy girl came out of the back of the shop. She was the antithesis of the woman at the counter. Pale, in a dull dress and laced-up shoes and no makeup at all – but what made Clara gasp was the yellowing bruise on her face.

'Hello, welcome to the Merryknowe Tearooms,' said the young girl, then walked Clara to the corner table by the window.

'This is my daughter Rachel – she will take care of you. I have to go to see Mrs Crawford at the post office and general store.'

Mrs Crawford must be the sour-faced woman who had just sold her an overpriced dustpan and brush.

The woman left as Rachel came back with a tall black linen-covered menu that looked like it should be in Claridge's but when Clara opened it, there was only a small selection of items printed onto the paper, which was fastened inside with sticky tape.

'What do you recommend?' asked Clara, noticing her bitten nails, but her eyes were drawn back to the bruise.

Probably a boyfriend did it, she thought angrily.

'Are you a sweet or savoury person?' the girl asked in a small voice.

Clara laughed. 'A bit of both, depends on which way the wind is blowing.'

The girl didn't smile. 'I can bring you some pinwheel sandwiches and a plate of iced fancies for afterwards?'

Clara paused. 'I think something hot would be nice, what sort of pies do you have?'

Rachel looked around as though someone was listening. 'I have a chicken and leek pie out the back you might like. It's a new recipe.'

'Oh delicious, perfect. And I will take an eclair afterwards.'

The girl disappeared and Clara checked her phone. Nothing from Piles or Judy. Traitorous bastards.

'Hello.' Clara heard a voice and realised it was the old woman behind her.

'Good morning,' said Clara with a smile and went back to her phone.

'Come and sit with me,' the woman said and Clara sighed. Old people and children loved her; it was just the ones aged in between who broke her heart.

'Oh, I don't want to intrude,' said Clara politely.

'Intrude on what, my dear? My general decaying? That will happen whether you are here or not. I would like the company.' It was as though the woman had decreed that she wanted Clara's company and she didn't have a choice in the matter. Clara found herself standing up and picking up her bag.

She moved to the woman's table and put her hand out. 'Clara Maxwell. New to Merryknowe. Regretful owner of Acorn Cottage, just near the church.'

The old woman's eyes narrowed as she spoke and seemed to turn darker as she looked at Clara closely.

'Tassie McIver. Former schoolteacher when the village still had a church and now the oldest resident of Merryknowe.

I live across the road in the house with the geraniums in the window boxes.'

Tassie put her hand in Clara's and she was surprised at how strong the grip was for such a tiny hand. She had pale pink hair, pink lipstick and pink nails and eyes as dark as ebony.

The old woman spoke in a frail voice. 'Acorn Cottage. I knew the woman who lived there. Sheila Batt. Like name, like person. She was an old bat. Died in her bed upstairs. I am surprised they didn't find her hanging from the eaves by her toes.'

Clara made a face of horror but Tassie shrugged. 'We all have to go sometime. Better to be in your bed than on the toilet like Elvis.'

Clara burst out laughing as Rachel brought over the tea and then the pie, which smelled like heaven. Clara cut it open and the creamy filling oozed onto the plate a little, then she tasted the first bite.

'Best pie in the area,' said Tassie. 'Unfortunately no one knows about them.'

Clara had to agree that it was truly the best pie she had ever eaten. She demolished it quickly, wishing there was more of it on the plate.

Tassie leaned over the table and whispered, 'She's a sad thing, that girl. Her mother is something else. Breaks my heart to watch the way she's treated.'

Clara nodded as she watched the girl moving about behind the bakery counter. She was anxious and nervous. Clara knew those behaviours; she had seen them in her own mother before they left Clara's father. Constantly trying to be ahead of the criticism, constantly trying to make improvements to the minutiae of life. Clara wanted to tell her that it would never be perfect enough for who she was trying to please.

She tried to guess the girl's age. She looked like she was in her early twenties but dressed like she was seventy and she sighed as though she was about to take her last breath.

'Does she have a boyfriend?' she asked Tassie who shook her head.

'No, no, the mother wouldn't allow it.'

Rachel cleared the plates and then brought Clara an eclair, so Clara seized her moment. 'You know, I'm new here. I've moved to the village today, at Acorn Cottage up past the church. Do you know it?'

The girl suddenly lifted her head, as though surprised at Clara's words.

'No, I don't,' she said, but Clara thought she was lying. She glanced at Tassie who raised a painted-on eyebrow.

'I'm the new owner and I don't know anyone here; it would be lovely if we could be friends. I'm Clara, Clara Maxwell.'

The girl paused. 'Rachel Brown,' she said. Her voice was low and careful, and Clara felt a shiver up her back.

'Perhaps we can have a drink sometime? Go to the pub? Here's my number.' Clara had written it on the back of a receipt from her purse and she pushed it into Rachel's hand. Rachel scuttled away as though she had been handed an illegal substance, shoving it into the pocket of her apron.

'She won't call. She never asks for help,' said Tassie. 'They came fifteen years ago when the father died. Never quite made a go of it. The village was bigger then and the shops were all filled up but now, there is barely anything. I rely on deliveries as I can't get into Chippenham. But they're so expensive to have sent up here.'

Clara wasn't really paying attention as the eclair was such a delight but she was trying to understand who gave the girl the bruise. Not her mother, surely? There must be a boyfriend. Probably a cheating, lying, absolute shit of a boyfriend who would ruin her life, like Piles tried to ruin hers. One who Rachel kept secret from her mother.

'Who gave her the bruise?' she asked Tassie, who looked over at the door as it opened, the bell giving a hollow tinkle in the echoing space.

Clara looked at Rachel as the mother came back into the shop and then she saw the flicker of fear that she had seen in her own mother's eyes before they fled for London.

And that's when she knew it was the mother who gave the bruise to Rachel.

'You realise the mother is abusing her?' she asked Tassie. 'I do.'

'Can't we do something?' A thousand ideas ran through her head but Tassie shook her head at her.

'We can't do anything as Rachel is an adult and Moira is her mother. All we can do is be her friend and try and help when she lets us.'

Clara watched the mother busying about the shop and putting on a show for Clara and Tassie, all airs and graces and being super sweet to Rachel.

Oh yes, Clara knew all of these behaviours and she felt the hairs on her arms rise and her jaw set.

Doing nothing wasn't in Clara's nature but she also knew it wasn't her place to interfere.

She left the old woman and the bakery and drove back

to the cottage, but she couldn't stop thinking about the girl in the bakery. No, this wouldn't do, Clara simply had to help Rachel; she felt it in her heart that girl would need her one day and that day was coming soon... but first she had to fix the hole in her own roof.

8

Acorn Cottage was Rachel's dream house when she was a young girl. When she first moved to Merryknowe and was at school in the next village, she would get off the bus at the road that led to the cottage behind the church and walk through the graveyard to the cottage.

Rachel imagined coming home to the house and sweeping the pathway and tying back the roses on either side of the front door.

She would have put in pink flowers in the front garden and had a pie cooling on the kitchen windowsill like they did in old movies and her mother would be nowhere in her life.

Over the years she had visited Acorn Cottage less and less as the bakery and her mother were too demanding, but it remained in her heart, a place of escape and a place to dream. She had always wondered why she loved it so much, why it drew her to it every afternoon growing up. Perhaps she would own it one day, she had thought.

Except now it belonged to Clara Maxwell.

Clara was older than her, probably about thirty or so, and she was so smart-looking with her striped T-shirt and jeans, with a straight dark brown bob and blue eyes with eye makeup. She had curves and wore silver sneakers. Mother never allowed Rachel to have makeup. She said it made her look cheap, but Mother's dressing table was groaning with shadows and powders and lipsticks. Mother looked cheap. Clara looked wonderful.

And Clara wanted to be her friend. Clara who looked like an angel when she walked into the shop. There was sunlight on her hair and a prism-like rainbow followed her from the concave window. Clara gave Rachel her number. She invited her to the pub. Rachel had never set foot inside the pub because of Mother, who said Rachel was not mature enough to drink – except Mother drank gin and wine and then slurred her words and got angry with Rachel for things she didn't do.

Rachel tried to imagine going to the pub with Clara and failed. She didn't know what she would wear or what the inside of the pub even looked like.

That night Rachel did exactly as Mother asked, and didn't mess anything up. When Mother wasn't looking, she put an extra sleeping tablet into the warm cocoa she made every night. This was a last resort and she had to be careful as Mother sometimes counted the tablets, but Rachel needed time to think.

When finally Rachel was alone in her room, and Mother was snoring loudly in her own room, she thought about how she could be Clara's friend. Mother would never allow it but she needed something more than this life.

Maybe she could go and visit Clara tomorrow but how would she do it?

It was impossible. She lay on her bed and stared at the dull, oatmeal-coloured ceiling.

'Dad?' she whispered. 'If you can help me escape Mother, to visit Clara and the cottage, I would be so grateful. I look after Mother the way you would have wanted. I do everything for her. Please help me, Dad.'

She felt her eyes fill with tears.

She missed her father but he was a sad man. A weak man, her mother said, but Rachel understood why he did what he did. Sometimes she thought about doing the same thing but then where would Mother be? She would have no one to help her get in the bath and make a living for them.

Clara made herself a cup of cocoa with extra sugar because Mother wouldn't allow it usually, and she ate a Hobnob and watched *The Graham Norton Show*.

It was perfectly lovely and she felt herself relax. Then after Graham Norton had finished, and she had washed her cup, put it away and turned off the lamps, she heard the door to Mother's bedroom open.

'What are you doing, you little bitch?'

Rachel felt cold and she rubbed her arms. 'Nothing, Mother, let me help you back to bed.'

Mother stared at her with a snarl on her face.

'I'm going to bed soon,' she said bravely to Mother, to try and show her she was doing what was expected.

'You will do nothing without me saying so. You're just like your father.'

Rachel stood still. Sometimes this strategy worked, as Mother's attention would be drawn to something else that was wrong that she could abuse but tonight Rachel thought it wouldn't.

'I have to check the locks downstairs,' said Rachel. She had already checked them but if Mother was in a mood, it was best she avoided her and took her time in the shop so Mother might go back to bed.

'Leave it,' her mother hissed. 'I'll go. You'll probably leave them open and I'll be raped and you murdered and they'll leave with all the money.'

Rachel wanted to scream, 'WHAT MONEY?' but said nothing as Mother weaved towards the door leading to the stairs down to the shop.

'I can go, Mother,' said Rachel, watching the way her mother swerved in her satin-like nightgown.

'You can't do anything, you stupid child, so stop pretending. I think something happened to you as a baby. God knows what. Perhaps they dropped you when you were born,' Mother said as she opened the door and started down the stairs.

Rachel wondered if they had dropped her, as she wasn't good at so many things, but surely her mother would remember if she had been dropped since she was the one who gave birth to her.

She could hear Mother muttering on the stairs, and Rachel stood still, unsure what to do. Should she just go to bed and avoid her mother or should she wait and receive more abuse when Mother came back?

Then the sound of thumping was heard and a scream came from the stairs and more terrible sounds like a bag of flour had been thrown. Rachel rushed out and saw Mother lying at the bottom of the stairs in an awkward position that made her body look inhuman.

'Mother!' She ran downstairs.

There was a cut on her head and blood was gushing out and one of her legs was at a peculiar angle.

She moaned and Rachel ran to the phone in the shop. She called triple nine and gave the ambulance service the address. Rachel sat on the bottom step and looked at her mother. She knew she should do something to make her comfortable but her leg was almost twisted behind her back and there was blood everywhere on the floor surrounding her head.

Rachel started to rock as she sat on the stairs. It was comforting but Mother often told her when she did, it proved she was the village idiot like everyone said she was.

She wondered what Clara would do in this moment. One thing was for sure, she would know what to do. Rachel carefully stepped over her mother and, pulling the number from the cash register where she had hidden it under the tray, she dialled and waited.

Clara answered almost immediately. 'Hello? Clara speaking.'

'Clara? It's Rachel Brown, from the bakery. I hope I didn't wake you.'

'Oh hey there, how nice that you rang. No, it's only nine-thirty. How are you?'

Rachel paused. 'I'm okay but Mother fell and I'm waiting for an ambulance. I was wondering what you would do in this situation.'

'God, is she bleeding?'

'Yes, from her head. There's quite a lot of blood.'

Even to Rachel, her voice sounded very calm, almost uncaring, but that couldn't be right – she was supposed to care about this moment. Perhaps she was in shock, like they said in the books she read.

Clara was speaking. 'I'll be there in a moment.' And then there was silence on the end of the line.

Rachel put the phone down and looked at Mother. She was pale, she looked almost blue and there was a large pool of blood spilling out onto the lino floor.

She knew she should do something, but she wasn't entirely sure what. More than that, she didn't know if she wanted to do anything for her mother ever again. For a brief moment, she wondered if her dad had pushed her down the stairs so she could be friends with Clara, just as she had asked.

9

Clara – aged 10

*C*lara had a ritual she would run through before her dad came home from work.

If she washed her face and hands and brushed her hair, then he would come home on time.

If she did all her homework, he wouldn't be drunk.

If she cleaned her bedroom and tidied up the papers from the kitchen table before Mum came home from work, then he wouldn't be mean to Mum at dinner.

And if she did her reading without missing a word, then Mum and Dad would sit and watch television and she would go to sleep with the sounds of Strictly Come Dancing *instead of yelling and the thump of Mum hitting the wall.*

Checking the time, she worked out how long she had before Mum came home from the grocery store where she worked. Sometimes she brought home sausages from the delicatessen that hadn't sold, and she would fry them up with eggs and beans and toast and HP sauce and Dad would tell jokes that made Clara and Mum cry with laughter.

Other times, when Mum brought the smoked cod home, and there was a letter from the bank on the table, then Dad would just make them cry.

Clara couldn't remember a time when her mum and dad didn't fight. Sometimes she wanted to run into Mum and tell her to not argue with him, that she would never win. Why did Clara know this but her mum didn't understand?

She would worry about it in school and if she had a test the day after a big row she would barely pass. Other days, when Dad told jokes and told her she was his clever Clara, she would score a ten out of ten.

It was so confusing.

Especially in the mornings when she woke up and Mum would be making Dad eggs on toast and coffee, and they would act like nothing had happened, as if Mum didn't have a black eye or a split lip.

Sometimes she wondered if it was a dream or if she was imagining what had happened the night before. But the hole in the wall was evidence it wasn't a dream and the broken cups in the rubbish were as real as the mouth ulcer that Clara kept putting her tongue into when she was nervous, which seemed to be a lot more lately.

So, Clara created a new ritual. At night, in her bed she would lie in the dark and work out a plan to get her and Mum away from Dad and they would only see him when he could be nice to them.

She would save all the money she found, and she would buy them a little house, just like in the book she was reading with the girl who found an abandoned cottage and made it her home. Clara had so many dreams of her and Mum leaving in the night-time, bags packed, being quiet so they didn't wake Dad. His drunken snores were a sign he was out for the night but you couldn't be too careful. Once she thought he was asleep but when she walked past him, he grabbed her on the arm so tightly that he left finger marks and Mum was called into the school to explain.

Last night Dad and Mum were yelling because he was flirting with a girl at the pub. She hated it when they talked about things like that. Once she had seen Dad with a lady she didn't know at the park, and he was holding her in a way she hadn't seen him ever hold Mum. She knew not to say anything to Mum though; that sort of thing was for adults, not for children to tell secrets about.

But Clara didn't like to think about those times. Instead, she imagined a little thatched cottage with a little dog all of her own and chickens in the yard, and she and Mum making cakes in the kitchen.

She would have a best friend like the little girl in the book she read who lived down the road and they would have all sorts of adventures together.

Oh yes, this was the perfect plan. She just had to work out a way to escape from Dad somehow.

So, night after night, Clara planned their escape, writing it all down in a notebook by torchlight under the covers. Her Safety Book, she called it, hidden away behind the skirting board where Mum or Dad couldn't find it and where all of Clara's wishes lay, waiting for her to make them come true.

10

Clara had been lying in her cold bedroom on her mattress with her old wooden bedframe lying outside on the long grass when Rachel called. Clara prayed the rain would stay away but English summers were always unpredictable.

She had cleaned the bedroom as much as she could, which meant she'd swept, dusted, washed the windows and sills and skirtings, and scrubbed the bathroom as much as she could but the pink tiles and pedestal basin needed better cleaning products than what she had. Thankfully the last owner (Sheila Batt, according to Tassie) had put a working toilet inside, the one she hadn't died on as Tassie reminded her. Clara had cleaned it but it was certainly not the dream space she had imagined.

There was no television, no internet, and Henry and Pansy had retired for the night into their van. Henry had offered for her to stay in the van but honestly, she had no idea where she would fit, and besides, she didn't want to intrude. No, she had made her bed, so to speak, and she had to try and sleep in it.

Henry had popped off to the local chippie and brought back a selection of fried treats for dinner and served them all in the little van. Pansy was thrilled about the dinner, telling Clara that she thought that when she grew up she would own a fish and chip shop.

The van was cute, with a little bunk bed for Pansy and a double bed for Henry below. There was a galley kitchen and a sofa, which Henry said turned into a bed, and a sweet little bathroom. The style was cute and homely and probably was put together by Henry's wife.

'Your van is what I would like my cottage to look like,' she admitted, after Pansy was in her bunk with the iPad watching her favourite TV show before bed.

'It was all Naomi,' he said and Clara inwardly acknowledged her instinct for seeing the woman's touch. It was in the cushions and the rugs and the sweet curtains and the teacups with pink polka dots on them.

Clara sipped her beer and ate a chip.

'How did she die?'

'Ovarian cancer; it was quick and it was ruthless. Spread everywhere. She thought she was pregnant at first but it was already on the march when she was diagnosed.'

'What a shit of a disease,' said Clara shaking her head. 'Completely rubbish, isn't it? You think about all those idiots who are wasting their time in life and then you think about your wife, and the snuffing of her candle far too early when she probably had a lot she still wanted to do.'

'She did,' said Henry leaning forward over the small booth table. 'She had so much left to do – we had things to do together.'

Clara nodded and sipped her beer. 'Life brings some absolute turds sometimes, doesn't it?'

Henry laughed. 'It has its moments.'

They were silent for a moment, and Clara felt something

shift between them. She wasn't sure what it was but it was something unusual and special, a connection perhaps. Nothing too big but at least it was an understanding.

'I should go to my crumbling castle now, and you said you were giving me a quote and list?'

Henry went to the pile of papers on the small desk and pulled out a folder with embossing on the front.

'Take it and read it and we can chat in the morning,' he said.

Clara touched the front of the folder.

HENRY GARNETT AND DAUGHTER

THATCHER, HANDYMAN, ARTIST, GARDENER.

'Do you do all of these?' she asked, looking up at him.

'Pansy is the gardener and artist but I hold my own.' He smiled.

Gosh, he was lovely, she thought later when she was sitting in her bed, wearing a parka and her boots, even though it was summer. No insulation in a place will do that, Henry had told her. Clara opened the folder and read the list he had written of everything he would do in the cottage.

Not only had he written an exhaustive list, he had also drawn little sketches of the cottage and watercolours of what it would look like after the garden was planted and in bloom.

It was the most exquisite thing she had ever seen and

she pored over the drawings of the rooms and the new roof, and the furniture suggestions. It was as though she was eleven again and she and Mum had briefly escaped and she was drawing pictures of her perfect house in her diary for one day. Someday. Maybe that day was now.

Choosing not to look at the prices yet, she had been lying in the cold imagining Henry's vision for her cottage when Rachel had rung.

She immediately dressed and ran out the door. As she turned on the ignition, she saw Henry's door open and he came to the side of the car.

'Everything okay?' His beautiful face was concerned.

'The girl at the tea shop – I gave her my number. Well, she called me; her mother is hurt. I'm going to wait with her.'

'The one with the bruise?' he asked.

'Yes!' said Clara. 'You saw her also?'

'I thought she must have a dodgy boyfriend.'

Clara turned on the lights of the car. 'No, I don't think it's a boyfriend. I'm going down to see if she's okay and wait for an ambulance with her. Something about her worries me.'

Henry nodded and then waved as she drove down the lane and onto the road.

The roads were dark and she thought the lights of her Mini weren't strong enough. She turned on high beams and saw a fox run across the road.

'Christ, fox, get off the road,' she murmured as she headed towards the village and then pulled up at the front of the bakery.

She used the flashlight on her phone and banged on the glass with her hand.

'Rachel? It's Clara. Turn the lights on so the ambulance medics can see the shop.'

The lights turned on and then the door opened, the bell sounding incongruous in the night and the surroundings.

Clara stepped inside and saw Rachel's mother lying on the floor with blood everywhere and her leg looking very much broken.

'Oh God, is she dead?' asked Clara without thinking.

'I don't know. I don't think so – she was moaning,' Rachel said in a monotonous voice.

Clara rushed behind the counter and pulled out a stack of tea towels and handed them to Rachel. 'Put theses against her head, try and slow down the bleeding.'

Rachel stood helplessly so Clara moved quickly and took them off her. She gently lifted the woman's head and put the tea towels underneath the wound, hoping it would stem the bleeding.

'Go and get a blanket for your mum. We need to keep her warm so she doesn't go into shock.'

Thankfully Rachel responded and went upstairs and came back with a wool blanket and Clara instructed her to use it to cover her mother.

The sound of the ambulance broke the still of the night and Clara watched Rachel, who was standing on the bottom stair, biting a nail.

'She will be okay,' she said gently to Rachel. She wondered if for a moment Rachel looked disappointed at this news and briefly entertained the thought that Rachel had pushed her mother down the stairs. If it was Clara, she would have pushed a woman like that, and for a moment, the memory of the last night with her father came back to her – the sounds of his screaming in the kitchen, and Clara's blind rage at what he'd done. It took all her might to push these memories back down where she kept them, guarded by the dragons of her childhood that had kept her safe.

Clara stood back as the paramedics rushed inside, did their work on Moira Brown and then loaded her into the back of the ambulance.

'We can follow in the car,' said Clara. Soon, she and Rachel were driving to Salisbury, the ambulance lights far ahead in the distance.

Rachel was silent as they drove in the car, speeding along the dark roads, and Clara respected that but wondered what was going on in the girl's mind. She knew this silence. She knew the fear this girl felt, and she knew the relief that the person who'd hurt you had been stopped – but at what cost had that come to Rachel? She hoped it wouldn't be the price that she had paid so many years before.

11

Henry was concerned he had done too much with the sketches and the watercolours for Clara but he was a visual person and sometimes a one-line quote description did not do justice to the work he could envision for a home.

It felt ironic to Henry that he was so brilliant at conjuring up what a house needed and wanted, as though it whispered it to him as he carried out repairs for the owners, and yet he travelled in a van on wheels.

If anyone else looked at Acorn Cottage, they saw a shrivelled old maid but Henry saw a great beauty waiting to be unveiled. With the right amount of care he could make her so pretty and elegant again, bringing the garden to life and the charm back to the home. Rethatching the roof was laborious and necessary but he would source the best water reed he could for Acorn Cottage, then he would paint the cottage inside and out. Perhaps a pink wash for the outside to pick up the light in the mornings and evenings. He wanted the cottage to look like a cloud at any time of the day.

The inside would be the colour of clotted cream and he would build furniture and fix things that were already inside, and find pretty items for the rooms in local second-hand shops and paint them with flowers and polka dots and everything Naomi had wished for and that Clara loved.

He imagined roses and larkspur and delphiniums as tall as Pansy, and the wisteria would be trained to run along the fence, like the frill of a skirt. The rose along the fence would keep trespassers out, and there would be a vegetable garden with a picket fence around it and a funny scarecrow wearing an old straw hat.

Henry had renovated many houses and thatched twice as many again, and he had worked in some of the most beautiful homes in England but Acorn Cottage had him bewitched like nothing before. He swore he could hear the cottage tell him what she needed and most of all what she needed was company.

Henry understood this need, as he knew what loneliness felt like. Some nights he wondered if he was going insane from lack of conversation, so it was no wonder Pansy spoke like a small adult.

After Clara had gone to help the girl in the village, he had walked to the front of the house and looked at the gate that was lying on the ground in the dark.

It was a simple fix – a few new hinges and tighten the latch and it would be right again.

Before he knew it, he had his lamp out and his electric drill and had lined up the hinges and rehung the gate. Pansy was asleep inside the van, used to the sound of the drill. Henry opened and closed the gate, listening to the satisfying click of the latch as it closed.

He took the sign off the front of the gate, which had the words Acorn Cottage carved into it, and ran his fingers over the words.

He found two small indentations.

The acorns.

He took the sign into the van, found an old cloth and wiped back the sign and held it up to the light. Yes, definitely acorns, he thought. The sign would once have been painted.

He went to the back of the van and found the old box of Naomi's paints and opened them. He hadn't seen the paints since she had died but the smell, the nutty scent of the oils, some smelling like a pine tree, some like flaxseed oil, the poppy oils and oil of cloves that she mixed into the paint to make it last longer, filled his senses. He picked up an old rag she used to dry her brushes on, disturbing the lavender and rosemary oils she had used as solvents and held it to his face.

When would the pain ease?

He missed her more than he could have thought possible. People said he should start dating again, meet women, get married, have another baby, but how could he start again when Naomi was supposed to be his ending?

Naomi had painted the furniture Henry made in bright colourful folk-art styles and they sold them to clients. Her deft hand and wonderful understanding of colour worked on the pieces and while not many people would think saffron yellow and turquoise would work as a pairing, in her hands and with her mixing of the hues, it did.

He searched for the right colour for the sign. A pale pink sign with green writing and the little acorns painted in brown and green would look lovely, and if Clara painted the house pink, it would work perfectly.

He painted the first coat and let it dry and then got ready for bed.

He wondered if he should text her and see if she was okay with the girl from the bakery. Naomi would have helped that girl, he thought, and she would have had the situation sorted and that girl safe in a moment.

He wondered how Clara was doing with the house. She'd seemed a bit vague on the details and not really aware of the enormity of the renovation required.

He texted her using the number she had given him.

You okay? How is the girl?

A text came back faster than expected.

I'm fine but Rachel is in shock. Her mother is in an induced coma as she was very combative when she was in hospital, maybe a brain injury they think, and has a broken hip and femur. They are sending her for surgery. I will stay with Rachel at the bakery and then come home tomorrow.

Henry put the phone down, got into his bed and lay in the darkness. The scent of the paints filled the air and he rolled onto his side where Naomi used to lie. He put his hand on her pillow. 'Say yes,' he remembered her saying.

Three years on and he still didn't know what he was supposed to be saying yes to in life. Surviving was enough for him but there was something in him that was shifting and he wasn't sure he remembered the feeling. It felt something like anticipation, or waking up – he wasn't sure but it wasn't familiar.

*

In the morning, he had finished painting the sign, and Pansy, excited to see the paints out, had demanded her own sign stating *Pansy's Room*. Not that she had her own bedroom but she still insisted he paint it and then draw pansies on the wood and paint them too.

When it was done, he left it on the sill of the window of the van to dry and walked out to the cottage.

Clara wasn't back yet, and she hadn't told him if she wanted to go ahead with the quote, so he wandered through the garden, seeing its potential.

Naomi had once told him he could find the potential in a concrete bunker but she was prone to exaggerating, he'd said to her, though she had replied that she 'never, ever, ever exaggerated'.

Pansy came into the garden with her pram and dolls and pushed them under the oak tree where moss was growing and the long grass had not reached.

'Lovely spot,' said Henry as Pansy looked up at the tree branches.

'Do you think there are owls in that tree?' she asked.

'I don't know. What makes you ask?' asked Henry. Pansy had never really been interested in animals before, more caught up in the world of fairies and make-believe. 'Do you like owls?' he prompted.

Pansy shrugged. 'I don't know any owls so I can't say if I like them or not but last night I dreamed Mummy came and sat in the tree and she was an owl.'

Henry felt a shiver run through his body. Pansy had never spoken of dreaming about her mother before. She was so little when Naomi died and even though Henry had tried to keep Naomi's memory alive, she was almost an imaginary symbol in Pansy's life, like Father Christmas or the Easter Bunny.

'Mummy was an owl? How nice,' he said, trying to keep his tone light. He hadn't dreamed about Naomi in over a year, and he missed her, but the pain when he woke and realised it was a dream was almost like going through the death all over again. He missed dreaming about her but was also grateful he didn't dream so much anymore and for this, he felt guilty.

'Yes, she was an owl and she was watching us.' Pansy stated this as though it were a completely normal event in her life as she wrapped a baby doll in a blanket.

'Were we also owls?' He smiled.

'No, silly Daddy, we were here as people, and the house was pink.' Pansy laid a doll's blanket out on the moss. 'My babies and I are playing vets now, so you can go and do your work.'

Henry watched his daughter line her dolls up and put a collection of plastic animals on the blanket with a toy doctor's kit.

She must have seen the sketches and watercolours he did for Clara, he thought, because how else would she know he thought the house would be perfect painted pink?

Children were funny little things, he told himself with a shake of his head. Nevertheless, he found himself looking up at the oak tree to see if Naomi was an owl in the tree, watching over them.

12

Rachel woke with a start. The sound of the kettle whistling was unfamiliar. Usually she was the one awake first, making Mother's tea and taking it into her bedroom and then going downstairs to start the day before dawn. Baking and kneading and preparing what Mother told her to sell for the day.

The memories of the night before began to stir. She remembered Mother at the bottom of the stairs and watching Clara come back after the hospital – Clara, who knew how to get bloodstains out of the linoleum. She didn't ask how she knew, as Clara seemed very focused on her task and was barking orders for baking soda and vinegar so Rachel did as she asked.

When the floor was clean, they went to bed. Rachel was glad Clara had stayed. She didn't want to face the stain or the memories alone.

Rachel pulled on her dressing gown and opened the door to her bedroom and went to the little kitchen, where Clara was dunking tea bags with enthusiasm, spilling little drops of tea onto the counter.

Mother wouldn't like that, thought Rachel and then she remembered Mother was in hospital.

'Hello,' she said to Clara, feeling ashamed of her having to be here to help her when they hardly knew each other.

Clara turned around and tucked her hair behind her ear. 'Good morning. I let you sleep. I put a sign up on the door of the shop.'

'What time is it?' asked Rachel, noticing the sun coming through the kitchen window.

'Eight,' said Clara. 'Milk, sugar?'

Mother didn't like her having either.

'Both, thank you,' said Rachel and watched as Clara spooned two sugars into the mug and a splash of milk, a quick stir, then handed it to Rachel.

'Shall we sit?' asked Clara, gesturing to the sofa.

They sat in silence, the heater warming their toes. Rachel wasn't usually allowed to have the heater on in the mornings and she felt her toes wiggle in appreciation.

'I've rung the hospital; your mum is going into surgery this morning. They said they will ring you when you can go down.'

Rachel nodded and let the mug warm her fingers as she sipped her tea.

She didn't want the hospital to ring. She just wanted to forget it ever happened but more than that, she didn't want her mother to come home.

Clara's eyes on her felt like X-ray vision, as if she could see everything Rachel was thinking. She stood up quickly.

'I need to open the bakery; I will just do some sandwiches for the day and some shortbread and scones.'

'You will have the day off,' said Clara firmly.

'I never take a day off. Mother said holidays are for lazy people.'

Rachel noticed Clara's eyes narrow slightly.

'Did your mother work in the bakery?'

'She did all the accounts and paperwork upstairs.'

Clara raised her eyebrows now and Rachel bit her lip. She knew what Clara was thinking but she couldn't be disloyal to Mother, not after all she did for her.

'Rachel, I want to help you,' said Clara, draining her tea and putting it on the table.

'You already have – thank you so much for coming when I called last night.'

And Rachel meant it. She was grateful. She wasn't sure what she would have done if she didn't have Clara's number. Or maybe she was sure and she didn't want to admit it yet.

'No, I mean about your mother. She seems to be very domineering – perhaps it's something you can speak to someone about.'

'She loves me,' said Rachel, knowing she sounded flat though she tried to mean it. 'She really loves me.'

'But she hurts you.'

Rachel was silent in the face of the truth.

'Love shouldn't hurt, Rachel. I know this. My mum went through it with my dad. I was lucky – she protected me and got me away from him, but there is no one to help you here.'

'I don't need help,' said Rachel defiantly.

'Then why did you call me, of all the people in this village, why me?' Her question was asked so gently yet it felt like Rachel had been knifed in the stomach. She bent over and sat down on the sofa again and started to cry.

She felt Clara's hand on her back, rubbing along her spine, as she cried.

'I don't have any friends,' she said.

'You do, you have me now,' said Clara. 'We're new friends.'

'Mother thinks I'm useless, and gets upset with me. She says everything I do isn't up to scratch.'

'You, Rachel Brown, are miles above scratch,' said Clara. 'You are beyond scratch. You are in the stratosphere of brilliant. Look at everything you do. The shop and the baking and caring for your mum – you are amazing.'

Rachel had never heard these words before. They made her feel like she was wearing a coat that was too tight for her body, tight on the arms and shoulders. It felt foreign and she tried to shrug it off.

'I'm not. Mother says I would be in a home for women who aren't very smart if it wasn't for her.'

'I don't know what century your mother lives in in her head but there is no such home for women like that, so she is wrong and you mustn't listen to her.' Clara sounded cross and Rachel was sorry she had been disloyal to her mother.

They sat in silence as Rachel's tears subsided and finally Clara spoke.

'I don't want to leave you here alone today,' said Clara. 'You should come and see my cottage and meet the man who is going to fix it up for me. He has the funniest little girl who says the funniest things. I think she will be just the tonic for today.'

Rachel looked up at Clara.

'You think I should take the day off?'

'I do. I think you should come and have a drive and see the place and we can mooch around together and then I'll drive you to the hospital when the hospital rings.'

Rachel was silent and she stood up.

'I'll get changed then,' she said, smiling a little at Clara. 'Thank you.' She wished she could do more for her new friend.

'You're welcome,' said Clara and her smile was so warm that Rachel burst into tears again.

'You have to stop being kind to me; it makes me cry,' said Rachel.

'Nope, you deserve kindness and you are allowed to cry and that's the end of that. Now have a nice warm shower and use all the water until it runs cold and then we'll pop over to mine and play house, okay?'

Rachel nodded at the helpful instructions and did exactly as Clara said.

They drove to the cottage in Clara's red Mini Cooper with the top down. She had music playing that Rachel didn't recognise but she liked the beat and she liked when Clara sang along, not knowing the words, so sort of making them up.

Clara was exactly like Rachel imagined a fairy would be in human form and she even forgave her for taking the cottage for herself.

Clara told her about her horrible cheating boyfriend and Rachel agreed to hate him also, because that was the right thing to do as a friend. Clara told her she wanted Rachel to teach her how to bake and for the first time in twenty-five years, Rachel felt free.

It felt like everything that had happened up until they got into the car had been imagined and now Rachel was really living her life. Her best life, as Tassie McIver had said to her the other day.

'Find your best life, Rachel Brown, because it isn't with your mother,' Tassie had said as she paid for her lemon cake and tea. Rachel hadn't understood what she meant but now she did. She could feel the wind in her hair, which she had worn down, and hear Clara singing as they passed the sheep munching in the fields. Rachel wanted to scream at the blue skies that she was free for today.

'I want to renovate the tearooms,' she said out of the blue, surprising herself as they drove.

'Do you? You should,' said Clara. 'What would you do? I love this idea by the way.'

Rachel paused, thinking about her ideas that she dreamed about at night in her room.

'I would make them cosy and cute, like the inside of a little old-fashioned parlour. Bookshelves with books and games for people to read and play. There's a fireplace behind the wall, and I could have a fire and armchairs. And flowers and wooden tables and a pink wall and peacock feathers...'

She gasped at her thoughts being spoken aloud. It felt like she was betraying her mother by saying the words to Clara.

But Clara was nodding excitedly in agreement.

'I can see it. It would be amazing, really. Just wonderful, you can do all of that and more.'

But Rachel was silent as they drove down the bumpy lane towards the cottage.

She wondered if that would ever happen. Probably not while her mother was in her life and in the tearooms and bakery. She had never imagined her mother not controlling everything about her existence, until now. Clara made her feel that maybe it was all somehow possible, as though she could make magic happen and could help other people find the magic inside them.

What could she be without her mother? As the cottage came into view, Rachel had an idea.

13

Henry and Pansy were in the garden when Clara returned with Rachel to the cottage.

Within moments of meeting, Rachel and Pansy were firm friends, with Rachel joining Pansy under the oak tree to discuss potential market spots for the fairies who lived in the trees, and what sort of special biscuits they would make for the fairies.

Clara watched them as Henry joined her side.

'She okay?' he asked in a low voice.

'Unsure. The mother is abusive but she's an adult so what can I do?'

'Is she an adult though?' asked Henry. 'She seemed very young emotionally.'

'She's so sheltered she has no self-awareness and her self-esteem is next to nothing,' sighed Clara.

She turned to the cottage. 'Now, about this, I need to get your quote. I'll go and read it now.'

'Then I'll make us tea and we can sit in the van and discuss.'

Clara smiled at him and went inside to get the quote he had provided her. The house was still a mess and depressing.

She found the papers and went back to the van where Henry had left the door open for her.

'Come in,' he said.

Don't get a crush on the thatcher, she reminded herself as she sat at the little booth and opened the folder of papers.

'I love these sketches and colours,' she said, running her fingers over the drawings.

He shrugged. 'Just letting the imagination run wild – it's your place, you don't have to do any of that at all.'

'But I want to, it's perfect.' She looked up at him and smiled, then found the list of things he thought she needed to do, her eye running over the tasks.

Painting.

New roof.

Update the bathroom.

Insulation.

Fix flooring in living area.

Clean fireplaces.

Chicken house.

Tidy garden.

The list seemed endless until she found the numbers at the bottom.

It was more than she expected but not as much as she had feared. She could pay for it all but she would need to work within the year. But that was for future Clara to think about.

Henry put the tea on the table in mugs with daisies painted on them.

'Cute mugs,' she said.

'Naomi painted them.'

'She was very clever.'

'She was far too clever to be with me but she was and here I am, without her.' He smiled at her and Clara knew then she was done for. In her mind's eye, the crush she had been avoiding came crashing over her like a wave, dunking her into the sand, until she resurfaced spitting it from her mouth and trying to wipe it from her eyes.

'The quote is fine,' she said, knowing she was turning red.

'Which part?'

'All of it,' she said. 'I want to live here, so make it liveable. I want you to do to it exactly what you would do if it was yours.'

Henry laughed. 'That was the easiest deal I've ever made. You're not even trying to whittle down the price.'

'Why would I? You say it will cost this much, you live in a van with a child, you have mugs with daisies painted on them by your late wife, and you painted my sign.'

She gestured to the sign drying on the windowsill.

'I did paint it,' he said. 'You're very trusting.'

'Not really, I'm just a realist. And I have a gut instinct around money – I guess it's my bank manager background. I know who is a good bet and who isn't.'

Henry banged his hand on the table, making Clara jump.

'I'm excited. And that is rare. I never get the chance to do a whole place from top to bottom and the garden. I have to order the thatch. We have to get paint samples. We need to discuss the garden.'

Clara laughed and finished the tea.

'I am glad I can make you excited,' she said, before realising the double meaning and put her hand over her mouth.

'Sorry, that was inappropriate and a mistake.'

'It's fine.' He laughed and shrugged. 'I don't get excited much anymore.'

There was an awkward pause and then Clara knew she was bright red.

'I'm going to go and check on Rachel.'

'I should check on Pansy,' he said and they both moved towards the door at the same time.

'Sorry, you first.' Henry opened the door and Clara noticed a flush on his neck.

Oh God, he wanted to run away from her. She had been far too forward by mistake and he thought she was making a move.

This was terrible and not at all what she wanted for either of them.

'For the record,' she said, her words tumbling over each other as she spoke, 'I don't like you that way, I mean I don't know you, you know? Sometimes I say things without thinking, so pay no attention to me.

Henry nodded. 'Sure, absolutely, never thought that for a moment.'

Clara went down the steps of the van and walked briskly

to the garden but Rachel and Pansy weren't under the tree anymore.

'Rachel? Pansy?' she called, walking around to the back door.

They were sitting at the old kitchen table, with Pansy's tea set laid out on a beautiful embroidered tablecloth.

'This looks lovely,' said Clara.

'Rachel found the tablecloth in the cupboard,' said Pansy. 'We are having make-believe marble cake and lemon madeleines.'

'In the cupboard?' Clara asked Rachel, who looked embarrassed.

'I shouldn't have opened the cupboards. I'm very sorry.' Her head hung down, her lank oily hair falling forward over her face.

'You don't have to apologise at all. I wasn't aware there were many things in there. I thought the owners had cleaned it out. I actually haven't had time to look or maybe I've been avoiding it in case animals jump out at me. Henry thinks there was a fox living in here.'

Rachel looked up. 'There are things in the drawers and in the attic. Lots of things.'

'You looked through all the drawers and the attic in the twenty minutes I was in the van?' Clara was confused.

'Rachel knows the house because she used to come here when she was little,' said Pansy, as she balanced a small pink plastic plate on her head.

'I thought you didn't know the place?' Now Clara felt very confused.

'I thought you meant a different house,' Rachel said feebly.

Clara sat at the table with them.

'Why did you tell me you didn't know it when you did? When you have been inside the house? I'm not angry, I just don't understand why you didn't say anything to me.'

Rachel looked up. 'Because I didn't know if you would tell Mother. She never knew I used to come here. I would come inside and pretend I lived here, but if Mother knew, she would punish me. She used to beat me with a wooden spoon on the back of my legs.'

Clara was silent as she tried to understand. She saw Henry stood in the doorway, his face showing he'd heard what Rachel had shared.

Tipping the plate off her head, Pansy caught it and looked at Clara and then at Rachel.

'Your mum sounds like a mean old cow. You should tell her to find a new house to live in.'

Clara tried to stifle her shocked gasp and Henry called out her name but Rachel looked at Pansy and nodded, smiling a little.

'You know what? She is a mean old cow and I hope she finds a new house to live in too.'

Clara and Henry exchanged a glance and smothered smiles. Sometimes children had the perfect understanding of life and it was the adults who made life complicated. Very complicated.

14

Clara opened the gate at the front of Tassie's house and carefully closed it behind her. Everything about Tassie's garden was perfect, from the carefully edged lawns to the lavender hedge left long on top, with bees lazily cruising between the flowers.

She lifted the brass knocker shaped like a fox and rapped on the door, remembering the fox she had seen the night of Moira Brown's accident.

Just as she finished the last knock, the door opened.

'Oh gosh, were you already at the door?' asked Clara.

'No, I knew you were coming. I was expecting you,' said Tassie. 'I got the Ladybird in my tea leaves again and I knew the nurse wasn't coming today.'

'Goodness, how spooky, are you sure you're not a witch?' she half joked.

Tassie rolled her eyes at Clara. 'I saw your red car, but I did think something was in the air today, as I had a very itchy left eyebrow.'

Clara peered at Tassie's eyebrows, which were drawn on with an eye pencil.

'What if the right one was itchy?' she asked.

'Left is a lady visitor, right is a gentleman visitor. I don't think the right one is even functioning anymore.'

Tassie wiggled it and Clara burst into laughter.

'I like the fox door knocker. I saw a fox the other night. It ran in front of my car when I was driving to help Rachel,' she said, making conversation. 'And Henry thought a fox was living in the house when I moved into the cottage.'

Tassie looked at her closely. 'You will uncover a great secret then,' she said.

Clara shook her head. 'Pardon? What do you mean?'

'Foxes crossing your path are leading you to reveal a great secret.'

Clara shrugged. 'I have no idea what that would be, I don't have any secrets.'

Tassie seemed to look at her longer than usual but it was hard to know because she was very old and perhaps she was merely trying to focus, thought Clara. Then Tassie spoke and the mood became lighter.

'Come in, pet – drink tea with me and have some lovely gingerbread that Rachel brought me yesterday. I don't get much company besides the nurse, who I could take or leave, although the cleaner sent by the council, Nahla, is always welcome. She's a lovely girl – you should meet her.'

Clara followed Tassie into the little kitchen. It was exactly what a kitchen should look like. Little checked curtains framed the window, lemons sat patiently on the windowsill, a cheery tea towel on top of the counter, an old double ceramic sink all set off by pale pink cabinets. Against one wall was a large Welsh dresser, displaying a large collection of mismatched china from Cornish ware to chintz teacups and pretty eggcups and jugs of all sizes and colours.

'A pink kitchen? Oh wow, this is perfect,' said Clara as she looked around. 'That dresser is incredible.'

'That was my great-grandmother's,' said Tassie as though it wasn't anything important.

Clara tried to imagine having anything that old in her life, passed from generation to generation, but failed to find the image or the feeling of having that much history. Clara had never delved into her family history, on either side. Some things need to be left alone; nothing good had come of her family so far, there was too much to forget, not celebrate.

'Do you want me to make the tea?' asked Clara as she saw Tassie put the old kettle onto the stove and then light a match underneath.

'No love, this will be the most exercise I'll do today, so I'll be sure to sleep tonight.'

Clara wasn't sure if she was joking or not, so she sat at the table while Tassie moved about slowly.

Tassie carefully placed the gingerbread on a plate with a faded pattern of pink roses and gold edging, and carried over the pot of tea when the kettle had boiled.

'Let her sit,' Tassie said, nodding at the teapot. 'She needs to stew.'

Tassie put down a small jug of milk and sat opposite Clara. A heavy sigh escaped as she sunk into the chair.

'Now you've come to talk about Rachel and her mother. I saw the lights of the ambulance, wasn't sure if Rachel had finally lost her head and did Moira in, not that anyone would blame her.'

Clara sighed. 'Mrs Brown fell down the stairs, terrible hip and leg injuries. I mean I feel awful for her but I'm glad

Rachel gets a break from her. But I don't know that Rachel can keep living with her mum. I just don't understand why she would be so awful to her daughter when they don't have anyone else.'

Tassie turned the teapot and then poured them both a cup.

'Some women are mothers and some aren't. Even if you grow a child within you, you can still fail them once they're out in the world. And you can be an exceptional parent and not have ever even conceived a baby.'

'Did you have children, Tassie?' asked Clara.

Tassie shook her head. 'Never did. We tried but no babies. In the end we just had dogs and chickens to care for. But I was the local schoolteacher when there were children in the village. I had more than enough little ones to care for and teach to read and how to say please and thank you.'

Clara smiled. 'That might be me, minus the schoolteacher part. I don't think I will have children.'

'You don't get to choose if you have a baby or not really. The baby chooses you. Some women aren't ready to have them and that's fine and some yearn for them so much they scare them away. I yearned. Still do sometimes, even though my insides are now pickled and George has been dead for thirty years.'

A shadow crossed Tassie's face and Clara felt guilty for disturbing old memories in an old woman.

'I want to help Rachel, but I don't know what else I can do,' said Clara changing the subject.

'Rachel needs someone to believe in her. Any praise you give her sits so uncomfortably on her shoulders that she'd as soon shrug it to the floor and ask for a beating than hear in detail why she might be brilliant. Abuse does that to you. You begin to believe it until you become it.'

Clara looked down at the table and touched the gold-edged plate as a vision of her own mum came into her mind, and she closed her eyes for a long moment.

Tassie continued. 'She needs time away from the abuse and the abuser, and then she needs to learn to trust. I had a rescue dog like her once. Took two years for her to allow George to pat her but then she would sit on his knee of a night and look at me as though I was the mistress and she was the wife.'

Clara laughed. 'I don't know that Rachel will ever get to that stage but I would just like her to have a little more confidence in herself and in her skills in the bakery.'

Tassie nodded. 'I agree, and that will come, but you have to show her you can be relied on, and small movements, no big gestures yet. She shies away easily.'

Clara wasn't sure if Tassie was talking about Rachel or her old pet dog.

'Tell me about the cottage,' said Tassie. 'I seem to remember there was a lovely climbing rose, pink, very fragrant. Sheila used to bring me bouquets when she came by the village.'

'I don't know much about gardening,' admitted Clara. 'I need to learn.'

'You'll learn by being in it,' said Tassie. 'The soil will be fine after all this time resting – it's ready for love, it's fertile. Put things in it, let them grow, create a little place where you don't worry about anything but the shoots coming up from the earth, and the thrill of the new buds on a branch.'

Clara thought back to when she was a child and the book she had loved.

'Like Mary Lennox in *The Secret Garden*,' she said.

Tassie smiled. 'Mary was a girl after my own heart. I would have slapped that terrible screaming Colin also.'

'You know, I am so glad I met you, Tassie. You just might be the perfect person. I think I'm going to aspire to be like you in my life.'

Tassie laughed and banged the table with her hand. 'Well, you might want to aim a little higher, love, but I will agree: I am a good place to start.'

Clara picked up a piece of gingerbread, took a bite and sighed. 'It's exquisite. That girl sure can cook.'

Tassie nodded. 'She needs to be on one of those baking shows they have on the telly,' she said to Clara.

'But her mother would be trying to get on camera instead. Claiming it was her recipe,' Clara answered.

Clara chewed her delicious treat and sipped her tea. Tassie was absolutely right, but how could Clara protect this girl from the one person who was supposed to love her?

If she knew the answer to that, then her own life would have been very different.

As though reading her mind, Tassie spoke. 'Sometimes the only thing we can do is survive. We can go through life showing people we are coping and functioning but inside us, we know we're only pretending and we hope that no one else will ever find out.'

She paused before continuing. 'Until there is something that changes us and we know we can't go back to living like that anymore. We have to move forward. We make a huge change. We do something drastic. For some women the first sign is cutting their hair. For others it's letting go of everything and by everything, I mean every cup and saucer, every shred of responsibility in life. They climb mountains or open an orphanage, or plant a garden. But they are changed and they know they can never go back to that life again.'

When Tassie finished speaking, Clara felt a tear fall from her eye but she didn't brush it away. It was soothing in the warmth of Tassie's kitchen.

'I don't want that life anymore,' she heard herself say aloud.

'Of course you don't, pet, that's why you're here; it's good to know what you don't want, so then you'll know what you do want when it comes.'

Clara wondered why such a strange sentence felt so right.

'Shall we do a reading?' asked Tassie as she spun her cup a few times and then turned it over on the saucer.

'What do I do?' Clara wondered why she felt like she was dipping her toes into a forbidden pool.

'Leave a little tea in the cup, not too much more than a sip, and spin the cup three times and turn it upside down.'

Clara did as Tassie instructed and stared at the cup for a minute.

'Now, turn it over,' said Tassie and they turned theirs over together.

Tassie looked inside her cup and shrugged. 'Nothing interesting.' Then she took Clara's cup and peered inside.

'A man and a goat,' she said and shook her head slowly.

'Is that good? Is Henry bringing a goat home?' Clara laughed.

Tassie put the cup down. 'A visitor who won't be welcome is coming. I suggest you be ready.'

Clara frowned and peered into the cup. All she could see were a few leaves with no distinct shapes.

'I'm not expecting any visitors, so I don't think it will come true. What does yours show?'

Clara went to grab Tassie's cup who moved it away.

'Nothing to see, love,' she said quickly and Clara wondered what Tassie had seen in her cup.

But she was more curious about who the visitor would be who wasn't welcome. She couldn't think of anyone, and dismissed it as quickly as she had entertained the idea. Tassie was an old superstitious lady who was clearly a worrier, and Clara decided to ignore her worries, lest they became hers.

15

Henry buttered the bread and then filled the sandwich with salami and cheese and cut it into triangles.

He used to ask Pansy if she preferred triangles or squares, but that was when Naomi was alive.

Now he put the sandwich on a plate in front of Pansy and sat down opposite her in the small booth in their van.

'You must stop saying rude things to people, Pansy.'

Pansy shrugged and chewed on her salami and cheese sandwich, leaving the crusts on the plate. 'It's not rude if it's true.' She spoke almost to herself, as though chewing the idea over as she ate.

'Sometimes saying the truth is rude, and it can hurt people's feelings,' said Henry as he glanced out the window at the cottage, wondering what Clara was doing.

'But you tell me to always tell the truth. Make your mind up,' Pansy muttered.

'Eat your crusts – they makes your hair curly,' said Henry.

'My hair was curly when I was born.'

'That's because your mum ate her crusts and you then inherited those crusts so you got curly hair.'

Pansy looked at him suspiciously. 'Sometimes I think a

lot of what you say is not true. Sorry if it's rude but I think you're a fibber.'

Henry burst out laughing. 'Oh, do you?'

'Yes, this is why I have to go to school. So I can learn what is true and what isn't.'

Henry swept some imaginary crumbs off the table onto his plate.

'I am teaching you everything you need to know,' he said, knowing he was being defensive. Pansy rolled her eyes and he thought she had never looked more like Naomi.

After lunch, Pansy went back to the cottage to be with her new best friend Rachel. If she was stating that a woman in her twenties who had a horrible mother was her best friend, then she did need to go to school and make friends her own age, he thought.

He had taught her the alphabet and she could count and they were doing simple word-recognition games. Naomi had said she would home-school Pansy when she was born and he wanted to honour her by ensuring he did educate his daughter but it was harder than he realised and he had to work.

Besides, school required a home address and they didn't have one.

He looked at the house plans and mentally calculated how long the renovation would take. Probably close to four months, maybe a little longer, depending on the weather. They were in the summer now but the rain still came and storms that could stop all roof work.

School seemed problematic because once Pansy was in the system they would have to stay in the system and what would happen when they had to leave Merryknowe for a new job? She would have to change schools again and make new friends and this could continue while he chased jobs around the country.

If he was honest with himself, he was tired of travelling. He felt like he was on the run from something or someone and now he needed to rest. He wanted to sit in a garden and feel good about the work he had done that day. He wanted a room with doors and some adult company. He wanted a little house like Acorn Cottage.

Henry rubbed his temples, wondering what he should do, and he looked at the shelf where Naomi's ashes sat patiently in a box she painted before she died. Tiny flowers and animals and colours like jewels covered the box, and even though he had looked at it a thousand times and more, he saw for the first time a little white owl on the side of the box.

The owl was no bigger than his smallest fingernail yet there it was, showing itself for the first time since Naomi had died. Was that where Pansy had seen the owl? Had she been looking at the box?

'Tell me what to do, babe,' he said to the box. 'Tell me what Pansy needs.'

A knock on the van door made him jump and he opened the door to see Clara.

'I'm taking Rachel back to the bakery. She doesn't want to see her mother, even though the hospital rang to say she went through surgery and is stable.'

'Okay,' said Henry. 'That's a good outcome for Mrs Brown but I can understand why Rachel doesn't want to see her. I wouldn't either.'

'Me neither,' said Clara. 'It's so awful. Also, Pansy wants

to come to town with me. I said I would have to ask you. You might like an hour to yourself.'

'You don't have to do that,' he said.

'I know, but she wants to see Rachel's bedroom. Can I use her booster seat for the car?'

'I don't think Rachel's bedroom will be quite what Pansy thinks it will be.'

'I know but hey, the company would be nice and she's an excellent mood lifter for Rachel.'

Henry laughed. 'You're right about that. After Naomi died, she was just a light energy and sometimes I felt guilty for laughing at her antics and conversations but she really did get me through that time with her spirit.'

'She's pretty special, Henry; you and Naomi should be proud.'

Henry felt his eyes sting with tears and he lowered his face away from Clara's.

'Sure, go for it. I can make some orders while she's out. And don't let her con you into buying her anything.'

Henry tried to think of the last time he'd had time away from Pansy. He couldn't remember; she was always there. He realised he was always making sure she was safe and out of harm's way.

He helped put the car seat into Clara's car and waved goodbye to them all, Pansy so excited to be in Clara's red car.

Henry made his phone calls and put some orders in and then went into the cottage.

It needed a good clean. He went back to his van and found the industrial vacuum and sucked up the dust and the mess from the hole in the roof. He went upstairs and sucked up the mess on the stairs and the skirting as he went and then went into the bedroom.

Clara's mattress was on the floor. He had seen the bed frame downstairs on the grass but hadn't said a word as it wasn't his place. The room looked grim, like somewhere a squatter would live.

He vacuumed the floor and then went downstairs and outside to the wooden bedframe. It was easy enough to pull apart and four trips later he had all the pieces upstairs and had managed to put them back in order and set up her bed. It looked better but still dull.

Downstairs in the living room, he had seen a small three-legged witches' table that would be perfect next to her bed. With three carved legs, it was actually a lovely piece of furniture, he thought as he wiped it down with a wet cloth and found, under the dust, some faint flowers painted on the top.

Naomi would have loved this, he thought as he carried it up to Clara's bedroom. The room needed something else though. He went downstairs and out to the garden and saw what he wanted down the side of the house.

A pink wild rose, messy but still thriving. He used his knife to cut off a few blooms and inside he placed them into a teacup with water and put them by Clara's bed.

Naomi had loved flowers by her bed when she was sick. God, she would have loved Acorn Cottage. He closed the door to Clara's bedroom and went outside again.

But Naomi was gone, and he had never felt more alone since she had died. It was as though the world was taunting him with the cottage and the dream that he couldn't have now. This was what they had wanted and here he was, a widower with a van for a house and a child who he was holding back because of his own failings. He needed to step up but the problem was, he didn't know how.

By the time Pansy and Clara returned, he had made all the orders and had a plan for the work to be done in sequence. And on top of it all, he had made a lovely chicken stew for dinner with rosemary potatoes and fresh beans.

Pansy came dancing into the van with a plastic tiara on her head and fairy wings.

Clara shrugged at him and threw her hands up in surrender. 'I know you said don't buy her anything, but they were at the pound shop in the next village. I went to get a few things for cleaning and she told me she had to have them, as her life depended on it. And I didn't want to return her on the cusp of death because she couldn't get a tiara and wings.'

Henry laughed. 'She seems to have a lot of things that her short life has depended on so far, so it's lucky she is so aware of her survival needs. How is Rachel?' He gestured to the empty seat in the van, as Pansy danced about the small living area.

Clara shook her head. 'I don't know. She seemed relieved but guilty. She refused to see her mother and wanted to go home and make plans for the bakery for tomorrow. She seemed almost excited to be alone.'

Henry lifted the lid on the stew and stirred it. 'You would be though, not having your abuser around – it would be like winning the lotto.'

Clara was silent, he noticed, staring into the distance,

her mind far away. He noticed how pretty she was and wondered why she wanted to live so far away from people when she was so young. She should be out dating and dancing and having holidays with friends.

'How old are you?' he asked.

'Twenty-nine, why?' Clara frowned. 'Do I look older since I've come here?'

'I didn't know you before here so I can't say but no, I was just wondering why a person your age wants to live in a tiny village in a tiny cottage with no social life or even a boyfriend.'

Clara smiled ruefully. 'I don't know either but I'm here now and I will make it work. I make everything work with a few minor adjustments here and there.'

'But shouldn't you be out at clubs and bars, dancing and going to cool restaurants?'

'I could do those things but it's never really been me,' Clara answered. 'My whole life I wanted something like this. I want a slower life, one where I know what I'm eating and doing and making something instead of buying it. I guess I just want something that means something to me, and being here in Merryknowe, even after a few days, meeting Tassie and Rachel and you and Pansy, it's the most exciting time I've had in a long time, which is either really sad or it's really wonderful. I'm going with wonderful.'

Henry listened to her speak then nodded. 'I get it, I really do.'

They smiled at each other and he felt the warmth of friendship and shared understanding between them.

'Whatever you're cooking smells amazing,' Clara said as she stood up. 'I should go and get organised for my dinner.'

'Stay,' he said suddenly. 'I've cooked too much and I would love some adult company.'

Clara paused. 'I really don't want to put you out. I was planning on cooking tonight anyway.'

'Oh? What? I don't think the Aga works yet.'

'Cheese on toast,' she said. 'The breakfast, lunch and dinner of champions and students across the world.'

'I think I can do better than that. You can set the table if you like and I'll pour us wine. Everything is in the drawers under the table.'

Clara opened the drawers and set out the placemats and cutlery. 'The way you use the space is amazing. Did you buy it ready-built or make it from scratch?'

Henry opened a bottle of red wine and sniffed the inside of the neck. 'It's not a prestige wine but it's drinkable.'

'I wouldn't know the difference anyway,' said Clara with a shrug.

'We bought the van as a basic model but Naomi and I made it our own with the bathroom, the extra cupboards and drawers and Pansy's little space above ours. We tried to make it like a home.'

Clara accepted the wine that he handed her. 'You both did an amazing job,' she said. 'It's my dream space really, just not on wheels.'

'Well, your little cottage is going to be amazing.' He smiled. 'I can see what it will look like when I stand back. It's going to be something special.'

Clara sighed. 'I hope so. I have no idea what I'm doing actually, so I'm hoping it works out.'

Henry sat opposite her. 'So why this cottage and why Merryknowe?'

Clara turned the glass by the stem on the wooden table and then looked up at him.

'I got drunk and bought the place as a massive F-you to my ex who was cheating with my ex-best-friend.'

Henry was shocked. 'Oh God, that's awful. What a huge betrayal by both of them.'

'Yes, it was... is. And it was a week after my mum died when I found out, and that was also terrible because Mum and I had always hoped one day that one of us would get this dream of the country cottage. Mum had a tough life, and I really wanted this for her and for me. I wanted to share this with her.'

Clara's face clouded with memories of her recent loss. Henry put his hand on hers as he saw a tear fall onto the table.

'I am really sorry about both those awful events in your life, deeply sorry. Life certainly isn't fair, is it?'

Clara looked up at him. 'It is what it is. I don't think there is such a thing as fair. I think people are just selfish and they don't think about what they do to others. That's what upsets me the most. My ex, my ex-friend, Rachel's mother, my...'

She stopped speaking and Henry wondered who the other name was that she swallowed instead of saying aloud.

'Do you speak to the ex or your friend now?' he asked.

'Nope.'

'Then tell me about your mum,' he said, trying to redirect the energy away from those who had hurt her so badly.

Clara laughed. 'My mum was the bravest woman I have ever known. And she was the most direct and straight up person I have known, which is where I get it from, I suppose. I'm not really one to hide from what I'm feeling.'

Henry looked at her closely. 'Really?'

'What?' Clara put her wine glass down.

'Before, you nearly said a name and stopped yourself...' He immediately regretted his words. Clara looked angry or upset or both.

'I don't know you, so why would I share that with you?'

'I was about to share my chicken stew,' he joked, wishing he hadn't mentioned it.

But Clara wasn't laughing. He had touched a nerve and he wished he hadn't.

'I'm sorry, I shouldn't have said that; your life is your life, and I overstepped. I guess I thought we were sharing.'

Clara looked at him, holding his stare.

'I accept your apology. I need to go to bed now. I'm tired from no sleep and from helping Rachel.'

Henry nodded as Clara stood up.

'Goodnight, Pansy,' she called out.

Pansy popped her head out from behind the curtain that was around her bed.

'Goodnight, Clara. Thank you for my fairy things.'

Clara nodded at Henry. 'Night then.'

'Goodnight, Clara' he said, feeling sad but unsure why. Clara shut the door to the van and he could hear her walking to the cottage.

He hoped she didn't take the setting up of the bed the wrong way. He hadn't touched anything besides the bed frame. He sat in the van wondering what she thought and wondering why he felt the sudden and intense need to kiss her when he hadn't had that need since Naomi. He also wondered whose name she had avoided saying aloud when it clearly was such a big trigger for her.

16

Clara stormed inside and stomped up the narrow staircase to her bedroom. Throwing open the door and turning on the light, she closed her eyes and groaned. Oh God, she thought. The bed, the little table, the roses. *Damn you, Henry Garnett. You might be the perfect man and I was just rude and didn't thank you for offering me dinner and had a tantrum because I couldn't be honest about myself.*

Clara sat on the edge of the bed, enjoying the fact it was no longer on the floor, and picked up the teacup of roses. She examined the perfect buds and open flowers and inhaled the heady scent of the sweetness of summer tickling her nose.

She needed to apologise but Clara wasn't very good at apologies. Her mum had told her it was her cross to bear and she would have to learn how to offer them or she'd spend the rest of her life learning until she grew up. Clara had ignored her. Besides, saying sorry didn't fix the unfixable in life. Sometimes things happened that couldn't be forgiven, like Piles and Judas.

Clara left unfinished business because she wouldn't or couldn't say sorry. She left friendships, she left jobs and she left home with apologies floating round her, waiting to be delivered, but there was something about Henry that made her think she didn't want to leave him without one or thinking less of her. Perhaps she was growing up.

She thought about Judas and Piles. She didn't owe them an apology; they owed her one.

She thought about her mother. She had tried to say she was sorry at the end, but did she hear? It was too late then. She was unconscious on her mother. She should have said it earlier when they first left him, when they ran away into the night.

She should have said sorry to the friends she'd never called back or contacted after she and Piles had split. She should have said sorry to her co-workers instead of not going back without a word. It wasn't that she thought people didn't deserve to hear her apologies. It was that Clara didn't know how to say them. Ever since her father, she couldn't apologise to anyone and she knew it was time she learned or her mother's prophecy was right – she would spend her life trying to say sorry to people.

Clara picked up her phone and texted.

I am sorry I was rude. I overreacted. I'm sorry I ruined the dinner. Also, thank you for putting my bed together, and for the roses and the table and really, thank you for everything. You're so lovely and I was so rude.

She pressed send and lay on the bed. It felt entirely different now she was off the floor, and the task of fixing up the cottage didn't seem so immense after all.

Her phone chimed with a return text and she picked it up and read it.

Check by the front door.

Clara nearly ran downstairs, wondering if Henry would be there but when she opened it there was darkness – until she looked down and saw a plate of stew with a candle next to it, some cutlery wrapped in a napkin, and a glass of wine.

Picking up the items, she carefully balanced them and carried them into the cottage and put them on the kitchen table.

It was the most caring thing anyone had done for her since before her mum became ill.

Giles had never cooked for her, claiming he was all thumbs in the kitchen. In fact, he didn't really do anything in the home. She had done the washing and the cleaning, because in the end it was easier than arguing and she had decided that arguing over whose turn it was to iron was not the hill she wished to die on.

Clara sipped the wine and sat at the table, the candle flickering in the darkness. The stew was simply delicious and the wine a lovely pairing, with a hunk of crusty bread to soak up the rosemary-laced gravy from the stew.

As Clara ate, she felt a warmth inside that she hadn't felt since before her mum died. Her eyes stung as she walked upstairs with the rest of the wine and the candle and climbed into bed in her clothes.

She missed her mum more than she could explain and Henry made her feel cared for, as though someone loved her for the first time in a long time. Someone looked out for her and had her back.

Clara finished the glass of wine and then sent a text.

That was so perfect and undeserved. You are a truly
lovely person. Thank you.

A text came back.

You are too hard on yourself. You've had very little sleep,
have helped a relative stranger and been dealing with
a child who might be a future world dictator. It was my
pleasure to feed you. Goodnight, Clara.

Clara felt her body respond to him using her name when
he wrote goodnight.

She imagined him lying next to her saying that very
phrase.

'Goodnight, Clara.'

'Goodnight, Henry,' she would say.

And they would sleep with their feet touching and in the
morning they would lie tangled together, his finger tracing
patterns on her skin until they kissed and...

The phone chimed again.

I need to talk to you.

She looked at it with hope for a moment and then saw it
was from Piles.

He wanted to talk to her? Her fantasy of Henry had
been broken by this absolute traitor of a man telling
her she should speak to him, as though that should
mean something.

In fury she typed back.

Never text me again. Go and be with my ex-best-friend.
I hate you. I'm now blocking you.

And she did block him because Piles and Judas could
go to hell. She lay in the dark trying to summon the vision
of Henry next to her until she fell asleep just as their
feet were touching.

17

Rachel was up earlier than usual. She had slept deeply and dreamed of cakes and a wedding and Clara and Pansy. It was nice to have someone else to dream of and think about as she slept and worked. She used to dream about her mother a lot and they were anxiety-filled dreams, with a recurring one with Mother chasing her through a forest.

Last night Mother wasn't in her dream at all and she woke up humming a tune that Clara had played on the radio. She showered and dressed, then put on a pair of sneakers that she had bought in Chippenham with Clara. They were so soft and felt spongy when she walked, as though she was walking on actual sponge cakes.

The sun was slowly waking up still, when a knock at the back door of the bakery interrupted Rachel. She was kneading the pastry for the rhubarb and strawberry tarts she was planning on making for the day.

The mini carrot cakes with little iced carrots on top were ready and there were butterhorn rolls to go with the lovely pea and ham soup or minestrone she had for lunch.

After wiping her hands on her apron, she opened the door, to see Joe the butcher standing in the dusk, the champagne light wrapping around him as though he was wearing it as a cloak.

'Morning, Miss Brown,' he said, not looking her in the eye. Joe was a shy redheaded man who was a few years ahead of Rachel at school. She doubted he remembered her but she remembered him because he had been kind to her when others were not, and he always pushed back on Mother when she tried to barter on the meat prices.

'Your mam said you wanted lamb backstraps.' He held out the packages in white paper.

'No, I want braising steak and kidneys,' said Rachel.

'Your mam didn't tell me that.'

'I'm telling you now,' said Rachel, feeling stronger than she should. 'I will take these for tomorrow but if you have any steak and kidney I would appreciate it. I can pay you cash.'

There were so many options to make for the bakery and tearooms and without Mother telling her to buy the cheapest cuts and put the plainest sweet items on the menu, she felt as though she could finally use her skills in the kitchen.

She knew people thought she was stupid; she wasn't, but fear of being hurt made her quiet, taught her how to hold her tongue, taught her how to turn away at the last minute so the back of her head caught the slap so it wouldn't leave a mark.

'Actually, can you return the lamb back to me minced, and I'll make cottage pies with it, and bring me the steak and kidneys, Joe? I'm sorry if it's a lot of trouble,' she said politely. She hated the way her mother had spoken to people who she deemed were beneath her, which was everyone but herself.

'Mum not around today?' he asked, peering over her shoulder into the kitchen.

'She's in hospital. She hurt her leg,' was all the information she offered.

Joe nodded, seemingly satisfied with her answer, and went back to his van to drive to the next town to fill her order and bring it back.

Rachel set about finishing the tarts and then carefully wrote on the blackboard outside the bakery, telling everyone who passed the specials in-store. Before, her mother had not bothered with the blackboard but Rachel thought it was a lovely chance to wish everyone a good day, so she went and checked the weather and then came back and carefully added the weather forecast and wrote:

Have a wonderful day.

She stood back and smiled at the sign, pleased with her work.

It was entirely too exciting, she thought as she placed the cakes and tarts into the glass cabinet. It felt like she was starting a new life.

Joe returned with her order and she had the cottage pies in the oven in no time. Soon they were browning beautifully and ready to be served with the special tomato chutney she had from last summer, all labelled and preserved in the pantry.

The bakery opened at midday but Rachel was ready twenty minutes before, so she opened it anyway, ready for the customers she hoped would come.

She had even brought Mother's radio downstairs and put

it on in the tearoom, playing classical music that Dad used to play before he died.

She remembered the music about the planets. Jupiter and something else. She would ask Clara, *she* would know. Clara knew everything.

Rachel picked up the phone in the bakery and dialled Clara's number and heard it go through to voicemail so hung up again.

She didn't want to leave a message. What would she say? *Call me back about some music my dad used to play?*

The sound of the bell above the door stirred her from her worrying about messages and music and there stood a woman and what looked to be her elderly father.

'Hello,' said Rachel brightly. 'Can I help you?'

'We would like some tea and an early lunch,' said the woman.

Rachel seated them, glad for the soft shoes she wore instead of the laced-up ones Mother insisted she wear, and talked them through the soups and pie options.

With an order of pea and ham soup and a steak and kidney pie, and a pot of tea stewing, Rachel thought she couldn't be happier.

As the afternoon wore on, she was busy and sold everything but two cottage pies and a steak and kidney and two carrot cakes.

She had over-catered but perhaps she had meant to, and when she closed the shop at just after three and cleaned up, she saw the hospital had called four times.

Instead of calling them back, Rachel packed up the food, put it into the basket on her bike and rode up to Clara's cottage.

Clara was in the garden when she arrived, Henry was on the roof pulling down the thatching in one area, and Pansy was running on the lawn with dolls set up in a row as though to watch her.

She rang the bell on her bike as she jumped off. 'Hello,' she called.

Clara looked up from pulling weeds and smiled as Henry waved and Pansy greeted her with a cartwheel.

The three of them smiling and looking so happy made her heart sing. There was something about this she loved but she couldn't put her finger on it. It felt like everything was right with the world.

When she had visited Acorn Cottage in her teens, this was what she had hoped for but now, it all made sense. That was when she realised she had to make Henry and Pansy stay and Henry simply had to fall in love with Clara.

'I brought some things from the shop to say thank you,' she said standing outside the gate, holding the package.

She noticed the sign on the front had been painted and looked fresh compared to the rest of the cottage. Henry must have done it, she thought.

'Come in,' called Clara, pushing up from the ground and stretching. She was so pretty with her dark bob and her large blue eyes. She looked like Snow White, so it was perfect she lived in a cottage.

Rachel unsnapped the gate and stepped inside.

'Did you bring cake?' Pansy asked as she ran towards her. 'I love cake, it's my favourite.'

Rachel laughed at Pansy. 'I did, I brought carrot cake.'

'Carrot cake? It sounds like it's cake for rabbits.' Pansy made a face.

'Pansy, don't be rude. Say sorry to Rachel.' Henry sighed.

'Sorry for being rude about your rabbit cake,' said Pansy, dancing away.

Clara laughed. 'Come in, mind the mess though. I've been trying to work out what goes where, and I have a man coming to put on the internet so I can be a modern person.'

Rachel followed Clara inside, stepping over unrolled rugs and boxes half unpacked.

The kitchen was looking disorganised and very messy, with paper everywhere and bubble wrap on the floor.

'How's your mum?' asked Clara as though it wasn't a big deal.

'Fine, doing well,' said Rachel with a smile.

She avoided Clara's searching look.

'You've been gardening?' she said, changing the subject, looking at Clara's hands.

'Yes, the cottage seems too overwhelming and the sun is so nice. I love being outside.' Clara looked out the open front door, as though she was dying to get out again.

Putting the items on the table, Rachel looked around.

'Can I unpack your kitchen? I love organising and I want to help you after what you did for me the other night.'

Clara looked taken aback. 'Really? That seems like a very big ask; I mean people hate unpacking and organising.'

'Not me, I love it. Yes, really. I do like that sort of thing.' Rachel hoped Clara would let her because it was true, she did love an organised kitchen.

Clara laughed. 'If I don't have to do it, then go on ahead. I trust you completely.'

Rachel smiled. 'Go on then, into the garden with you.'

So Rachel Brown went to work, finally fulfilling her

dream at Acorn Cottage, but this time it felt better doing it for Clara, as though she finally had some value, and she could feel the little cottage humming with purpose again. *That's all we ever want in life*, she thought. *To have a purpose.*

18

Rachel not only cleaned Clara's kitchen, but she also unpacked the remaining boxes of kitchen items and put things away in cupboards and drawers and made the kitchen feel loved and warm, and as though it made sense. She'd found all manner of things left by the previous owner including tablecloths that just needed a wash, some mismatched plates and cups, a collection of buttons in a large jar, which she knew Pansy would love to play with, and a mousetrap with the skeletal remains of a long-passed creature.

It was nearly Clara's favourite room in the house but right now it was the bedroom because Henry had been in it and had placed the roses there, and it was where she imagined their feet touching every night.

After Rachel had finished her work, they had all had afternoon tea together, set up by Rachel again, who had put out the cakes and cups and saucers and they all had a lovely time. Pansy had declared the Rabbit Cakes yummy and not just for rabbits.

Henry had asked Rachel about schools. Pansy had looked at him in shock and then choked on the cake until Clara had patted her back until it passed.

School? Was he staying? God, she could hardly bear to think about what that meant. Why did he want to stay? How long would he stay? So many questions but gosh, she had a huge crush on him.

Nothing had changed between them but he was in her thoughts all the time.

And Rachel. She was in her thoughts too but in a different way. The girl she met the night of the accident was not the girl who excitedly showed her where the mugs and tea were kept close to the kettle.

Rachel rode her bicycle home and Pansy had waved from the laneway until Rachel was out of sight, and Clara and Pansy went back inside to tidy up.

Henry's face peered through the door. 'Hi, you want to bring the pies to the van for dinner later?' he asked.

'Love to, what time?' Clara smiled at him. God, she wanted to kiss that mouth.

Henry nodded. 'Six-ish? I need to have a shower.'

Don't even think about him in the shower, she told herself.

'Your van has everything, doesn't it, even a shower?' Clara wiped her hands on the tea towel that Rachel had hung on the hook next to the dish rack.

'Nearly everything,' he said, and she wanted to ask what it didn't have but she knew she was blushing.

'Do you promise not to storm out again?' he asked.

'I promise,' she said, shaking her head. 'I am sorry about that. I was thinking about something else at the time and misunderstood what you were saying.'

'Then tell me about it at dinner?'

'I will try.'

She took a bath in the claw-foot bath. She lay in the foamy bubbles and washed the gardening dirt and sweat away then dressed with more care than usual. So far Henry had only seen her in jeans and some horrible sweatpants that she had been gardening in today.

The air was still warm, almost muggy, so she slipped into a red sundress that she had once worn on holiday in Spain with Giles and Judy. She wondered now if that was where the affair had started. She had food poisoning and told them to enjoy the time together while she was sick in the room for three days. It was after those few days things had changed. Where once her boyfriend and best friend had seemed to hate each other, then they had private jokes and a need to say Spanish words as though they were in an Almodóvar movie.

Then three months later the traitors were holding hands while Clara set fire to the dinner table and threw a breadstick at Giles's head.

And then he had the nerve to text her. It made her furious to think about and she sprayed extra perfume and put on a slick of red lipstick as a sort of revenge moment.

Too much? She wondered as she looked in the tiny bathroom mirror.

Who cares? she heard her mum's voice in her head. *Who cares if the boys like you? Who cares if you want to wear the pink stockings and red shoes? You be you, Clara Maxwell.* When did she forget how to be herself? She knew when and she didn't want to remember. Only for a short time had she been herself when she was a child. That was when they left in the night, her mother with two suitcases and her father passed out on the floor.

Clara pushed the memories away and went downstairs

and out of the cottage. Henry's van was lit up and the door was open.

He was leaning against the door as Pansy was skipping in the summer twilight, singing a rhyme as she jumped the rope.

'Robin Hood, dressed so good, got as many kisses as he could. How many kisses did he get?'

She started to count as she jumped the rope.

'One, two, three, four.'

Clara looked at Henry who was smiling at Pansy.

'Henry Garnett, wish he'd stay, he could take as many kisses as he may,' she whispered to herself.

'Clara, watch me skip,' called Pansy.

Clara saw Henry look up at her and his eyes sweep over her in the sundress. She held it out and did a small curtsey, knowing she was blushing.

He did a silly bow but she didn't feel it was too much; it was just enough. He was more than enough.

She walked towards Pansy, clapping her as she made it to ten without stopping and then starting again.

It was thirty-six steps to Henry's van – she counted. She smiled as she looked up at him.

She wasn't going to excuse the dress or try and make it less than it was.

She hated when women made excuses for looking nice. She never heard men do the same. 'I just felt like dressing up tonight. No reason other than needing to remember I like nice dresses.'

'That dress suits you,' he said.

'Thank you,' said Clara, feeling a knot of pleasure in her stomach.

'Clara, watch me,' demanded Pansy. So, she watched as Pansy struggled with the rope, flicking it over her head.

The close proximity of Henry made her skin burn with need and she wondered if she was just projecting onto the first single man since Piles or if she was really as into Henry as her body was telling her right now.

'Wine?' asked Henry and she heard his throat catch.

'Yes please.' Henry almost automatically handed her a glass.

'The service is wonderful here.' She laughed, turning her head to him, over her shoulder.

Henry laughed back but seemed flustered. Was she flirting? Was it too much?

He was hired to fix her cottage, not to take her to bed, she reminded herself.

Pansy walked towards them, panting dramatically, 'I am knackered from that skipping,' she said.

'Come inside and you can have a sit-down while I run a bath for Miss Foulmouth.'

'You have a bath?' Clara shook her head. 'This van is like Mary Poppins's bag. It seems to have more room in it than meets the eye.'

'Come and see,' said Henry. She went inside and behind a nondescript-looking door, was a little bathroom complete with a half-sized claw-foot bath, and subway tiles. Ferns swung from macramé holders and a basket of bath toys was next to a sink and a toilet.

'There is everything here, isn't there?' Clara looked in amazement at the quality of the workmanship on the panelling of the walls and the tiling; even the macramé was beautifully done.

'Nearly everything,' said Henry as he turned on the bath and put in some rose-scented bubble liquid.

'Where is the water coming from?' she asked.

'I have a water tank on top and a small water heater,' he said, as his hand stirred up the bubbles as the tub quickly filled.

'Pansy,' he called and she came running.

'Go away, I'm going to be in the bath,' she said, shoving a laughing Clara out of the way.

Clara waited in the van, adjusting her dress and trying to be casual. Why was she treating this like a date? It was just a simple early dinner with a man and his kid, nothing more.

Henry came into the space and sat opposite her and raised his glass. 'To Acorn Cottage and its beautiful and clever owner, Clara Maxwell. May you find exactly what you want in this lovely spot of the world, and may you find the peace you need in your mind and forgiveness in your heart.'

Clara raised her glass to his and they touched them and then sipped the wine.

'Thank you,' she said and, from that moment, Clara wondered if Henry would ever find someone to share his life with. It seemed an enormous waste to have him all alone in the world.

19

Clara – aged 13

The first time she and Mum left was after Dad had hit Clara. It was an accident, he said. She'd got in the way. But Clara had screamed at him that he shouldn't have been hitting anyone and this time he hit her on purpose. A smack across the face that spun her into the wall and while she was clutching the side of her head, he grabbed Mum by the throat and held her up against the wall.

'Never, ever argue with me about money. I decide where it goes. I make it, you don't. Understand?'

Clara had seen Mum nod, while gasping for breath. Dad had stopped her from working, even though they didn't have enough money. He said the money wasn't worth it and she needed to do a better job around the house.

Now he was talking about Clara leaving school in a few years and working to help around the house.

After his suggestion, Mum had a look on her face that Clara hadn't seen before. For the past few months, Mum had been doing more ironing than usual for the ladies up the road. But Clara knew not to say anything and Dad was so stupid he didn't realise she was being paid.

She had seen Mum put the money into a coffee tin and

bury it around the side of the house and again, Clara knew not to say anything.

And one night, when Dad was out at the pub, and Clara was doing her homework, Mum came to her with two suitcases packed. She had told Clara she had only ever used the suitcases once before, on her honeymoon with Dad to the seaside. Now she was using them again.

'Get your school things – we're going,' said Mum.

Clara could see the fading yellow bruise on her mum's neck. Last time Dad had held her against the wall, she had blacked out and that's when Clara knew she hated her father.

Clara swept her things into her bag and ran into her room and saw it was cleared out of nearly everything personal and she came out to Mum again, excited and scared about what Mum was finally doing for them. For herself most of all.

'Your grandmother's house,' said Mum, not looking at Clara.

'My grandmother?'

Clara had never heard she had a grandmother, and she wondered what she was like but knew not to ask any questions yet.

Knowing when to speak and when not to speak was a skill that Clara had learned from her father. And as they shut the door behind them, Clara crossed her fingers that Dad wouldn't come home from the pub early and see them at the bus stop.

20

The next morning, Henry woke earlier than usual. He was looking forward to the work ahead for the day. New roofing reed was coming and then he, Clara and Pansy were travelling into Chippenham to look for bookshelves and get paint samples for the inside and outside of the cottage. But most of all, he was looking forward to seeing Clara.

She had made him laugh so much over dinner, telling stories of loan applications for bizarre things at the bank she used to work at. She had coloured in a fairy book with Pansy and took Pansy's bossy instruction about which colours to put where with good grace. And she looked so beautiful in her red dress with her dark hair that shone under the lamplight.

The strap of her dress fell from her shoulders periodically and it was all he could do not to gently lift it back, wanting to feel her skin with his fingers.

But he didn't. He kept himself busy, serving, cleaning, pottering and when Pansy was in bed, they took their wine outside with his outdoor chairs and sat in the semidarkness telling stories about themselves.

He lay back in his bed now, remembering her closeness to him, the stars bright above them.

He had told her about Naomi's death. She listened. She asked questions about Naomi people had never asked him.

What was her favourite film? Who did she hate? What was she most grateful for in life?

He knew all the answers.

The Great Race.

People who used religion as an excuse for being cruel to others.

She was most grateful her Mum had time to say goodbye instead of her death being swift and sudden, leaving loved ones bewildered and in shock.

He told her he thought he would die when Naomi died but the morning after she died, Pansy asked for pancakes and he made them because there was no one else and they ate pancakes and got on with living because that's what Naomi would have wanted.

And she told him about her mum.

She was eleven when they left the first time. The beatings and drinking were too much. Then she was thirteen when they left again. And then fourteen. And then finally they left for good when she was fifteen.

Her mother had to learn how to do everything again as Clara's father had controlled the money, the food, even what to wear.

No wonder Clara felt compelled to help Rachel escape her mother.

Henry showered and then changed into his work clothes and checked his phone.

Pansy is here, eating rabbit cake for breakfast.

He laughed and walked over to the cottage. He found Clara and Pansy sitting in their pyjamas eating cake and drinking tea.

'Have a look at you two,' he said. 'You look like absolute old women nattering and too lazy to get dressed.'

Pansy ignored him, but he noticed Clara blushed. She looked gorgeous in her flowery PJs and messy hair.

Stop, Henry, he reminded himself. *She's a client. You're lonely, that's all. Having a crush on your boss isn't going to help anything, especially when it's not reciprocated.*

He hadn't dated at all since Naomi had died, it wasn't even a consideration, but Clara made him wonder if he was ready. Except he didn't want to date anyone. He just wanted to kiss Clara. He realised she was all he thought about now, which was a nice change but it made him feel like a teenager again and he hadn't enjoyed his teen years once, so he definitely didn't want to go through it again.

'What time are we heading off?' asked Clara, pouring him tea and pushing a mug reading *Keep Calm and STFU* at him.

'When you're ready,' he said, sitting down and taking some cake and raising his mug in a toast with Pansy.

'What does your mug say?' asked Pansy.

'God, sorry, I shouldn't have given you that,' said Clara.

Henry glanced at the cup and then at Pansy, 'Keep calm and eat your crusts.'

'It does not,' said Pansy, looking at him suspiciously.

'It does so,' said Henry.

Clara laughed. 'I'm going to get changed.' Clara left the kitchen and he heard her running upstairs.

Clara seemed to rush everywhere. She had more energy

than Pansy at times, and never complained about tiredness. He wasn't sure if her energy was contagious but he felt alive when he was around her, more alive than he had felt since Naomi died.

Perhaps part of him died with Naomi but with Clara a new part of himself had been born. He was excited and laughed more easily and was always thinking about the next day instead of getting through the current one.

He washed up the teacups and hummed a song he wasn't sure how he knew or what the name of it was.

'If you marry Clara, then I can stay here and go to school and we can get a dog,' said Pansy leaning on her hands and peering at him.

'Oh really?' He laughed. 'Clara might have other ideas.'

'I don't think so,' said Pansy. 'She asks a lot of questions about you.'

'Does she?' Henry felt pleased and confused and like that dammed teenager again.

'What sort of questions?' He tried to play it cool.

'About our house and about me going to school and about if you have a girlfriend and if you liked medium steak or something.'

Henry tried to stifle a laugh and failed.

'Maybe she's just trying to get to know me through you – I mean you know me better than anyone.'

'I wasn't sure if you liked steak, but I told her you like sausages and so do I. I think I will have to know you better also, Daddy.'

He looked at his serious little daughter and he was filled with such love for her. He leaned down and kissed her curly head.

'That's okay, we have plenty of time to get to know each other. Now, go and get dressed and we'll head off for the day.'

Pansy ran out to the van while he finished the dishes and washed them and put them in the drying rack.

'I'm ready,' he heard, and turned to see Clara in jeans and a white shirt and pink blazer. She put a foot up to show her silver sneakers. 'I have my sensible footwear on, so we can go traipsing through the shops.'

'Excellent,' he said, feeling awkward. 'I did the dishes.' Why did he say that? Was he wanting praise? What a stupid thing to say. *She can see you did the dishes, you idiot.*

'Thank you,' Clara said. They stared at each other for a long moment.

'Clara,' he began to say.

'Yes?' she answered quickly, almost breathlessly.

'I'm ready,' yelled Pansy, jumping through the door in a party dress, gumboots and fairy wings.

'Perfect shopping attire,' said Clara as she held Pansy's hand and twirled her. 'Let's go and show Chippenham how the cool people dress for shopping.'

The drive to Chippenham was lovely. Pansy chatted in the car and then fell asleep, and he and Clara sat in comfortable silence, occasionally commenting on a cottage they passed or a farm or a lovely view. The countryside seemed greener and brighter than Henry had remembered it before.

The music on the radio played softly and sometimes he and Clara would sing along as though to themselves but not really. They could hear each other and there was no self-consciousness. They were just in complete unison.

When they arrived in Chippenham, Henry took them straight to the paint shop.

'We need to find the perfect pink for the outside,' he said. He was holding Pansy, who was still dozing, her head on his shoulder.

Clara picked up a selection of pink cards. He stood close to her, as she shuffled through them. He could feel her shoulder against his arm and it made his heart beat faster.

She leaned against him slightly or was he imagining it? He wasn't sure. Pansy was heavy in his arms, but he couldn't put her down. She was anchoring him, because being this close to Clara made him feel like he would float away.

'Kiss me,' he heard Clara say and he felt dizzy.

'Sorry?' he said to her.

'The paint, this colour, it's called Kiss Me. Do you like it?' she asked.

'Perfect,' he said trying to get his thoughts straight. 'Absolutely perfect.'

And he wondered why he felt like he was cheating on Naomi.

21

Once Rachel had hated the bakery and the tearooms, seeing them as a prison from which she couldn't escape. Mother was the warden and the daily baking was a punishment, but now Rachel was ready to go earlier than ever and she had so much energy and so many ideas.

Now the bakery opened at eight in the morning and the tearooms at ten, because Clara and Henry said people wanted morning tea and an early lunch and they were right. It was only half past nine and the bakery was humming with customers wanting their fill of Rachel's baked items.

Today she had filled the glass cabinet with fondant fancies iced like a deck of major arcana Tarot cards that Tassie McIver had left for her, thinking she might like them.

Rachel didn't understand the cards but she liked the drawings on them: the Sun, the Moon, the Lovers, Justice, The Chariot.

It was fun to ice them when she was awake before the sun was up. Joe called in with some lovely lambs' kidneys and she showed him her work.

'That's very clever – you could be an artist,' he said seriously. He looked at Rachel as though she truly was an artist and she knew she blushed at his words.

It had been so long since Rachel had received a compliment she wasn't sure what to say but somewhere she remembered Tassie McIver telling her years before to not brush away good energy and to say thank you because if you disagreed with the person, they might think you think them stupid.

Rachel had said thank you and had given him the fancy with The World iced on the front, which he was very chuffed about. He seemed to turn red as he looked at it closely.

'She's naked,' he said almost to himself.

Rachel hadn't meant anything by giving him the one with the naked woman on the front but she wondered if she should have given him The Fool instead but that would be taken the wrong way also.

'I remember at school you were always good at art and things like that,' he said, and she noticed a blush on his thick neck.

'You remember me from school?'

Joe had been kind to her but then it seemed Joe was kind to everyone. He always said 'Hi', and always opened the door if they arrived at the same time at school.

'I do. I remember you very well.'

Rachel frowned. 'You've been coming here for years. Why didn't you say anything before?'

'Your mum didn't make it much of a social visit,' he said wryly.

Rachel nodded slowly, thinking of all the times her mother scared people away from her and the bakery itself. Her customer service wasn't a strong feature of the Merryknowe Bakery and Tearooms.

'I actually have something of yours, from school,' he said, not looking her in the eye.

'What?' Rachel felt nervous at what was to come.

'My mum bought it from the art exhibition they had; you put in a drawing of a wedding cake. She loved it, said it was the prettiest thing she had ever seen. We didn't have much art at home but she loved that. Got a frame from Chippenham and had it on the wall of her bedroom. She said she could always see something new in it every time she looked at it.'

Rachel gasped at the memory of the drawing. She had not thought about it since she left school. There were a few pieces bought by parents but Mother told her no one wanted her piece, and she had already left by the time the exhibition was on. She never knew what happened to it, but she remembered drawing it now.

A painstaking drawing of a six-tiered wedding cake, each tier the theme of a love story. The couple meeting in a park with their dogs. Their first date at a movie, a dinner and a dance, then the proposal and finally topped with the wedding.

She had hand-drawn it in ink and then filled it with watercolours. To know Joe still had it on his family home wall was astonishing.

'That's amazing your mum loved it so much,' she said, feeling shy.

'We all love it, me and Alice, my sister.'

'I remember Alice,' said Rachel. 'How is she?'

'Looking for a part-time job over the holidays, so if you need any help, she's great with change and friendly with customers.'

'That would be perfect. Can she come by tomorrow?' asked Rachel.

Imagining her mother having a pink fit at Rachel hiring someone made her smile. The phone rang just then. Rachel picked it up and cheerily answered.

'Merryknowe Bakery and Tearooms, can I help you?'

'Is this Rachel Brown?' asked the person on the other end of the phone. She could hear the sound of a tannoy announcing a Code Blue in Ward 3 South, and cold water ran through her veins.

Rachel knew who it was as soon as they asked.

'No, she's busy in the bakery – I work with her. Can I take a message?'

'Can you tell her that her mother is hoping she will come and see her soon and that she needs a few things from home?'

'I will,' lied Rachel and she hung up the phone.

Joe looked at her, his brow furrowed. 'Who were they after? I thought you were the only one here?'

Rachel paused. 'Someone for Mum, and I didn't want to have to explain.'

Joe nodded, seemingly in understanding.

'See you tomorrow when I drop Alice off?'

She nodded, waved goodbye to him and pushed her mother from her mind.

It had been over a week since the accident and Rachel had never felt happier. The bakery had new cakes every day, and people in the village even asked her what she had planned for the day, so they could get in quick for the jam-filled sponges and hummingbird cakes.

Joe had brought her rabbit and chicken and beef,

which she had turned into wonderful pies. She had paid him on time, which he was very grateful for as apparently her mother had always quibbled over the bills and then paid late.

But Rachel would never pay late. She would never do anything her mother had done. It was now her life purpose to not be anything like her mother.

Instead she wanted to be like Clara. Clara with her chic haircut and easy laughter. Maybe she would get her hair cut today. She had the money and she could borrow Mother's car. She hadn't driven it often but she knew how and thought she would probably be more confident without Mother criticising her constantly from the passenger seat.

Rachel looked up the name of a hairdresser in the next village. She didn't want to go to one she knew Mother had visited. Instead she chose one with a European-sounding name that she knew would be too expensive for Mother to attend, and besides, she didn't like anything that she couldn't pronounce, which is why she refused to allow Rachel to make any French pastries.

But today Rachel had made *millefeuille* with raspberries and a dusting of chocolate and they had sold faster than any of the other items on the shelf, and she had put up the price.

Tomorrow she was planning on making *nonnettes*, a French gingerbread, to go with the coffee she had ordered, and she would make it a spiced combination for the coming of autumn in a few weeks.

Rachel finished the afternoon and considered her transport options again. She had a driving licence but Mother rarely let her drive, insisting she was too stupid to understand the road rules. But it was too far to ride her bicycle, and besides, what was the point of having a driving licence and car and not using them?

Rachel made her decision and carefully drove the car out of the garage, checking both ways before she turned onto the road. She had the day's takings in her purse and she was ready for a new-look Rachel.

Driving carefully and exactly on the speed limit to Chippenham, she even managed to parallel park outside the salon, something Mother told her she wouldn't be able to do successfully. But she had done it easily for her driving test; she just couldn't seem to do it when she was in the car with her. Mother made her nervous whenever she tried anything, from driving to baking new cake recipes, to wearing brightly coloured jumpers.

Rachel stood outside and looked at the salon, all white and crisp with elegant writing on the window reading *Belle de Coiffeur*.

She was ready for the new Rachel and she took a deep breath and pushed open the door to the shop.

The salon was warm and busy with a girl on the phone at the front desk, who tapped away at a computer with nails that seemed far too long for the task at hand.

She looked at Rachel. 'Can I help you?' But she was friendly and didn't make Rachel feel small, which seemed to be very easy for some.

'I'm Rachel Brown. I'm here for a four o'clock?'

Every part of Rachel wanted to run away but she stood still, determined to follow through. She had never been to a hair salon before. Her mother had always cut her hair before.

'Come through, Rachel,' said the girl, and she stopped by a series of hooks and held out some sort of kimono wrap. 'Pop this on.' Rachel put her bag between her knees and slipped her arms in the jacket and the girl tied it firmly at Rachel's waist.

It was such a simple gesture but it made Rachel feel secure as she was led to a comfortable-looking chair.

She sat down and the girl left briefly and returned with a stack of magazines, all with bright colours and celebrities on the front.

'Coffee? Tea? Champagne? Water?' the girl asked.

Rachel tried to think. 'Water?'

The girl brought her back sparkling water in a green bottle with a label in Italian and in it was a red and white paper straw that reminded her of her dad.

She hadn't seen one like this since they used to go to the cafe before he died and she would order her a lime spider and himself a malted milkshake.

She touched the straw and sipped the cold water that tingled her tongue.

'Rachel?' A man stood behind her and smiled and he was so handsome she was lost for words – so she merely nodded instead. He was tall and swarthy and slim-hipped like a pirate turned musician.

'I'm Sean. Now what did you want me to do today?'

He picked up her limp hair and let it run through his fingers and she thought she might die of pleasure.

'I don't know, I just don't want to look like me anymore,' she heard herself saying.

'Who do you want to look like then?' He laughed but not unkindly.

'I don't know, I just don't think I like this and want to look like a better version of me.'

Sean nodded and beckoned to another girl.

'Take Rachel for a wash and head massage and use the volume treatment.'

Rachel was directed to the basin where she lay down on the recliner and looked up and saw a television on the ceiling, playing videos of models walking the catwalk in heels and then behind the scenes of hair and makeup.

It was fascinating, she thought as she watched a woman have tiny diamond stickers placed along her cheekbones.

The girl had tucked a towel around her neck and soon warm water ran over her head. The touch was gentle and Rachel felt her eyes closing. She wanted to watch the models but the girl was now massaging her head and it was better than anything she had ever felt.

She felt tears fall from her eyes and slide down into her ears, which tickled, but her hands were trapped under her kimono and cape, so she let them be.

She couldn't remember if she had been touched tenderly since her dad had died. He used to hug her when she was small but that was all she could remember.

It was as though the girl now running her hands through her wet hair had unblocked her need for touch.

'Are you okay?' asked the girl very softly in her ear.

'I am,' choked Rachel.

She wasn't sure what happened after but somehow she was in her comfortable chair and the girl was combing out her wet hair very gently and then Sean was behind her and the girl whispered something to him. Sean smiled at her in the mirror.

'Are you ready, Rachel?' he asked.

'For what?'

'To become yourself.'

22

The radio played as Clara pushed the roller in time to the music, and back and forth in the tray, just as Henry had showed her. She had to get enough paint on it but not too much and then she lifted it to the wall.

The interior paint was called Frangipane, which she thought Rachel would like, and as she started to paint the wall in the hallway, she felt incredibly pleased with the new fresh look. She worked happily, not thinking about anything as she covered the old walls of the cottage.

I wonder what this cottage has seen, thought Clara as she worked. Two hundred years of births and deaths and marriages and fights and love and hate and everything in between. Life came down to these moments, and this was a beautiful moment.

She could hear Henry on the roof, putting up the new reeds, while Pansy was sitting at the kitchen table playing with play dough that Henry had made in the microwave and had coloured a very bright red.

In one of the kitchen drawers, the previous tenant had left scone cutters and some shapes for gingerbread people, which was what Pansy was making now, while she sang little songs to herself about the red people and how they liked to only eat cakes and red wine.

It was a sense of peace Clara hadn't felt before. She wasn't trying to keep Giles happy, or Judy, or the people at the bank, or even her mum, she was just painting a wall.

Henry walked in through the front door. 'Looks nice – don't forget to cut in at the edges with the brush.'

Clara poked her tongue out at him. 'Don't forget to wear your bossy boots.'

'But I'm always wearing them.'

Clara made a face at him and went back to the painting task.

Something had shifted in the past few days, since the trip to find paint and bookshelves, which they had successfully done.

There was a lightness, maybe even a flirtation… or was that just Clara flirting? It had been a long time since she had flirted and she wasn't very good at it when she last tried, so she wondered if it was even registering with Henry.

She was eating with Henry and Pansy every night, and it was getting harder to leave to return to her cold bedroom and lie in bed alone.

She missed them both when she wasn't with them. The way Pansy would come and talk to her and hold her face sometimes when she needed to make a point.

She missed the way Henry laughed at her jokes and didn't frown when she used a swear word, making sure to never use one in front of Pansy.

And she missed the conversation. She and Henry could have talked about everything and anything forever she thought. Trying not to compare him to Piles was a daily battle and one she always lost.

It was as though she was more herself than she had ever been and yet she was so far removed from her old life.

Did anyone miss her back in London? Judy hadn't called, not that she wanted to think about her anymore.

Judy was her past, Giles was her past but were Henry and Pansy her future?

She kept painting as Henry was talking to Pansy in the kitchen. The last time she had painted was with her mum when they left her father for the last time. Her grandmother had said Clara could paint her new bedroom, and Clara had insisted on a buttercup-yellow feature wall, like she had seen in a magazine. So, she said she would paint it but then, like most things, she lost interest and her mum had to finish it off.

That was before that awful night. The last time she saw her father.

She shivered as Henry came back into the hallway. 'You're cold? It will be warmer when I get the insulation into the roof, I promise.'

'It's okay, just a shiver.'

'Someone walking over your grave, huh?' Henry laughed as he left to go back to the roof.

Pansy walked into the hallway, her hands filled with play dough. 'Daddy said I can go to school next week.' Her little face looked both pleased and worried.

'Oh wow, Pansy, that's amazing. You're going to love it. I loved school.'

'Daddy said he will sign me up tomorrow. And I can have ribbons for my hair.'

'Ribbons are a must. I wonder what colour the uniform is?'

'Daddy?' Pansy ran outside and Clara put down the paint roller and followed her. 'Daddy? What colour is the uniform?'

'I don't know,' said Henry. 'Clara, I was going to ask if we can use your address for the mail? Just until we get sorted.'

Clara felt like doing a cartwheel similar to the one that Pansy was attempting.

'Of course, anything you need,' she said trying to be casual as she wandered back inside and then in the solitude of the hallway she did a little happy dance.

He was staying. Pansy was going to school. He wanted to use her address. God, it was so exciting.

The sound of her phone ringing interrupted her solo dance fest and she fished it from her handbag and answered.

'Hello? This is Clara.'

'Clara Maxwell?'

'Yes?'

'You brought in Moira Brown last week… umm on Tuesday evening last?'

'Yes, I did, can I help?'

Clara was looking at the wall, thinking how much better it was looking. It really brightened the area… or was that because she was glowing with happiness at the thought Henry and Pansy were staying forever?

'We are trying to get on to her daughter, Rachel Brown. We have left several messages but she isn't returning our calls and we have asked for several things to be dropped off for Mrs Brown but she hasn't visited either.'

Clara paused.

'Let me speak to Rachel and find out what's happening, okay?'

'Mrs Brown has had major surgery and is very alone and worried about her daughter. She is facing a lengthy recovery, at least three months in rehabilitation, and then the occupational therapist will have to come and assess the house to see what modifications will have to be made.'

'She lives above a bakery,' said Clara. 'There are stairs – the stairs she fell down.'

'That's not for me to assess. That will be the rehab team's job when Mrs Brown is ready to be released.'

Clara thought for a moment. 'Let me talk to Mrs Brown's daughter and I'll let you know the next steps.'

'Thank you, Mrs Brown will be relieved to hear you are helping.'

Clara put down the phone and picked up the roller.

She knew Mrs Brown was hard work but how bad was it if Rachel refused to even take calls from the hospital?

She would head to the bakery tomorrow and find out exactly what was happening, but in the meantime, she needed to finish the painting in the hallway and then she was planning on cooking in the Aga for the first time. A roast chicken with all the trimmings and a lemon self-saucing pudding with cream. It was exactly what Granny used to make before everything happened, and she wanted to make Pansy feel like she had felt as a child when she was at her granny's house. Warm, safe, cosy and loved.

She never wanted Pansy to feel fear like she had felt as a child and it was then she realised she loved the little girl. She wondered if she loved Pansy like she was her own daughter, would she fall in love with Henry?

Henry knocked on the doorframe.

'You need a hand with anything before I go back to the

van to shower? Pansy wants to stay here till dinner but if that's too much, let me know and I can lock her in a cage, also known as the van.'

He smiled at her and she felt herself smile back. Oh, all bets were off, there was no doubt she would fall in love with Henry Garnett. It was hurtling at her like a freight train and she felt like she was tied to the tracks and there wasn't a single thing she could do about it.

23

The sun streamed into Clara's curtainless windows and she stretched, wondering if Henry was awake. He seemed to be the first thing she thought of and the last when she was in bed. The fantasies went from basic domestic ones where they cooked and chatted about plans for the day, to intense passionate intimacy that made her blush to think about when she was around him.

All this time she'd thought she wasn't into sex but in fact, she realised, she had never felt real desire. Nine years of average sex and not saying what you need in life or in bed will do that to you.

But she felt it now when she was around Henry. The ache in every part of her body, needing to be touched, filled, sated.

If she could rate her favourite things about Henry, it would be his arms, his hands, his thighs, his legs, his forearms, his smile. Oh, it was everything. She climbed out of bed, and wandered to the window to peer at the van.

The door of the van was open and Henry came to the door, a tea mug in hand. She could see the steam rising from it. He looked up at her window and smiled and waved.

Dammit, she thought. Now she looked like a creeper, spying

on him in her ugly Justin Bieber T-shirt that Judy had given her as a joke present. She didn't have a washing machine and was running out of clothes and refused to ask Henry if she could wash her knickers in his machine, so to speak.

He had offered at dinner when she mentioned it in passing but she refused his help because she already had taken too much from him and washing was so intimate.

Pulling on jeans and a sweater with tiny ribbon bows in different colours sewn onto it that her mother had given her before she died, and one she had never worn because of those tiny bows, she dashed downstairs and outside.

'I need to go to the village and see Rachel about her mum, and then I need to buy a washing machine.'

'Cup of tea for your troubles?' He stepped back into the van and handed her a mug.

'You are almost perfect, you know,' she said as she took a sip of the strong tea at perfect drinking temperature.

'Oh? What would make me perfect?'

She wondered if this was him flirting. Clara tried to think of a flaw but couldn't. 'I don't know but you are pretty clever at things and you know how I like my tea.'

'Before you get a washing machine, you'll need a plumber as you don't have any taps for a machine.'

'Oh God, do you know a plumber?'

'I do.' He nodded. 'I can call them and see if they're around.'

'That's wonderful, thank you.' They sipped their tea in comfortable silence.

'It's so peaceful here.' She looked up at the trees and their green canopy.

Pansy popped her head out, around her father's back.

'Can I come and see Rachel?'

'Not today, darling, we're heading up to see about school, remember?' Henry said to her.

Pansy disappeared singing a rhyme about school and Clara smiled at him.

'So... school? Does this mean you're staying in Merryknowe for a while?' she asked carefully, not wanting to tread on any toes or fragile feelings. She knew this was a big deal to Henry and she also knew it would be arrogant to think it had anything to do with her.

Henry shrugged. 'For the time being. There is a lot to do on the cottage and she's going to be behind if I don't start her soon.'

'She will love it,' said Clara.

'I hope so.'

They looked at each other. A thousand things came into Clara's head that she wanted to say to him, but instead she said, 'I blocked Piles.'

Henry raised his eyebrows. 'Sorry?'

'Piles, I blocked him; he rang me and said he missed me and I blocked him.'

Henry started to laugh. 'Piles?'

'Oh, it's Giles but he's such a pain in the arse I called him Piles.'

Henry laughed even harder.

'And I blocked him, because I don't love him anymore. Not sure I ever did.'

'Okay, that's good. A wise decision,' said Henry nodding and wiping his eyes.

Clara felt her cheeks turn hot and she handed back the tea. 'Anyway. I need to dash.'

She ran back into the house and grabbed her phone and dialled the bakery.

'Rachel? Hi, can I come and see you? And can I bring my washing?'

She gathered her washing, which was rather a large amount, and dragged it out to the car in a moving bag.

'Do you need a hand?' Henry asked, as he was gathering the old reed from the roof from the garden and putting it in a pile on the outside of the fence.

'No, thank you,' said Clara, not looking at him. The words, 'I blocked Piles' rang in her ears. Seriously, she needed a muzzle when she was around Henry. She just said everything and nothing all at once.

'Where are you taking your washing?'

'To Rachel's. She said I can borrow her machine and dryer.'

'I would have done it for you,' he said. 'I have a machine.'

Clara looked up at him. 'I just said I blocked Piles. The last thing I need is my knickers in your machine. I mean I'm really overstepping boundaries here.'

'You are honestly the funniest person I have ever met.'

She sighed. 'That's the trouble. I don't try to be, I just think I don't have a filter.'

She opened the car door and pushed the box of clothes inside onto the back seat, using her bottom for the final push, and then got into the driver's seat.

'I don't think you're mad, I think you're fantastic, and you were right to block Piles. He sounds like a huge idiot to let you go.'

Clara felt butterflies migrate inside her and she gripped the steering wheel.

'Be careful, Henry, a girl might think you're giving her ideas.'

She turned on the ignition and backed out into the laneway and drove up towards the village.

Too much? Oh whatever, life was short and she really couldn't embarrass herself any further than she already had. She had a crush on Henry and like most crushes it would deflate when he did something stupid or wore a horrible hat or something. She just hoped it came soon before she was head over heels in love with him.

When Clara arrived, Rachel was serving in the bakery. Clara nearly didn't recognise her with a new haircut but it suited her so much. It was shorter and with layers that made her fine hair seem thicker, and showed off her lovely neck. It was so different that Clara felt her mouth drop open in surprise.

'You hate my hair,' Rachel stated, and touched it somewhat self-consciously.

'Not at all actually. It looks amazing. When did you get it done?'

'Yesterday,' said Rachel as she let Clara through the back door and showed her through the kitchen to the washing machine and dryer.

'I just wanted a change.'

Clara smiled at her. 'It's a lovely change. Really suits you.'

Rachel flushed pink with pleasure. 'Thank you.'

'You don't mind if I do some washing? I need a machine and Henry has to put taps in or something before I can get one.'

'Help yourself,' said Rachel as the bell on the door of the bakery rang and she rushed off to serve the customers.

Clara put on the first load of washing and went into the bakery where she saw Rachel buzzing around and customers waiting.

People were coming in the door and sitting at the tables. Clara saw how flustered Rachel was becoming as she tried to serve, use the till, bag items up and get to the people at the tables.

She looked around and saw an apron hanging on a hook. She pulled it on and tied it up behind her waist and stepped out next to Rachel.

'I'll do the tables; you do the serving here at the counter.'

Rachel looked up at her. 'Oh gosh, thank you. It's never been this busy. Joe's sister Alice is going to help me but she can't start till tomorrow.'

'It's okay, I'm here,' said Clara and she moved from table to table taking the orders for the coconut sponge, or the coffee cake, or the steak and kidney pies with chutney.

It was busy in the tearooms and bakery but while Clara worked, chatting to customers, helping Rachel behind the counter and warming up pies and serving generous slices of cake, she stopped thinking about anything else but work. She missed talking to people, she missed the business and she wondered if she could live in the cottage with no company and no real work besides the house and whatever she made of the garden.

After the final customer left, Rachel and Clara sat at one of the tables, eating the last pie and piece of coffee cake.

'Thank you for helping me today,' said Rachel, and she slid over a fifty-pound note.

Clara slid it back over the table. 'It was fun and it was interesting, but I don't need the money. Save it for Alice.'

'I know, but Mother always said we never needed help before so I'm unsure of the procedures.'

'I don't think your mother ever saw the place as busy as it was today. Hiring someone is good and it will help Alice and help you.'

Rachel was silent and Clara cleared her throat before speaking.

'The hospital rang me this morning about your mum.'

Rachel stayed silent.

'They said you haven't seen her yet.'

Rachel toyed with the fork on her plate.

'I don't judge you for not wanting to see her, Rachel, but you will have to make a decision about this, because she will return here eventually unless you make some hard decisions.'

Rachel looked up at Clara; her eyes were wide and her face pale.

'I can't see her again. This time without her has been lovely. I hate her but no one will understand. You're not supposed to hate your parents but I do. I hate her with everything I am. I wished she'd died the night she fell down the stairs.'

Clara took Rachel's thin hand in hers. 'I understand and I don't judge you. Just because she's your mother doesn't mean she was good enough for you to love unconditionally.'

Rachel frowned and pulled her hand away. 'I don't want to see her again.'

'I understand.'

'How? How can you understand?' Rachel glared at Clara.

'Because I had a father I hated. I hated him so much and it changed who I was. It changed me and I don't want you to have that pain.'

They were silent for a while.

'So, what do you want to do about your mum?' Clara asked.

'I don't know, I can't think about it. I have to clean up and get the orders in to Joe for the meat tomorrow. I was thinking of making a curry pie. That would be popular, don't you think?'

Clara could see a faraway look in Rachel's eyes. She knew that look. It was the look of disassociating from the situation. It was too much for Rachel to think about and Clara understood that pain. She finished another load of washing and drying, and helped Rachel clean up, sweeping and mopping the floor. There was only one thing to do: she would go and visit Mrs Brown and see if she couldn't solve this whole mess herself.

24

Rachel had spent years trying to understand her mother's hatred of her. It didn't matter what she did, it was wrong in her mother's eyes, and eventually Rachel drew further into herself until she felt like a little turtle, peeking out for signs of danger and then hiding away when her mother was around.

But if you stayed hidden long enough, you forgot how to be in the world. You forgot how to make conversation, or even the sound of your own voice. If it wasn't for the shop, Rachel would never have spoken to anyone besides her mother.

She couldn't remember having friends when she was at school, but she also couldn't remember being bullied or shunned. She was mostly overlooked in life, a shadow of a girl who should have been going to parties, having sleepovers, trying on her best friend's clothes and wearing makeup and kissing boys.

Instead she was a slave to the bakery, told to leave school by her mother because she wasn't smart enough, even though Rachel's home economics teacher said she was creative and could make anything in the kitchen and with the sewing machine.

Mother told her that home economics was a useless skill but that was all she did in the bakery. Measuring, budgeting, planning, mending the curtains on the windows because Mother wouldn't pay for new ones.

But Rachel's inner life was rich and filled with imaginary friends, dancing and perfumed nights with handsome men who vied for her kisses and more.

When her face stung from a slap or her upper arm ached from the bruising, she would lie in her bed and dream up intricately detailed scenarios where she would find herself being wooed and loved beyond anything she had ever imagined. In her imagination was a wardrobe of delicate and beautiful dresses, sexy outfits, demure outfits, and a perfect figure. She would turn heads when she walked into a room, and would charm women and men with her kindness and warm wit.

In her dreams, she was exactly what Clara was in real life.

Rachel opened the back door of the bakery, to take the rubbish out as Joe the butcher's van pulled up.

'Hello,' he said, jumping down and rushing to her, taking the rubbish bag from her hands and easily throwing it into the bin.

'Hi,' said Rachel, wondering why he was there. Had she ordered something and he'd forgotten to deliver it earlier?

'Good day?' he asked, shoving his hands into the pockets of his denim jacket. She was used to seeing him in his striped butcher's apron, which he always wore when delivering the meat. He looked less... She tried to think of the right word. Less butcherish, she decided, and much more handsome.

Joe was nice-looking, in his own way. Copper hair with

bright blue eyes, and while he wasn't tall he was strong-looking; he had a strong back and arms and thick thighs and neck.

Rachel tried to think of something to say when Joe spoke first.

'Alice said she likes working in the shop.'

'She's great with the customers,' Rachel said, meaning it. Alice was smiling and happy and exactly the sort of friend Rachel wished she'd had when she was at school.

Joe shuffled his feet.

'Do you want to go out sometime?' he asked.

'With Alice?' Rachel was confused.

Joe's face turned red. 'No, I mean me but if you want go out with Alice, I can ask her.'

Rachel took a moment to take in his words. 'Me?'

'Yes,' said Joe.

'Why?'

'What do you mean?' he asked.

'Why do you want to go out with me?'

Rachel wasn't testing him, she was genuinely curious. She knew she wasn't beautiful, or witty, or even interesting, so she wondered what he saw in her.

'Because I think we should be friends,' he said. 'There's not a lot of people around here our age – we should stick together.'

'Okay.'

At least he was honest and didn't pretend there was anything about her that was compelling.

'And because I like you. I don't know you very well but that's not because I didn't want to – your mum made it sort of hard to chat, you know?'

Oh, how she knew, but instead she just nodded. How much had her mother taken from her for all these past years?

'That would be nice – to go out,' she said.

'We can have an early pint and roast at the pub if you want?'

She thought for a moment. She was hungry and she hadn't eaten much today and someone else cooking sounded like a dream.

'I would like that very much,' she said, meaning it. 'I'll go and get changed.'

She glanced down at her work clothes. 'I can't wear this to the pub.'

'Why? You look fine,' he said. 'But if you want to get changed, then I'll wait.'

Rachel thought about her idea of what she should wear in her imaginary wardrobe. A dove-grey chiffon cocktail dress with satin shoes like she had seen an actress wear in an old movie once. It was so elegant and perfect. She didn't think she would be wearing some old pants and a flowered print shirt, and sneakers. But then, hunger and curiosity took over.

'Let me grab my keys,' she said. She ran inside, ignoring the ringing phone, and slammed the door behind her.

25

When Clara returned from Rachel's, Henry was talking to an older man outside the cottage. Clara dragged her washed and dried clothes in the large box from the back of the car and left them on the ground, as Henry came to her side.

'Let me get that,' he said as he touched her shoulder for just a second longer than what would be an accident.

His touch ran through her body and landed in her stomach again and then further down.

This was ridiculous, she thought. As she was about to speak he gestured to the older man.

'Michael, this is Clara Maxwell, the owner of the cottage.'

The man nodded. 'I put your taps in.'

'Sorry?' She looked at Henry for translation.

'The taps for the machine. He put them in the kitchen, so there is room for a machine.'

'Oh wonderful, thank you!' said Clara, meaning it. The idea of trekking into Rachel's to wash her clothes wasn't something she could foresee doing weekly.

The man turned, grunted and handed Clara a piece of paper, which she looked down and saw was a handwritten bill for his time and materials. He then walked to a truck that had *The Friendly Plumber* stencilled on the side.

'That's false advertising – he's about as friendly as Eeyore,' said Clara, pointing at the words as he drove past them.

Henry laughed. 'He warms up eventually.'

They walked into the cottage together.

'Do you want this in your room?' he asked, looking at the washing.

'Um, yes but I can take it.'

'No, it's too heavy, let me.'

Clara ran up the stairs ahead of him, trying to remember if she had made the bed and if there was any underwear lying on the floor.

She opened the door and kicked a sad bra that had seen better days under the bed.

'Just pop the box down on the floor,' she said casually.

'You don't have any drawers or a wardrobe,' he said, looking around.

'No. That's on the to-do list. Along with one thousand other things.' She swallowed, trying to not show her nerves at him being in her room.

Get it together, Clara. He's not here to undo your bodice and ravage you, although you wouldn't say no, but seriously, get it together, girl.

Henry was measuring an area of space with his hands and then walking in weird robotic-style steps and counting.

'Are you okay?' she asked.

'Just working out where I can put a chest of drawers and a wardrobe.'

'You don't have to worry about that,' she said.

'But you need somewhere to put your clothes.' He seemed genuinely confused.

'Henry, you are doing so much for me already, I can't ask you to manage my clothing situation.' In her head, she heard a pithy comment about him managing her undressing situation but didn't say it, even though she was thinking about how clever she was.

'If we were closer, I could but I respect your boundaries.' He pretended to tap a cigar from the corner of his mouth like Groucho Marx.

'What on earth are you saying, Henry?'

'Nothing, nothing.' She saw him turn ever so slightly red.

They both knew what the other was thinking, she realised, and she started to laugh and then so did he.

'God, there are so many double entendres going through my head.'

'Me too, sorry.'

'You want my knickers in your drawers,' she said, having trouble getting the words out when she was laughing so hard.

'I want to open your drawers,' he said wiping his eyes.

'I want you to manage my clothing situation, and by that I mean unclothing me.' She screamed with laughter.

'I want to kiss you,' Henry said suddenly.

The laughter stopped and they stood facing each other.

'I want you to kiss me,' she said, feeling the familiar ache in her body when she thought about him.

Henry moved towards her, and she met him halfway. Still not touching, her eyes searched his face.

'You're gorgeous,' he said.

'So are you,' she whispered.

'I think about you all the time, Clara.' His voice sounded tight and his words were rushed.

'I think about you too, Henry,' she whispered and moved closer to him.

He leaned down and she closed her eyes when she heard a huge crash and a scream.

'Pansy,' they both said then raced down the stairs and out of the cottage.

Henry went out the back door and Clara out the front door. They ran around the garden and saw Pansy standing pointing at the van.

'Oh fuck,' said Henry as he ran towards Pansy and scooped her up into his arms.

Clara looked at the van.

A huge branch from the oak tree above had fallen on the van, crushing the roof in the middle. It would have killed anyone who was sitting inside at the little booth where they had eaten the night before.

'Oh God,' said Clara. 'Oh my God! What if you were in there?' She started to cry and couldn't stop.

'But we weren't,' Henry said calmly as he walked to her side, Pansy still in his arms.

'But what if you were? Oh God.' Clara couldn't even fathom the disaster had they been inside the van.

'But we weren't,' said Henry again, putting his arm around her shoulders.

'And if we were, we would have smashed-in heads now,' said Pansy. 'So it's good we weren't inside and if we go inside we will have to wear a helmet like Rachel wears for her bicycle.'

Clara started to laugh through her tears. 'Yes, we will have to all wear helmets,' she said.

The three of them stood looking at the van, Henry's arm around Clara's shoulders and Pansy in his arms.

'Well, this puts us into a bit of a quandary,' he said.

'You will have to stay with me,' she said. She felt his hand on her shoulder tighten and then release.

'I don't expect you to do that,' he said.

'I know but you must. I have a spare room.' She said it as though it wasn't a big deal but it was a huge deal. It was a loaded gun and all Henry had to do was pull the trigger and he could be in her bed in a heartbeat.

Pansy jumped down from Henry's arms.

'I get to sleep in the cottage? In a house?' She ran inside and left Clara and Henry outside.

'I'll sleep in the spare room with Pansy,' he said. 'I'll try to grab the mattresses from the van, once I get the branch lifted off.'

His arm was still around her.

She didn't want him to move his arm away but he did and she felt the energy in her body dissipate.

'I'd better check on the van,' he said. 'I'll have to call the insurance company and take photos.'

Clara nodded. 'Sure, I'll go up and see how the room will work for you both.'

She turned to walk inside as Henry went to the van and opened the door and looked inside.

'Oh God,' he said. 'Oh Naomi.' He sat on the steps of the van and put his head in his hands.

Clara rushed over to see what he was looking at. She stepped around him and looked at the inside of the van. On the floor was a smashed wooden box and grey coarse sand was all over the floor.

Clara sat next to Henry on the step of the van and took his hand.

'I am so, so sorry,' she said. 'It's awful. Really.' She rubbed his back as he cried. He wept like she had never heard a man cry before, body-racking sobs that shook the van's steps as his head ended up on her lap. She stroked his hair until the sobs subsided, and she realised then that the crush had dissolved and had been replaced by a deep and real love, just like the love he still felt for his dead wife.

26

Clara brought Henry a plastic container from her kitchen, as he couldn't access any of the cupboards, and a dustpan and brush. He swept up Naomi and put her into the container with an orange lid with Clara's name written in marker underneath.

'I'm sorry, darling,' he said as he sealed the lid.

The beautiful box she had painted was shattered and beyond repair.

After he had cried, and Clara had held him, he realised he hadn't cried like that since the funeral but he was unsure if he felt any better. Some people claimed that crying helped you but now he felt embarrassed and guilty for keeping Naomi's remains in the van and not putting her to rest. And then when he was just about to kiss Clara the branch fell. She knew, he thought. Naomi knew and she'd dropped the branch on the van because she didn't want him to be with anyone. He knew it was ridiculous but he also half believed his superstition.

He and Naomi hadn't talked about what would happen to Henry after she died. They only talked about Pansy. About how to care for her, what she needed at that time but they weren't to know what she would need in the future because they were so focused on the moment. Time was running out and they needed to collect as many memories as they could.

He pushed down the lid on the container and walked to the cottage.

Clara and Pansy were talking in the kitchen and he put the container in the top cupboard above the stove.

'I'll try and get the mattresses out,' he said, not looking at Clara or Pansy. 'I've unhooked the van from the truck, so I can still get around. The insurance company have asked for photos, which I have taken, but I will need to get the tree off and try and get the roof pushed up so I can get all our things out.'

'Can we stay here, Daddy?' Pansy smiled up at her father. She looked so like her mother it took his breath away and he felt the tears threatening to fall again.

He looked up at Clara who seemed to be busy with the carrots she was peeling.

'Maybe I will try and get us a hotel.'

Pansy and Clara looked up at him.

'No,' cried Pansy. 'I want to stay with Clara.'

'Stay here, Henry, it's fine. It would be nice.' Clara seemed fine, maybe a little distant but she smiled at him warmly and he felt butterflies. Why was this all so confusing?

'I'm going to get the beds,' he said and walked outside to the van.

He managed to crawl into the space and drag out Pansy's mattress as it was smaller than his, along with her bedding, and he pulled it upstairs into the spare room.

Clara followed him up the stairs.

'I'll go and buy a spare bed tomorrow. I needed one anyway, so it's a good excuse.'

Henry sighed and turned to her. 'I am sorry about before.'

'Which part?' asked Clara but it wasn't combative. It was real and curious and he tried to work out which part he was sorry for.

'All of it,' he said.

Clara sighed and looked around the room. 'It's not perfect but it will do for now.'

'Clara, I am sorry I cried.'

She spun around to look at him. 'What on earth for? Why would you apologise for feeling emotion? You had a shock. Your wife's ashes were on the floor. It was awful.'

'It's not that I think men shouldn't cry; it's that only three minutes before, I was about to kiss you.'

She paused for a moment and he was worried what she would say next.

'I wanted you to kiss me,' she said, tucking her hair behind her ear. 'But it's probably best you didn't, you know? It would complicate things with you working here and so on.'

Henry felt disappointment flood his body. God, he felt like he was being unfaithful to Naomi and he was letting Clara down.

'Okay,' he said. 'You're probably right.'

Clara left him alone in the room. He made Pansy's bed up and went back to the van for some of her clothes and some of his. What a mess, he thought as he closed the van door after taking some more photos for the insurance company. What a huge, fucking mess.

Clara made them cottage pie and Pansy ate only the mashed potato and then rubbed her eyes and said she wanted to lie in bed and watch her TV show on her iPad about a talking dog.

Henry tucked her into bed and came back to Clara who was scraping the leftovers into a bowl and covering it with cling film.

'Thank you for dinner,' he said, feeling awkward.

'That's okay, cottage pie is always a good, filling option.' She filled the sink with hot water and dishwashing liquid and dropped the plates into the sudsy water.

'I'll wash, you dry,' she said, tossing him a tea towel.

They worked in silence for a while.

'Cottage pie was what broke myself and Giles up.'

'How?'

Clara rinsed a plate of the suds under the tap.

'I sent him to a golfing weekend with his friends. He said he was staying at a mate's house, and I knew it would be pizza and beers, so I made a big cottage pie and put it in a container and sent it away with him. Then months later, after he's told me he left the container at the mate's place in the country, I figure it's just gone, you know?'

Henry nodded as he dried a plate and Clara continued. 'Then I go to dinner at my best friend Judy's house and go to get something from the cupboard in the kitchen, and lo and behold, there's my Tupperware with the orange lid that has my name on it and was sent away with cottage pie in it, at her house. The one Naomi's ashes are in now. Sorry but that's all I had.'

Henry shrugged. 'That's okay, she would like to be a part of the drama. Go on. What happened then?'

'I confronted them at the dinner, and that's when Giles told me they were in love. So I set fire to the dining table by accident after throwing a breadstick at his head but since I don't believe in accidents and coincidences, I probably meant them to all burn in hell, and so I left with my container and haven't spoken to either of them again.'

Henry started to laugh and so did she. 'So, Naomi's ashes are now in the container that you once filled with cottage pie that then uncovered an affair? Oh, that's perfect.'

'Yes, sorry, I can try and find another container but that's all I had at hand.'

'That's okay, she would love it.'

They sat at the kitchen table and drank tea and talked late into the night. Clara was whip-smart and Henry was entertained by her humour and dreams for her future, which included chickens, a dog and an open fire and a Welsh dresser just like Tassie's.

But later when the lights were out and he was trying to sleep, half on Pansy's mattress and half on the cold wooden floor, he wondered if there was such a thing as Naomi's having a premonition, and her insisting he say yes. But to what? When they were first together, she would create elaborate treasure hunts with such obscure clues that even she would forget what they meant and they would have to work them out together, which he loved doing. But she had left him for three years wondering what he was supposed to be saying yes to and now she was in the container that had undone Clara's relationship and had brought her here, lying in the next room.

It was so ridiculous it was funny, but somehow it almost made sense. Almost.

27

Clara walked into the large and impersonal hospital, finding the floor and room where Mrs Brown was recuperating.

She knocked on the open door, put her head around and saw Mrs Brown lying in bed.

Gone was her tanned face and bouffant hair. She looked paler and older and without makeup, somewhat vulnerable. Clara nearly felt sorry for her.

She put a bag of grapes on the table next to the bed.

'Hello, Mrs Brown, I'm Clara Maxwell. I'm a friend of Rachel's.'

Mrs Brown glared at Clara. 'She doesn't have any friends, so who are you? A social worker?'

'She does have me as a friend. A new friend but she is a wonderful girl.' *Considering your abuse, she's bloody amazing*, Clara thought but didn't say.

Mrs Brown scoffed, 'For an idiot, she does okay. Why hasn't she come to see me? I need things from home.'

Clara pulled up a chair and sat next to the bed.

'I think Rachel is afraid of you,' she said and watched Mrs Brown's face, which gave nothing away.

'She is an ignorant child who would be living in a house for retarded women if it weren't for me giving her a job.'

Clara held her tongue at the poison coming from the woman's mouth. 'You shouldn't say that word.'

'I don't care, I say it as I see it, and she's not right.'

'How can you say that about your own child?' Clara could not understand how this woman could be so cruel.

Moira Brown looked nonplussed.

'Mrs Brown, did you ever think that your continual criticism and abuse made her so anxious she couldn't function properly?'

'Don't be ridiculous, I didn't abuse her.'

'You did! You hit her – I saw the bruise and according to others, this was a common occurrence.'

'When she can't take instruction, I do it to help it sink in.'

Clara could not believe this woman wasn't even denying her abuse to Rachel. God, now she wanted to push her down the stairs.

'You can't keep abusing her and holding her back. She's doing wonderfully at the bakery; it's never been busier.'

Mrs Brown laughed. It was a thin, brittle laugh that sounded like a glass splintering.

'I am selling the bakery and the tearooms. I'm heading to the Costa del Sol to live. Rachel can come to be my housekeeper. God knows she wouldn't get a job here.'

'Are you serious? That's how you speak about your own daughter?' Clara failed at keeping the venom from her own voice.

'She's not my daughter,' said Mrs Brown. 'She was my useless husband's child. The wife died and I had to take her on as well, and then Alfie died and left me with his lump.

I started the bakery to try and make a living but she can't cook very well and all I do is work.'

Clara stood up and picked up the grapes. 'You are a truly awful person. Really, and I knew someone who was awful, but this sort of abuse – and it is abuse – is not ever going to be allowed as long as I know Rachel. Goodbye, Mrs Brown, and I hope you break your other leg.'

She walked out of the room, her eyes stinging with tears in the face of such hate and loathing.

She remembered the words her father used to say to her mother.

You're an idiot. You can't do anything right. What is this slop you've cooked? Why didn't you die when you had Clara? Would have saved me having to care for you and for her.

Clara leaned against the wall and took a deep breath. *It's okay*, she reminded herself. *He's gone. You are safe.* But Rachel wasn't safe. There was no way she would let that bitch take Rachel to Spain and ruin what chances she had of having a life with joy and purpose and perhaps love.

She would do whatever it took to save Rachel from that woman and Clara thought she might have a plan.

After Clara had gone to see Mrs Brown and bought two single beds and bedding for the spare room, to be delivered that day, she drove back to Merryknowe and called in to the bakery.

'Hey,' she said to Rachel who was plating pies in the kitchen. 'Is that Alice working behind the counter?'

'Yes. She's much faster than me on the till and doesn't

need to use the calculator. She can do all the maths in her head. I'm jealous, I wish I could be that fast.'

'And I reckon Alice wishes she could make a raspberry pie as good as yours. We all have different skills. The world would be boring if we were all the same.'

'Joe said that to me also; you and him have the same ideas about some things,' Rachel said. 'You're both so smart.'

Clara smiled at Rachel. She was so sheltered and so abused that anyone who had normal views of the world was considered a genius in Rachel's eyes.

She noticed Rachel mentioned Joe more often than not lately.

'How is Joe?' she asked casually, remembering Tassie's words about not making any sudden movements around Rachel lest she scare her away.

'He's well. He dropped off some lovely middle bacon last night and stayed for a cup of tea. We had it with a Hobnob, which was perfect.'

Rachel left for the tearooms, pie plates in hand and a dreamy look on her face.

Clara watched the tearooms and bakery from the kitchen doorway, as the customers chattered to each other and Rachel and Alice served them pots of tea with Earl Grey cupcakes or coffee and pistachio cake. The pies for the day were an egg and bacon open pie or the leek and sweet potato, with a pretty lattice crust. They really were a work of art, thought Clara as she went into the kitchen and plated up some of the orders for the guests in the tearoom.

And that's when she knew what she had to do.

Rachel walked into the kitchen with some empty plates and put them on the bench.

'Can I see you after work today?' asked Clara. 'I have to go and do a few errands. A branch fell on the van and so Pansy and Henry are sleeping in the spare room, and I'm having some beds delivered so I need to be home.'

'Are they all right?' Rachel's hand was over her mouth in shock and her eyes wide. 'That's terrible.'

Clara touched her arm to bring her out of her panicked state. 'They are fine; they weren't in the van at the time, absolutely fine, just homeless.'

'Thank God.'

Clara paused. 'Can I come back around five? I have something I want to talk to you about.'

'Okay,' said Rachel, as Joe's sister Alice popped her head around the corner.

'More customers.'

'Coming,' said Rachel quickly, and she rushed back into the shop.

Clara slipped out the back door and drove back to the cottage.

Henry was talking on the phone when she arrived, and Pansy was sitting on the grass by the fence watching him.

'Everything okay?' she asked Pansy as she walked up to her.

'Daddy said shit, fucking joking and get off it three times,' Pansy reported.

Clara stifled a laugh, sat next to her and picked a daisy from the grass.

'Do you know how to make a daisy chain?'

'No?' said Pansy looking interested.

'My mum used to make them for me. When she was a little girl, her grandmother told her that wearing a daisy chain would protect her from lightning and from the Goblin King who liked to steal fairy children.'

Pansy's eyes widened. 'Can you make me one? I don't want to be taken by the king.'

'I will make you one and I will teach you how to make one, so you can be safe from all storms and evil kings.'

She thought about Rachel, who needed more than a daisy chain to protect her from that cow of a stepmother.

She deftly picked the daisies and made a slit in the stem and threaded another through and on and on until it was long enough to go around Pansy's head like a crown.

'You make one,' said Pansy. In the distance, Henry was pacing and still talking on the phone as Clara made herself a daisy crown and put it on her head.

'Now you're safe from the Goblin King,' said Pansy.

Henry walked over to them. 'You two look very pretty,' he said and Clara knew she was blushing.

'Who were you yelling at?' she asked, trying to be nonchalant.

'The insurance company. I have to wait to take the branch off till an assessor comes and sees the damage. But the assessor could be a week or more as there was a lightning storm in Trowbridge, which caused all manner of havoc.'

'They needed one of these,' said Pansy to Clara, touching her daisy crown.

'They did,' said Clara as the sound of a truck rumbled down the laneway and stopped.

'What's this?' Henry asked. 'Are you expecting anything?'

'I bought a few things in Salisbury,' she said. She got up from the grass and brushed her jeans of grass then went to the cottage and opened the door for the deliverymen to carry the beds upstairs.

Henry helped them, and then came down to Clara who was opening the bedding in the living room while the men put the bed bases together.

'You didn't have to do that.'

'I did and I have, so that's that.' She unfolded a red gingham duvet cover and held it up. 'I hope you won't feel like you're sleeping under a picnic blanket.'

'I don't mind what I sleep under as long as it's not on the floor. Pansy completely kicked me out of bed last night.'

Clara smiled as Pansy came in as she pulled out a kitchen chair.

'Daddy, I want to live in the cottage now. I'm over the van.'

Henry's face made Clara burst out laughing. 'You're over the van? Who taught you what being over something is?'

'I saw it on TV.' She sighed.

'I hate to break it to you, Pansy, but the van is our home.'

Clara picked up the linen and left the room for the living room, but she could still hear Pansy negotiating the change in housing.

'We can live here and I can go to school and we can plant Mummy in with the vegetables.'

She heard Henry pulling out another chair and sitting down.

'Pansy, this isn't our home, and Mummy said she wanted it to be our home when we put her ashes in the ground.'

'But I love Clara.' Pansy's voice broke a little and she felt deep love for the child.

'I know, I love Clara too but we can't stay here forever.'

Clara held the linen to her face, knowing it was red and her eyes were brimming with tears.

What did he mean? Did he love her? In what way? Was he trying to make Pansy feel better?

The sound of the deliverymen's feet on the stairs pushed her away from where she was eavesdropping.

'We're all done, Miss,' said one of the men.

'Thank you so much,' she said as Pansy came out of the kitchen at the sound of the voices.

'Want to come and help me make up the beds?' she asked Pansy who immediately ran upstairs.

Henry stood in the doorway looking at her and she looked back at him.

'Did you hear us talking?' he asked.

She thought about lying but she couldn't lie anymore. Her whole life she had lied to protect others but mostly to protect herself. If she was going to live a new life at Acorn Cottage, then she had to be truthful from the start.

She nodded. 'I did.'

Henry shuffled his feet, as though he was kicking the dirt, and he put his hands in the pockets of his jeans.

'I don't know how to be with anyone but Naomi.'

She said nothing.

'I have avoided everything, dragging Pansy around the place, not sending her to school, looking for Naomi in every place, avoiding the feelings. When I cried on the steps of the van it was the first time I cried since she died. I mean, it's been three years. I have just avoided feeling everything, but I can't avoid you. I don't want to avoid you. I just don't know how to do it.'

Clara sighed. 'Well, I don't know either, but I'm not

pushing you to be with me or away from me. I'm not going anywhere. This isn't a test or a demand. There are things I have to tell you one day, and you might not want to be with me after that, so we all have risks to take.'

Henry smiled. 'Did you murder someone?'

Clara looked him in the eye and paused.

'Clara,' came Pansy's voice from upstairs and saved her from answering.

'Gotta go, my queen is calling me.'

Henry walked towards her and she felt her stomach fall away as he was so close. He kissed her on the forehead. Lingering and soft, and he smiled down at her.

'Then why are you still wearing your crown?' he asked and then walked outside. Clara realised that whole time she had been wearing her daisy crown and somehow it all just felt so right.

28

Clara – aged 13

Clara could hear Dad taking off his boots by the front door. His words were slurred and she knew what would be coming next.

He called for her and she froze at her desk. She was working on her maths homework, trying to win the maths prize for the year. It was worth twenty pounds, and she would save it for when she and Mum escaped.

They had tried to leave again after Dad found them at the bus stop when she was younger. He'd dragged Mum home by her hair, huge handfuls of it coming out as Clara ran screaming abuse at him.

Nobody came to help them. Nobody called the police. They had nobody to help them, but Clara had found her grandmother's phone number and called her when Mum wasn't home.

Dad had told Mum she wasn't to call her mum or even see her because she hadn't wanted Mum to marry him. But Mum had secretly been sending her pictures of Clara for years and when Clara was a baby, she had seen her grandmother, not that she remembered.

Gran was nice and said she understood and that they

could come whenever they wanted to live with her. But Clara wondered if her mother would take up Gran on the offer and let them go and live there.

But the older Clara got, the more complicated she understood her home life was.

Nothing had worked to make Dad stop drinking and hurting Mum or Clara, and even through she got excellent marks at school and didn't do anything to worry her mum, she still felt like she was failing her mum by not protecting her from him.

They left him again when Clara was fourteen, and went to a refuge for women and children, but they couldn't sleep and at night some of the men came and yelled abuse at the women through the letter box of the door.

Dad turned up all shaved and in a fresh shirt and said he was sorry to Mum but Clara didn't believe him. She tried to get Mum to understand it would start again but Mum said she didn't have a choice, and she was sure he had changed this time.

It took three days and a bottle of brandy to show he hadn't changed and the next day, nursing a broken collarbone, Clara went to school and told her teachers and her principal and asked for help for the first time in her life.

29

Rachel had closed the shop and was waiting for Clara upstairs.

Alice had been paid and promised to come back tomorrow and Joe had called her and told her how much it meant to Alice to have a little job over summer and that he had a lovely new cut of topside she might like and would she like to go to see a film with him in Chippenham.

Rachel said she was happy to help Alice, and yes she would like the topside and would like to see a movie with Joe on Friday night.

That had been the best day they'd had in the tearooms, and so many of the villagers told her that her hair looked like something a French girl would wear. Perhaps she would even try some red lipstick like the girls in France wore.

Rachel wasn't sure she could be any happier as Clara walked upstairs and into the living room.

Clara didn't even say hello. She threw her bag down onto the sofa and sat down.

'I saw your mother today. My God, she's an absolute bitch. I don't think I have met a nastier female, and I went to a private girls' school for two years – trust me, there were some horrible girls there.'

Rachel gasped. 'You saw her? In hospital?'

Clara raised an eyebrow. 'I took her grapes but I took them back because that woman doesn't deserve grapes or anything from me or the rest of the world. I am surprised you didn't push her down the stairs. I would have.'

Rachel didn't know if she should cry or laugh but Clara was the bravest person she ever met for confronting her mother and for taking the grapes back.

'What did she say?' Rachel asked, grasping her hands together, twisting them and sticking her nails into the cushiony bit of her hand near her thumb.

Clara looked Rachel in the eye. 'Why do you call her Mother when she doesn't act like one? And besides, she's your stepmother.'

'What?' Rachel didn't understand. 'She's my mother. And she does act like one.'

'No. Mothers care for their children – they love them, they don't punish them for existing. They support them, and they do the hard work while you learn how to become a grown-up. Their love is a feeling of peace.'

Rachel sat back into the sofa. 'Not my mother? What do you mean?'

'She told me,' said Clara. 'But I need to confirm that it's true or if she's just saying it to stir up drama. Where does she keep all her papers?'

'What papers?'

'You know, birth certificates and things like that?' Clara said.

Rachel tried to think. 'There's a locked box in the cupboard in her wardrobe.'

'Grab it for me and let's have a look.'

Rachel left the room and came back and put the box on the table in front of Clara, who looked at the lock.

'Got a screwdriver?' she asked.

Rachel went downstairs and came back with a set of screwdrivers. Clara chose the largest one and started to jimmy the lock.

'What are you doing?' Rachel couldn't believe Clara's lack of care of what her mother – or stepmother – would think.

Clara ignored her and used the screwdriver to push in the lock and then Rachel heard a snap. Clara lifted the lid and looked at Rachel.

'This could be tough, Rachel. Do you want me to look first?'

Rachel nodded and Clara pulled out an official envelope and opened it and read aloud.

'Rachel Louise Brown. Born to Peter Brown and Sarah Brown.'

She handed it to Rachel then opened another envelope.

Rachel ran her finger over her mother's signature on the birth certificate extract. Sarah Brown? Why didn't they tell her?

Clara handed her another certificate.

This one was the death certificate for her mother. She was only nine months old when her mother died of an embolism. No wonder there were no photos of her as a baby before nine months. Moira had probably thrown them all away.

Her mother was twenty-six when she died. Only a year older than she was now. She felt tears forming and she started to cry.

Clara was next to her now, hugging her. 'All this time, I wondered how my own mother could do this to me, but now I know she wasn't my mother, and it makes it better somehow but also worse. I thought I couldn't be loved if my own mother didn't love me.'

Clara held Rachel closer. 'You are loved, you are wonderful, you are special and you never deserved what she did to you, Rachel, never – you understand?'

Clara pulled away and held Rachel's face in her hands.

'This was never about you, it was done to you, but it's about her. She's a truly awful person.'

'Who will come back and make my life worse,' cried Rachel.

But Clara was smiling and shaking her head. 'No, I don't think she will. Let me go through these papers but if she is as evil as I think she is, she will have done something that might just undo her.'

Clara went back to the box and picked up the rest of the papers and envelopes.

'Can I take these?'

Rachel nodded her consent, still in shock.

Clara leaned down and hugged her again. 'It will be okay, Rachel, I promise you that. I know exactly what I am going to do, but I just have to get the evidence to prove it.'

She left in a whirlwind. Rachel went to the box, and found an envelope from a pharmacy and opened it. Inside were old photos, and with her heart in her mouth she pulled them out.

There was Sarah Brown. Almost exactly like Rachel to look at, with the same short haircut she had now and with a broad smile, sitting in a park, Rachel on her lap. A photo of the three of them, her dad looking happier than he had ever looked with Mother. She mentally corrected herself. Moira.

More photos of them at a party, maybe her mother's birthday. Yes, there she was being held by Sarah in front of a cake with candles on it

She checked the date on the photo and the date on the death certificate and touched the photo. Months later her mum would be dead and Rachel would never know that love again. She lay on the sofa and cried for everything she had never known and most of all for her mother who had never known her daughter.

What Moira did was unforgiveable. She had taken everything from Rachel, including her confidence and her sense of worth, Clara said, but Rachel had one thing Moira didn't have. She had talent and she was determined now, more than ever, to make the Merryknowe Bakery and Tearooms a soaring success.

30

Henry tucked Pansy under the covers and kissed her goodnight on the forehead and then closed the door and went downstairs, where Clara was sitting in the kitchen surrounded by papers.

'Can I ask a personal question about what happened when Naomi died, in terms of paperwork and so on?'

'Of course.' He sat down opposite her at the table and turned the teapot he'd brought in from the van for them. Clockwise three times and anticlockwise another three, just like Naomi used to do.

'When Naomi died, did she leave anything to Pansy or does everything just go to you automatically?'

Henry rubbed his face where his beard was annoying him. He'd been thinking of shaving it off but autumn wasn't far away and then he would complain about the cold.

'Naomi had a life insurance and a policy from her parents, who died when we were first married. She left me the insurance money to care for Pansy and put half into an account for her schooling and half into a trust for her when she turns twenty-one. It won't be a huge amount but enough for her to buy a car, put a deposit on a little flat or something.'

'And you can't touch that?'

'No, it was in Naomi's will.'

He picked up a document and started to read and then looked at Clara. 'So what do you think happened?'

Clara picked up the papers and flicked through them.

'I wonder if he left a will,' she said.

'Not everyone has one.'

Clara clapped her hands. 'I can find out if her dad had one through the probate directory. I forgot about that. Maybe see if her mum had one also. You never know.'

He noticed that her eyes sparkled when she had a good idea. First it was the beds for the spare room, then when she said they should stay, and now with hunting down some justice for Rachel, a girl she hardly knew but who needed someone on her side for the first time in her life.

'What about your dad? Did he leave a will?'

The spark left Clara's face and she seemed to be searching for an answer.

'No. I mean it was complicated...' Her voice trailed away.

'How so?' Henry encouraged.

But Clara shook her head. 'I can't really talk about him – it's sort of hard.'

Clara seemed nervous but he wasn't sure why.

'Of course. But you know you can tell me anything.'

Clara looked down at the papers on the table. 'I know but I can't yet. I don't know if I ever can.'

'You don't have to do anything,' he said. 'But if you want to, if you feel it will give you some sense of ease if you put it down and share it with someone, a friend, instead of carrying it around, then I would like to take the load for a while if you'd let me.'

Clara said nothing and went back to her paperwork. He watched her work for a while, wondering what was so big that she couldn't share it with him. He had told her everything about his simple life and yet, he felt there was a huge shadow between them, something that stopped her from moving towards him.

'Clara?'

She looked up at him.

'Whatever it is you want to tell me, I will listen, and I won't judge you. I couldn't. So when you're ready to tell me, when and if you're ready, I will be here, okay?'

She nodded and he could see her eyes were shining with tears.

'I feel like there is nothing we couldn't tell each other.'

Clara put her head down. 'That's not true though – we all have dark secrets.'

Henry nodded. 'Yes, but some of them aren't so scary if we bring them into the light once in a while.'

He saw a tear drop onto her hand and his heart hurt.

'Maybe,' she said.

'Whenever you want to tell me, Clara, I will be here. I won't run, if that's what you're thinking.'

Her eyes lifted to meet his. 'Is that true though? Will you be here? What is even happening between us?'

He paused and thought for a moment.

'I don't know but I know I can't wait to start work every morning. I know you make me laugh and you make me think. I know I want to impress you and I know I haven't felt this way since I met Naomi.'

He saw her face soften.

'Is this really happening between us? Is it okay? Can it happen when I'm paying you?' she asked.

He shrugged. 'So don't pay me.'

'I'm not not paying you,' she said. 'That's ridiculous. That's not what I meant.'

'I know, I just wanted you to know that this—' he gestured to them both '—has never happened before. I have never, ever had feelings for my clients, except maybe harbouring bad feelings towards idiots but you are something entirely new. I don't know that I quoted for falling for you.'

Clara's mouth dropped open at his words.

'Did you just say you were falling for me?'

He nodded, almost surprised at his words. Clara made him want to tell her the truth. He just wished she could share her truth with him.

He saw she was blushing now and she bit her lip, stifling a smile.

'So, tell me what you want?' he asked.

'Now? Tomorrow? Sometime soon?' she teased.

'All of the above.'

Clara gathered the papers and put them into a neat stack and put her pen on top.

'Now? I want to go to bed and sleep. Tomorrow, I want to solve the issues with Rachel's father's papers and at some point in the future, as I have told you, I would like chickens and a pet dog.'

She walked to the door of the kitchen.

'Just for the record, I'm falling for you too, but I worry we are each other's rebound relationship.'

But Henry shook his head. 'You are not a rebound.

A rebound is when a person is using someone else to try and unlove another. I will never not love Naomi; she's the mother of my daughter. I could have dated, I could have sent Pansy to my parents and slept with random women, I could have done many things but I didn't because I didn't want to, because I didn't meet anyone who lights up my life like you, Clara. So, you aren't a rebound for me and since you never loved Giles, I don't think this is a rebound for you either, but it's worth exploring isn't it?'

He saw her hand grab the doorframe and then a slow smile spread across her face.

'You are something else, Henry Garnett, I tell you that much.'

'A good something else?' He laughed.

'Better than good,' was all she said before she left him alone in the kitchen.

31

The next morning, Clara was up and dressed and ready to face the day. Her moment with Henry the night before had given her a new energy that she hadn't felt before, not even with Piles.

Pansy was soon up, as was Henry, and the three of them chatted with ease in the kitchen. The electricity between her and Henry was addictive, and at times, she stood a little too close just to feel the friction. She wanted him. It was simple and yet complicated, as she knew Henry wasn't ready for the next move; him admitting he had feelings for her was huge in itself.

Part of her worried he would never be ready for them to be together but she had time, and she wasn't about to rush anything – besides, she had to help Rachel.

'I'm heading to Salisbury library today, and I thought you might want to come with me, Pansy. We can read some books and visit a very good toy shop they have there.'

Pansy pleaded with Henry to go, who rolled his eyes.

'I really don't think I have a say in it,' he said to Clara. 'I'll put her seat in your car.'

They caught each other's eyes and her stomach flipped.

'Thank you.'

Pansy was dancing between them, discussing what toy she might like to get before Henry told her to go and find her shoes and put them on.

'I haven't had any long periods of time without her since Naomi died,' he said. 'The other day when you went to Rachel's was the first time in three years we haven't been together.'

Clara felt herself frown. 'What do you mean? You've never been apart?'

Henry sighed. 'Never. At first she wanted to be with me all the time, which I understood, but then I guess I wanted her with me all the time also, so now we have this weird co-dependent thing and I know she needs to have other people. My parents have asked for two years to have her to stay but I couldn't do it.'

Clara nodded, trying to understand, and she thought of her own mother.

Piles had said they were co-dependent but when there was no one else to depend on, it made sense to want to only be with each other.

'I will look after her, Henry, I promise.'

He shrugged and put his hands up. 'I know you will. And she knows also – that's why she wants to go. She always says no to other people but she didn't even miss a beat today.'

The privilege of Pansy and Henry's trust wasn't lost on her and she took Henry's rough hand in hers.

'Thank you,' she said.

'And thank you for not judging me. I know it's not healthy but being here at the cottage, I don't know, it's kind of healing us both.'

Pansy exploded into the room with her shoes on the

wrong feet, a sun hat on her head and a pink feather boa.

'Wow, that's perfect for town,' said Clara. 'Exactly what I would have worn if I had a feather boa.'

Pansy looked smug as she walked out to the car and climbed into her seat.

Soon they were on their way to the village in Clara's car.

'We just have to stop in and see a friend of mine,' said Clara.

She parked the car and walked up the path and knocked on the door, which opened almost immediately.

'Good morning, Tassie, I'm heading into—'

'Yes, I know,' said Tassie. 'Let me get my handbag.'

The old woman shuffled to the hall table and picked up an old-fashioned bag. Clara smiled when she saw Tassie was wearing pink lipstick.

'How did you know I was coming to see if you wanted to come to Salisbury?' Clara asked, trying to see if Tassie had a hidden camera somewhere.

'I had an itchy stomach all last night and woke this morning to a bumblebee in the kitchen, so I knew something good was coming and I needed to be prepared.'

'I like your lipstick,' said Clara, meaning every word. The lipstick added much-needed colour to Tassie's tiny face and she had little pearl earrings on that Clara was sure she hadn't seen before.

'I thought I should look nice for whoever came to the door, even if it was the reaper – at least I would go dressed and ready.'

Clara laughed as Tassie closed the door and handed her house keys to Clara to lock it.

'We have another passenger. Pansy is the daughter of the

man who is helping me fix up the cottage.'

She opened the car door and helped Tassie get into the car then ran around to the driver's side and put Tassie's seatbelt on for her.

'This is a fancy car,' said Tassie to Pansy in the back.

'It's red,' said Pansy. 'Red cars go fastest.'

'That's wonderful to know,' said Tassie, sounding sincere. Clara saw Pansy nodding as though she knew a great many things she was ready to share with Tassie.

'Your man is the one with the little house on wheels?' asked Tassie.

'Yes,' said Clara amazed. 'How did you know? More and more I think you're the witch of Merryknowe.'

Tassie giggled. 'Don't be ridiculous, there are at least three of us in the county.'

Clara wasn't sure if she was serious or not but didn't ask.

They drove along the roads towards Salisbury, and Tassie told Clara the history of the druids in the area.

'They loved oak trees; would meet under them and do their druid business. You have a great oak on your land. There were many more oaks surrounding the cottage but there are only a few left now, aren't there? I haven't been to Acorn Cottage in years.'

Clara made a mental note to take Tassie to the cottage as soon as possible.

'A great oak?' she asked as she drove along the road, the sunshine lighting up the countryside so it looked like a postcard.

Tassie was still chatting. 'In olden times oak trees were thought to be magic. I remember my mother saying that some of the gypsy women would put acorns under their pillow if they wanted to have a baby.'

'Acorns under your pillow would be uncomfortable.' Clara laughed. 'I have to go to the library and then we can do what we like,' said Clara to Tassie as she found a place to park at the front of the library building.

Tassie smiled. 'I don't mind what we do. I haven't left Merryknowe for three years, so just seeing everything is marvellous.'

Three years without leaving the village was ridiculous, Clara thought as she wound down the windows of the car. Three years since Henry and Pansy had been apart. Three years since Naomi died. So much was happening all at once and Clara wondered why it was all happening now but she couldn't explain it and didn't want to try. It just felt right. She glanced at Pansy in the rear-view mirror.

Tassie was clutching her handbag on her lap and happily staring out the window as though everything was new to her eye.

Tassie's loneliness would be the next thing she dealt with after Rachel. Goodness, whoever said that life in Merryknowe would be boring was very wrong indeed. Clara came for a slow life and ended up being busier than ever and she wouldn't have changed it for the world.

32

After Clara and Pansy left on their adventure, Henry felt lost without them.

Their breakfast had been as cheery and chatty as ever, but there was a new energy in the cottage between him and Clara.

They stood close at the counter when they made tea, and sometimes, when she leaned across him, he felt the softness of her breast against his arm and he thought he might die of desire.

Was she teasing him? He wasn't sure but God, he wanted her. He ached for her. All night he had lain in the room next to her, wondering if she was thinking about him.

Now she was gone with his daughter and he looked around the cottage. He wanted it to be everything she and her mum had dreamed of and more.

Getting in the truck he headed out past Merryknowe and into the deep country until he found the turn-off and drove up a country lane and there was the white farmhouse. He parked the truck and walked up to the gate with a sign that said:

Please shut the gate as the chickens like to explore and
the foxes like it when they do.

He smiled and shut the gate behind him as a woman came out and waved at him.

'Hi, Henry, I haven't seen you in forever.'

'Hi, Julia, yes it's been ages,' he said as she walked up and embraced him for a long time.

Julia had been one of the palliative care nurses who cared for Naomi. She was there through the long nights and there at the end and had stayed in touch with Henry through emails over the years.

Since she had retired, she had started breeding chickens and ducks and had made a name for herself for breeding high-quality birds and all the necessary items for the chickens and ducks.

'How is Pansy?' asked Julia, after they hugged.

'Hilarious, never-ending energy, so like Naomi and so much herself if that makes sense.'

'I think of you two often. I wished there was a better ending for you all.'

Henry shrugged. 'It has been tough but things are getting better, or maybe they're just different.'

'So, have you finally settled down and found a place and want some birds?' Julia asked as they wandered towards the enclosure where the sound of the chickens grew louder. 'Naomi and I often talked about the chickens she wanted. I am glad you're doing it.'

'It's for a friend – she really wants some chickens. She's just bought a place in Merryknowe,' he said.

He felt Julia's eyes on him and he knew he was turning red. Would she think less of him if she knew his feelings for Clara?

Always intuitive, as most palliative care nurses are, she touched his arm.

'I am glad, Henry, you deserve a second chance. Naomi didn't want you to be alone your whole life.'

'Didn't she?' Henry was surprised. 'She never mentioned it to me.'

'It is quite common. She knew it was incurable and she knew she was close to the end but she was also very stubborn and didn't want to admit it.'

'You are so right about that,' said Henry, scuffing the ground with his boot.

'But she said she hoped you would find love again, because she thought you were very good at being married, and not everyone is. She said you like showing people love through actions.'

Henry shook his head. 'I wish she had told me this.'

'Would it have made a difference?' Julia asked.

Henry looked out across the fields and felt the breeze on his face and he scratched his beard. 'I don't know, but I am glad I know now.'

'When we are ready we find out what we need to know,' Julia answered and then clapped her hands. 'Now let's get your girl some birds.'

He didn't explain about Clara. He didn't need to explain her to anyone; he just wanted to make her happy and he knew this would make her more than happy.

Two hours later, Henry was back at the cottage with six hens, which were in a box, and he had started assembling the chicken coop.

It was shaped like a small castle, complete with a tower.

Usually Henry would have made something for the chickens but he knew the designs from Julia and the kits were perfect and whimsical for Clara and he didn't have much time.

The more he got to know Clara, the more he saw her magic. She had a kindness and need to improve people's lives but in a joyful way, not demanding they change for her benefit. She could make anyone laugh; she was straight, direct and still kind. She would have been an excellent bank manager but he was glad she was here.

He ran chicken wire around the bottom of the coop to protect the birds from the foxes and set up the nesting boxes, lining them with fresh hay.

Finally, the coop was finished and Henry put the chickens inside and closed the door.

One last thing – he went to the van and managed to squeeze under the crushed roof and pulled out Naomi's paint box. He went back to the coop and thought for a moment before he painted on the door with slow careful strokes and then stepped back and smiled.

The sound of the chickens pottering in their new environment made him smile and he looked around at the messy, overgrown, wild garden and the cottage with the blue tarpaulin on the roof, and a van with a tree crushing the roof, and thought he hadn't felt this happy since before Naomi became sick.

He checked the time and realised it was nearly mid-afternoon. He wanted to make Clara and Pansy dinner, so he went into the cottage and went up to shower, and soon he was back in the kitchen, pottering as he prepared dinner for them all.

Thankfully the tree had crushed the end of the van, so

he could get to the refrigerator and freezer. He pulled out some items for him to make his perfect vegetable curry with pappadums and coconut rice.

He turned on some music on his phone and put it in an empty glass to work as a speaker then chopped the sweet potato, cauliflower florets, carrots and tomatoes.

He hummed along to the music as he fried off the onion and garlic in the frying pan and opened a beer from the fridge while the vegetables sweated in the heavy pan.

He couldn't wait for Clara and Pansy to come home, and he occasionally checked out the front to see if they had returned.

When the curry was slow-cooking, he went to the front of the house, pulled a chair from the van and sat on the lawn, looking around him, feeling content. He was happy. It was a truly remarkable feeling, like remembering a name for something that you thought you'd forgotten, or having a drink of water when your mouth was so dry you couldn't feel your tongue.

The sound of a car coming up the unmade road made him jump up. He couldn't wait to see them but it wasn't Clara's red Mini that came into view.

It was a green car and it had a man at the wheel.

Insurance company, he thought with a wave.

The car stopped and the man alighted.

'Hi, thanks for coming out this far,' said Henry.

'Sorry?' said the man. Henry noticed he didn't have much of a chin, and he was wearing a business shirt with a woollen vest, even though it was warm.

'Aren't you from the insurance company?' asked Henry.

'No, I'm looking for Clara Maxwell.'

'Oh, she's not here. Can I take a message?' asked Henry with a sinking feeling in his stomach.

'I'll wait,' said the man and he went to the car and sat inside it, the air conditioner on and the windows up.

Henry went back to the cottage and tried to call Clara but she didn't answer. He didn't want to text her as he knew she was driving, so he sat in the kitchen with his phone in his hand and his heart in his mouth. *Please let it not be Giles wanting her back.* He had never wanted Clara more than now he knew he might lose her. He ran through scenarios in his head. Would she go, stay, kick Henry and Pansy out?

He called Clara again and this time he left a message.

'Clara, it's Henry. Hurry home. You have someone to see you.'

That's all he could do right now, other than wait for Clara to make her decision.

33

Tassie returned home from her trip with Clara and Pansy a happy woman. She'd had lunch at a pub where she ate a proper roast pork meal with crackling and apple sauce and had shared a lovely crème brûlée with Pansy. They took much joy in cracking the top together and sharing the toffee shards and creamy filling. Tassie chose not to read the leaves in her teacup at the pub, because the same symbol kept appearing and she wanted a day free of thinking about it, but she knew that she was buying time. The cup was never wrong. The first time she saw it was when she turned the cups with Clara. She was handing over to Clara, even if she didn't know it yet.

Her whole life she had worked to help others and and provided care for all of the children in the village, and beyond, over the years. The countless times she had stepped in to help a child when Mum or Dad couldn't, taking over a dinner or bread and milk, washing little one's clothes or calling the doctor or the police in Salisbury to step in when a child's safety was in danger at home.

Life was simpler now but there was still work to be done in the village and Clara would take care of it because she was the most capable person Tassie had met in her eighty-nine years. Clara didn't even know how brilliant she was, but Tassie did. Tassie had taught children for so long, she could see what they were capable of before they could even read.

Clara was creative and she could turn Merryknowe around. Tassie wanted to be around to see it come to fruition. *Not yet*, she thought as she looked out the window over her neat back garden. *I still have work to do.*

Merryknowe could be a wonderful little village again if people came to see it and then stayed. They could have a lovely life away from the city, perhaps the school might open again one day? They just needed something to bring them to the village or it would die slowly and painfully and Tassie knew there was nothing worse than driving through a once thriving place to see the shops closed and the churchyard overgrown.

Tassie pushed away the grim thoughts and remembered Pansy's smile and copper curls, entirely enchanting. She was also capable of so much if she could harness her spirit and sit still for a minute.

Tassie was filled with a sense of purpose she had forgotten existed.

It felt strange to have this after so many years of waiting for death. Now she didn't want to die, she wanted to help Clara find her path to her own truth and Rachel to believe in her own magic abilities but more than anything else, she wanted to teach Pansy to read.

Clara had said she was starting school but she was already a year behind and the little one probably didn't know her A's from her T's.

When Pansy had slept in the car on the way home, Tassie had asked Clara about the child.

'She's bright but I don't think Dad has really let her out of his sight since Mum died. This is the first time he's had a day without her, he said.'

'Goodness, that's not right for either of them.'

Clara had shrugged. 'I guess but I don't know what I would be like in the same situation and he's a good man; he just needs to see he and Pansy can be happy again.'

Tassie had sat, trying to think of the best way for Pansy to learn to read.

'If you bring her to me in the mornings, I can get her started for school,' she'd said. 'I still have some books and things that might help.'

'Oh wow, I will ask Henry, but it sounds wonderful.'

When they dropped Tassie off, Pansy had woken up and come inside to use the bathroom and then had come out and sat in Tassie's lounge.

'I like your house – it feels like Christmas.'

Tassie had looked around for any signs of last year's decorations but couldn't find any.

'Why does it feel like Christmas?' asked Clara.

'It feels like magic,' was all Pansy said and played with a small bowl of shells on a side table.

Later, ignoring the ache in her old bones, Tassie went to the room where she kept her old books and, searching through boxes on the shelves of the cupboard, she found the box she wanted.

Lifting the lid, she hoped nothing had eaten the old pages or notes but time had been kind to her and the box, and inside were the old school books she had kept for the past sixty years. The books were out of date but the cards with the pictures and words never went out of date. She shuffled through the well-worn cards. Flashcards, teachers called them now, but to Tassie they were her magical deck of cards that helped children to open the gates to a world of words and stories.

Moving back to the kitchen, she sat at the table and wrote the lesson plan out carefully.

Sounds. Letters. She would get some butterfly cakes from Rachel's bakery and she would make some homemade lemonade. Coloured pencils and a scrapbook of paper would be needed for writing the letters also.

Oh, there was so much to do, and for the first time since George McIver died, Tassie went to bed excited to wake up in the morning.

34

Clara was excited to see Henry as she pulled into the laneway and drove down to the cottage. She turned to park her car to find an unfamiliar car in the place her red Mini usually sat.

She turned off the ignition, opened the door and walked around to let Pansy out, who ran inside the cottage with her fairy doll and dinosaur egg toy that she had insisted to Clara she had needed above anything else in the world.

The green car's door opened and Giles stepped out.

'Hi, Clara,' he said, and she felt such blind rage it was all she could do to not walk over and slap his face.

'Why are you here?' She crossed her arms. 'I hope you didn't bring Judy with you.'

She stood very straight wondering where Henry was. This was terrible, she thought. Why would Giles come here? How did he know where she was?

'No, Judy is at home,' he said, looking down at his feet. He was wearing those stupid orange suede loafers that he bought in Spain with no socks. God, she hated that look – his attempt at Euro fabulous, she had teased at the time when he bought them. He hadn't laughed. She should have known then he wasn't a keeper.

Giles put his hands in the pockets of his trousers. 'I tried to call you but you blocked me.'

'Yes, I tend to do that to people who cheat on me.'

They stood in silence staring at each other.

'I'm sorry, Clara, it was really badly done on my behalf and Judy's.'

'Do not speak for her. You don't get to speak for her.'

Giles went to speak but she interrupted him.

'I don't want you back, Giles, so I have no idea why you're here. We are done. Over. You made your choice and if you're back to try and tell me now you miss me and you're sorry, well, I am sorry you feel that way, but I have moved on and if things didn't work out with you and Judas, that's on you, nothing to do with me.' Clara felt very proud of herself as she spoke.

'Judas?' asked Giles, looking confused.

Clara shrugged. 'Freudian slip.'

Giles cleared his throat. 'Actually, I am not here to ask you to take me back; I'm here to tell you in person that Judy is pregnant. We're engaged.'

Clara swallowed and bit the inside of her lip until she tasted blood and then she spoke. 'Why the hell did you think I needed to know that? Why did you think you needed to drive all the way here and stalk my new house and tell me that? What was your intention? To make me feel bad? To see my reaction so you and Judas can laugh about it later? Why?'

As Clara spoke, she felt tears fall but she knew they were tears of rage not sadness; of sheer frustration and anger that he dared to enter her world. Her perfect little world in Merryknowe that she was creating.

'You cheated on me, you hid your relationship with my

best friend for God knows how long and now you think I need to know your lovely plans with chinless babies and tacky weddings? What is actually wrong with you? You're a sad, pathetic man who is here to try and hurt me. Well, guess what? I don't love you. I don't think I ever did. I chose you because you seemed safe and non-threatening. I chose you because I didn't want to have sex with you and you didn't want to have sex with me either. I was sad and pathetic also, so don't think I don't know I settled for something less than I deserved. We are better off apart and you and Judas can have a lovely life together but please go now. I don't care about you. I don't think about you. It is as though my life before here never happened. Everything I want is here and I'm happy.'

Giles stepped back from Clara as though she had slapped him.

'Do you mean that man I met earlier, the bearded meathead drinking beer on your lawn? Your tastes have gone down. You like them burly and stupid, I see.'

'Why do you care what I want?' she asked, genuinely confused. 'You didn't want me, so why do you care what I want now?'

Giles shrugged and gestured to the cottage. 'Well, I am surprised you want this and him – it's all a bit of a step backwards, isn't it?'

Clara took a deep breath and then blew out the air slowly, trying to maintain her cool.

'He is one thousand of you, Giles. Maybe a million. He can do anything and he does it for me. And I love him. I think of him every minute of every day in a way I never thought about you. I want to make him happy but with you, I existed to try and please you but failed over and over again. The smallest thing I do for him, he is happy. I want that. I deserve that. I used to exist off the scraps of your love that you breadcrumbed through our relationship to keep me on the trail but this man, this man and his child have my heart in a way you never could. So please leave now or I will have my bearded meathead of a man throw you off my land.'

Shaking, Clara went to her car and picked up her bag and papers and the shopping bags then walked into the cottage, where she saw Henry and Pansy standing in the hallway. She knew they had heard every word.

'Something smells delicious. What's for dinner?' she asked cheerfully, putting down her things.

But she was still shaking. She felt Henry's arms around her and Pansy's arms around her legs.

'I love you,' she heard Henry say and Pansy mumbled into her bottom, 'I love you, Clara.'

Clara waited until the sound of Giles's car had disappeared before she burst into loud, noisy sobs, with Henry rubbing her back, and Pansy patting her bottom like she was a baby.

Finally, she finished crying and she pulled away and wiped her eyes with the sleeve of her top and Pansy handed her some toilet paper to blow her nose on.

'Thank you, sweet pea,' she said to Pansy, who nodded, her face very serious.

'I cry like that when I miss Mummy. It's good to cry, Daddy says.'

Clara bit her lip to stop from crying again and looked up at Henry.

'That was intense, sorry.'

'Don't say sorry for speaking the truth, my love.' His eyes were so kind, she felt dizzy with love.

'I have something to show you. I know it's probably not an ideal time, as emotions are high, but you will hear it later and wonder what on earth is going on.'

Clara looked up at him.

'I could do with something nice right now to take my mind off the murder I've been planning.'

She put her hand out to Pansy who took it, while Henry took her other one and he led them out the back door.

Clara's eyes adjusted to the light and then she saw the chicken coop.

'You didn't?' she yelled, jumping up and down.

'I did,' said Henry, looking worried. 'Should I not have?'

She and Pansy ran towards the coop and Clara burst into laughter at the door.

'What does it say?' asked Pansy, excited like Clara.

'It reads, Clara's Clucking Castle.' She turned to Henry who was standing with his hands in his pockets, looking both pleased and embarrassed.

'You are hilarious,' she said. Her eyes caught his and she smiled at him, seeing him flushed with pride at the reception to his gift.

She opened the door carefully and let Pansy in, then she followed. They went to the nesting box and Clara lifted the lid. A single egg sat on the straw.

'There's an egg,' squealed Pansy. She picked it up carefully and held it close. 'I will love this egg forever and ever,' she exclaimed.

'Or you can have it for breakfast tomorrow,' offered Clara.

'Can I, Daddy?' Pansy called and Henry nodded.

Pansy opened the door to the coop to run inside and Clara quickly closed it as Henry came to watch the chickens scratching about the ground.

'You did this for me,' she said. It wasn't a question but a statement, as though she had to say it aloud to be sure it was true.

'I did,' said Henry.

'Do they have names?' she asked, as the birds pecked around her.

'Not yet.'

She walked to the wire fence and put her fingers through the wire, and he touched them with his hands.

'This is perfect – you know that, yes?'

He gave a shy smile, and she realised he had been unsure.

'You said you wanted chickens,' he said. 'I took a chance.'

'I did, and this is generous and thoughtful and honestly, just perfect.'

'I want to kiss you.'

'Then come into my coop and kiss me,' she said.

'There's an offer I can't refuse.'

And he did. He kissed her in a way that she had never been kissed, with happy chickens pecking and clucking around their feet.

'Stay with me tonight,' Clara said when they pulled apart.

'Stay with me always,' he said and she kissed her answer back.

35

Clara stood in her bedroom, trying to work out if she would dress in her sexy underwear, still unworn from when she was with Giles, or if she should just wear her PJs and act as though there were no expectations.

When she asked Henry to stay with her in her room, she wasn't even sure she meant it as a request for sex. All she knew was that she wanted to be with him every moment.

She could hear him reading Pansy a story and him patiently answering all her questions about the characters and why Moon-Face had a slide in his tree and if they could put a slide in the tree outside.

Clara brushed her hair again, and then ate a breath mint, even though she had cleaned her teeth.

She got into bed, and then out again and then swapped her pyjama pants for tracksuit pants and pulled a sweater over the pyjama top.

Then she heard the door to Pansy's room close and Henry enter the bathroom.

The nerves felt like Bolshoi dancers in her belly, and she wondered if she should be casual and lie on the bed reading a book – except she didn't have any books in the room.

Before she could decide, Henry walked into the room and smiled at her and she laughed.

'I have been trying to work out the best way for you to find me. Should I be casual, or sexy, or chilled or indifferent? It's been a whole thing,' she admitted.

'Be yourself,' said Henry as he came and sat on the bed, kicked his shoes off and adjusted the pillow so he was sitting up.

Clara did the same and they sat side by side in silence.

'I haven't been with anyone else since Naomi.'

'Me neither,' said Clara. 'I mean, not that I was with Naomi but since Giles.'

God, why was she so awkward. *Stop talking, Clara.*

'We don't even have to do anything. We can just lie here and talk,' she said, and she meant it.

Henry moved his pillow so he was lying down and facing Clara and she did the same.

They looked at each other and smiled.

'We're a fine pair, aren't we?' he said.

'How do you mean?'

His feet found hers and they touched and she felt a shiver of pleasure run through her body as they rubbed each other's feet.

'I mean, we have both declared our love to each other. The first gift I have given you was chickens and a hen house, and we are living in a house with a hole in the roof and we have done nothing but had a few chaste kisses.'

'It's very Jane Austen meets Milly-Molly-Mandy.' She laughed then shivered as his foot ran over her ankle bone.

'You're cold – get in, under the covers,' he said, and they both hopped out and back in under the duvet.

He was still dressed as was she, but it felt intimate under the heavy cover and her foot found his again and they touched.

She saw the desire in his eyes and she leaned forward and kissed him. It wasn't a chaste kiss now. It was searching and filled with questions that he answered by pulling her to him.

His hands were on her hip and he pressed against her. She heard him moan as she pressed her hips back against him.

His tongue flickered in her mouth and she caught it, sucking on it, thinking she would die with desire. His hand went under her top and the touch of his skin made her gasp with pleasure. His hands were rough and demanding and she felt his thumb brush against the side of her breast. She moved so he knew she wanted more and soon his hands were everywhere.

She pulled him on top of her in the bed, feeling his hardness between her legs, and she moved against him.

God, I haven't made out like this since I was a teenager, she thought as her legs went around him.

It was exquisite pleasure and she didn't want it to end but she wanted more.

Henry pushed up on his hands and looked down at her.

'Tell me what you want me to do to you?' he asked and she saw he was very serious.

She paused, trying to think. She wanted everything at once. Him inside her, above her, behind her, over her, under her.

'Everything,' she simply said and he sat up and pulled off his top.

His body was lovely. Strong, with chest hair, which she tugged at, biting her lip as she smiled up at him.

'God, you're gorgeous,' he said.

'So are you.'

She pulled him down to her and bit him gently on the nipple. Then she rolled on top of him and pulled off her top and smiled as she undid the button on her pyjama top.

'You are seriously sexy.'

'Yes, pyjamas are very sexy – the boys love them.' She laughed as she shrugged the top from her shoulders.

'You could be wearing a cloak made of feathers and I wouldn't notice. I just want you naked.'

The desire he had for her was unlike anything Clara had known before. He was raw and primal and she felt intimidated and yet so special as he pulled her down and sucked on her nipple then rolled her over onto her back.

Within minutes, her pants were off, and he was between her legs. She grasped his head and pulled the pillow over her head to stop her cries waking Pansy.

He didn't stop, until she had come three times and then she pulled his head up and rolled on top of him. 'Now, inside me,' she moaned, wondering who this girl was in bed with this man.

Sex had been pleasant but perfunctory with Giles when it happened, which was rare. Before that there had been a short-term university boyfriend, who ended up being gay, which explained why he wasn't into sex with her, and a few boys from high school and university who she had sex with because she could, sometimes even when she felt she should but nothing had prepared her for Henry.

He was naked, between her legs. She looked down at him and felt as though she might die with desire.

'What do you want, Clara?' he asked.

'You.'

'Are you sure?'

Gone was the shy man and in his place was this bearded man who looked like he was going to claim her in every position and more and she couldn't wait.

'Yes, I'm sure. Fuck me,' she said, surprised at her words. Had she ever said that before? Perhaps she had said it because she was supposed to but this time she meant it with everything she had.

Henry paused, his cock running along her wetness.

'Don't stop,' she moaned.

'Oh, darling, I haven't even started yet,' and with that he pushed up into her, opening her, and she arched her back with a pleasure she had never known before.

36

The end of summer rainstorm was keeping the people away from the bakery and tearooms so Rachel took it upon herself to make a cup of tea and sit behind the counter on the stool she had brought in from the shed outside.

Mother had said sitting in the shop was lazy and Rachel had agreed but she was tired now it was so busy and besides, there was a lull between customers.

Joe had told her she needed a website, but since she didn't have a computer, he brought her the small one that his sister Alice used for school but she had recently upgraded.

It wasn't that she didn't understand computers or emails but her mother had a tablet and controlled it like everything in Rachel's life, not letting her use it for anything unless it served Mother.

Now, as she surfed through the pages and pages of recipes and photos and gorgeous inspiration for tearooms and more, Rachel felt a flicker of something unfamiliar. She started to download photos she liked, then picked up the notebook used for ordering and wrote ideas for baking as she read the pages.

The sound of the bell on the door made her look up and she saw Tassie from across the road.

'You're brave to go out in this rain. I think the creek will flood,' said Rachel as she closed the computer and stood up.

Tassie waved her hand at Rachel. 'No need to get up, my dear, I will find a seat.'

'Tea? Cake? Something warm?' offered Rachel.

'Bring your tea to me and show me what you are looking at on the computer. You seem to be lost in creative exploration. I could see the little sparks coming off you from across the street.'

'Could you?' She wouldn't be surprised. Tassie always knew what was happening in the village and more specifically in the bakery.

Mother had said she was an old busybody who didn't have a life so used other people's lives as a way of feeling important but Rachel had never felt that Tassie had overstepped any boundaries, not the way her own mother had.

Thinking of her mother's rules now made her shiver.

Not being allowed to lock the bathroom door, so Mother could rattle the handle when she walked by to ensure Rachel wasn't up to no good. She wasn't sure what she meant but as Rachel's body began to change Mother wouldn't let her look at herself in the mirror; she said Rachel's breasts were disgusting, and that she should avoid looking at or touching her private parts at all costs.

And it wasn't as though Rachel wasn't aware of sex or didn't have sexual feelings but she would never have been allowed to have a boyfriend with Mother in her life because it would take Rachel away from being her servant and providing money for Mother.

Rachel took tea and a butterfly cake to Tassie and then

carried her own mug of tea and the computer to Tassie and sat down.

'Show me how these things work,' said Tassie, as she peered at the screen. She took her glasses out of her bag and peered even more closely.

'I have been looking at tea shop ideas and interiors. I would like to spruce this place up a bit but I don't know if Mother will let me or if we can afford it.'

Tassie looked at the screen and pointed to a photograph of a tearoom with bookshelves.

'That's lovely.'

'Yes,' said Rachel. 'Can I show you what I want to do if I had the money and the freedom?'

Tassie sighed. 'Money and freedom. The wish of so many women of my generation, and still the wish remains unfilled.'

Rachel took Tassie through her ideas of the bookshelves and the open fire for winter and the tables with pretty tablecloths and flowers in vases.

'I think it could be a place to stop by for ten minutes or hours if you wanted. You could have book readings happen or get authors to come and do signings or artists to show their art. My dad wanted to be an artist but he became an insurance salesman instead. I want to create a place where everyone can come and be inspired.'

Tassie smiled and sat back then picked up her cake and took a bite, spreading icing sugar on her purple coat and leaving cream on her top lip.

'I think that's perfectly doable, more than doable. I think it's super-duper doable.'

Rachel sighed and closed the computer. 'I don't know.

Mother will have to come back. Clara said she had some ideas to help me but I haven't seen her lately.'

'I saw her a week ago when she took me and the little one to Salisbury. It was very nice indeed. But Clara will be back – she has some things she needs attending to right now.'

Tassie raised her eyebrows a few times and Rachel laughed. 'What does that mean?'

Tassie drained her tea and put down the cup and looked inside it.

'An important announcement is coming,' she said. 'My death notice might be in the paper, so I should check.'

The sound of the bell rang and Clara stood in the doorway.

'Hello, Ladies of Merryknowe,' she cried, waving an envelope in her hand. 'I have news.'

'There's the announcement,' said Tassie to Rachel.

Clara came to the table and sat down.

'You seem well,' said Tassie with a look that Rachel didn't understand.

'More on that later,' said Clara very firmly to Tassie, and Rachel noticed a blush climbing up her neck.

'So, last week I went to Salisbury and I looked into your dad's will, which wasn't with the other papers.'

Rachel nodded. 'Mother might have misplaced it.'

'She isn't your mother, Rachel,' said Clara.

'Old habits die hard, darling,' Tassie said to Clara in a gentle tone and Clara put her hand on Rachel's knee.

'I'm sorry, I just dislike her so much.'

Rachel nodded. 'I don't like her either but I don't have any power here. She is truly the wicked stepmother and I am the baking version of Cinderella.'

Clara laughed and threw her head forward so her dark hair fell over her face. When she looked up at them her eyes were sparkling and her smile wide.

'That's the thing. Your father worked in insurance, didn't he?'

Rachel nodded.

Clara slammed her hand on the table. 'Your dad knew what he was doing. He set everything up so your stepmother had an allowance but most of the money would be left to you. Instead she forged signatures and God knows what else and she took the money to buy the bakery because she saw you were cheap labour. What she didn't know was you were good at it, and she hated that. I think she kept you back from being creative in the kitchen because she didn't want you to draw attention to the shop. She got enough to keep it going but, Rachel, you own this. You own the shop and the tearooms. The whole thing.'

Rachel was silent as she looked around the shop and then she started to cry.

It felt like the sobs were coming from the earth and up through her feet and out her mouth as she wailed into the echo of the shop.

Clara was holding her hands now, and Tassie was rubbing her back as she cried until she thought she was going to be sick and then it slowed until she could breathe again and when she looked up, the sun was out, shining on Clara's black hair, making her look like exactly like Rachel had always thought of her – as her own guardian angel.

'You mean I can do the renovations?' Rachel asked. 'I can have a fireplace and a bookshelf and games and cards?'

'You can have it all, Rachel Brown, everything you've

ever wanted for your life,' Clara said. Rachel looked at Tassie and then to Clara and wiped her eyes with a napkin.

'You two are the best friends anyone could ask for. My whole life I was lonely and I used to ask my dad to bring me friends. Ones who could make me feel good about my life, who would help me get away from Moth... Moira, and here you are. I don't think I could be any luckier than I am right now and I want you both to know, I love you very much.'

Rachel saw Tassie wipe her eye and Clara was nodding and had tears in her eyes.

'We are a lucky three, aren't we?' Clara said and they held hands around the table, just as a huge crack of lightning went off overhead, making Clara and Rachel laugh and Tassie look smug.

37

Clara – aged 15

*T*he chickens were chatting among themselves when Clara arrived home from school. She dropped her bag in the back garden and went straight to them, opening the gate to the chicken coop and greeting the girls before she asked their permission to check for eggs.

She always felt guilty she was taking their hard-earned work for her breakfast but they seemed quite proud of their work and so Clara always praised them and thanked them.

Mum thought she was silly for talking to chickens but Gran understood the mutual respect.

Perhaps Mum had lost her understanding of respect after Dad abused her so many times?

Clara didn't have any answers but she also didn't have as many questions now they lived at Gran's house.

Once she'd told the teachers what was happening at home, they had contacted the police, the social workers and some lawyers who helped Mum leave Dad and they went to court and Dad wasn't allowed to come near them anymore.

Mum had said that Dad didn't even know where they lived anymore, so Clara stopped listening for him before dinner. Slowly she began to relax at home and at school.

She made friends and joined the football club and she liked a boy named Jamie.

But Gran was the best part of it all. She was like the grandmothers in books with warm cocoa and teaching her how to make cakes and painting faces on boiled eggs for her breakfast.

And Mum had a job at a nursing home working with old people. She would tell Clara and Gran stories over dinner while the heater was on and sometimes, when it was raining and they were cosy inside the kitchen, Clara thought this was almost as good as the cottage dream she had when she was little.

But the dream of the cottage hadn't died in Clara and Mum's minds, and when a new show started on BBC called Escape to the Country, they would watch and make notes of some of the villages they wanted to move to and the houses they liked.

Clara liked the thatched cottages but Mum liked the barn conversions or even a house with a water mill, which Clara told her would make her want to go to the bathroom all night.

Clara kept a new notebook this time, with all the notes of the villages and the houses they liked. She cut out maps of the areas and circled where she thought the houses might be and found old house magazines in charity shops and pasted in the pictures of rooms she thought looked like they belonged in a cottage.

Curtains with flowery sprigs and soft lamplight and open fires. Overstuffed sofas with dogs lying on them, with bunches of roses in teacups and violet-lined paths.

It was a perfect dream and Clara knew that she would

make it come true one day, because she had managed to do the hardest thing in the world, and Mum laughing at Clara talking to the chickens was living proof.

38

After they worked out a plan with Rachel at the tearooms, and the rain had stopped, Clara walked Tassie across the road back to her home, ensuring she didn't slip on the road.

'Have you asked Henry about Pansy coming to read with me?' Tassie asked as she opened the door.

'Not yet, we've been busy,' Clara said and Tassie laughed.

'I can tell. Don't forget school starts soon and Pansy needs to know her letter sounds at the very least.'

Clara paused. 'Do you want to come and see the cottage and ask Henry yourself? It might be better coming from you, otherwise I'll look like the evil stepmother trying to get rid of the child.'

'Are you going to be the stepmother?'

For a woman closer to ninety years of age than she was to eighty-nine, she didn't miss a trick, Clara thought as she felt Tassie's eyes try and bore holes into her mind.

'I don't know yet. I just like being with him and Pansy.' She smiled and corrected herself: 'Actually, I love being with him and Pansy.'

Tassie nodded in understanding. 'Then I should come to the cottage and see that all is as it should be.'

Clara laughed as Tassie closed the door and locked it. They went to Clara's car and drove to the cottage.

Henry was on the roof when they arrived and Pansy was lying on the lawn on a blanket, surrounded by her dolls and animals.

'Tassie,' Pansy cried, when Clara opened the car door and she ran towards them.

Henry waved from above.

'Henry, this is Tassie McIver, my friend who lives in the village,' Clara called up.

Henry waved. 'I'll come down,' he said.

'Come inside,' said Clara. She wanted Tassie's approval of not just Henry but also the cottage.

She opened the front door and Tassie walked inside and looked around. Then she walked to the living space, which was still a mess, and then to the kitchen and out through the back door.

'Don't you want to see upstairs?' asked Clara, as Henry joined her side.

'Stairs at my age are not my friends, dear,' said Tassie as she walked out towards the huge oak tree in the back garden.

'What a beauty she is,' said Tassie to the tree more than to Clara.

Clara and Henry stood back as Pansy went to Tassie and held her hand and looked up at the tree also.

'Sometimes I hear the tree whisper to me,' said Pansy to Tassie as though this was an entirely normal thing.

'Of course you do, pet,' said Tassie. 'What does she say?'

'She says that I am loved.'

'That you are.'

'And that Mummy is here with me.'

Clara felt herself tense at the mention of Naomi. Should she be jealous of a dead woman? There was nothing to be jealous of except the energy she left behind that still wrapped Henry and Pansy in its starry cloak.

'Of course Mummy is here, and Daddy and Clara and everyone,' said Tassie in a very no-nonsense voice.

Pansy was quiet for a moment. 'The tree also says that I should have ice cream more than once a week. And cake is good for breakfast and eating your crusts doesn't make your hair curly.' She turned and looked pointedly at Henry.

Henry burst out laughing and Pansy turned to glare at him.

'You don't know what it said to me,' she said to her father and turned back to the tree.

Clara nudged Henry who nodded.

'No, I don't know what it said to you Pansy. I apologise for being rude. I'm just jealous because the tree didn't talk to me.' And then to Clara: 'Shall we talk over tea?'

Clara felt nervous as she went into the kitchen and made a pot of tea and put out some shortbread she had bought in Salisbury.

Henry came and sat down at the table with Tassie.

'Clara talks about you often,' he said.

'As she does you,' said Tassie and she leaned over the table and patted his hand. 'Now, I would like to borrow your child.'

Clara put out the cups, trying hard not to clatter or clash them so as not to ruin the moment with clumsiness.

Henry seemed surprised. 'Borrow her for what? I'm afraid she would be a terrible scullery maid.'

'I am old,' said Tassie, and Clara noticed she was putting on a more tired voice than usual, or was she a little more tired than usual? 'And I want to spend some time with your little one and help her learn to read for school. I used to be a schoolteacher in the village. It would charm me no end to have some time to teach again.'

Henry crossed his arms.

'She's attending the school in Chippenham next month – they can teach her.'

Clara sat down. 'Oh I think Tassie knows that; she just wanted to give Pansy a head start because she's a year behind the others.'

'Are you saying I've held my daughter back?' asked Henry in a clipped tone.

'No, that's not what I'm saying,' said Clara but Tassie put her hand up.

'That's exactly what's she saying,' said Tassie. 'You have held her back to protect her and love her and ensure that she will be with you and untouched by the horrible things that happen in life but you can't do that forever, Henry. You will give her the best gift of all by letting her read and discover the world and start school with a joy for words and numbers and art and science.'

Henry was silent but Clara could see the muscles in his jaw twitching.

The way Tassie presented the situation was entirely reasonable and compassionate and she watched Henry process the information.

'Naomi wanted to home-school her,' he finally said.

'But Naomi is gone now, pet,' said Tassie. 'Sad but true and sometimes the old ways aren't for the new times. She will understand – you can ask her later. Do you love your little one with everything you have?' she gently asked Henry who nodded and Clara could see tears in his eyes, wetting his long lashes.

'Then let her discover the world with the wisdom of her mother and the bravery of her father to guide her.'

There was silence for a moment.

'And I would love the company of a little girl with a sharp mind and a taste for butterfly cakes to give me some purpose again.'

Henry sighed.

'How can I argue against any of that?' He looked at Clara. 'What do you think?'

Clara shrugged and smiled at him. God, she loved him so much but he was so lost when the task was emotional and not physical.

'I think it would be good for Pansy and I think it would be good for you. Practice for the longer days when she is at school.'

Henry sipped his tea and then ate a shortbread biscuit. Clara saw him looking at the cupboard where Naomi was.

'Okay,' he said and he got up from the table, pushing the chair out with his legs, and walked out of the kitchen. They heard him climbing up onto the roof.

'He's upset,' said Clara looking up at the ceiling.

'Not with you, pet, he's upset with life, because it gave him a bad hand the first time round but he will process it up on the roof. He's closer to spirits up there, so it won't take him long to understand.'

'I'm pretty sure you're a witch.' Clara laughed.

Tassie smiled and sipped her tea. 'And how are you sure you're not one also?'

Before Clara could say anything, Pansy came running into the kitchen.

'The tree said there are biscuits and I must have one.'

Clara looked at Tassie and sighed. 'This tree whispering is going to be an excuse for everything from now on, and I blame you.'

Tassie shrugged and held out the plate of shortbread to Pansy before looking at Clara.

'If you listen closely to her and the tree, you might learn a few things also.'

'Like what?' said Clara as she pulled Pansy onto her lap.

'Whatever it is you need to know, Clara Maxwell. Because you stopped listening to your inner Clara a long time ago, and only you know why. But I tell you this, if you don't start hearing the wisdom again, then it will roar in your face until you hear it, and that is never pleasant and it always comes with a strong dose of heartbreak.'

Clara sat very still with Pansy on her lap. 'What do you mean?' But Tassie shook her head at Clara.

'No more, you know what I am talking about. Now take me home, I have to get ready for my new student.'

39

Clara decided to immerse herself in her rural dream. She was ready to become crafty except she didn't know how to be crafty. For years she had read books on how to knit or sew or crochet but had never actually sat down and tried, so the following Saturday Clara arrived at Tassie's house after lunch with her needles and bag of cotton yarn.

This was Clara's knitting lesson and she was nervous.

Tassie had offered to teach Clara how to knit when she had seen the jar of knitting needles in her hall cupboard.

'I have a book but it's hard to understand,' said Clara.

'You don't learn from a book, you learn from a knitter,' said Tassie firmly. 'Now mind you, I haven't knitted in about ten years, haven't had anyone to knit for, but I will teach you how to knit dishcloths.'

'Dishcloths?' asked Clara.

'Nothing like having a dishcloth you have made yourself and they wash in the machine and they are very easy to make and long-lasting. I never bought those cloths when I was first married. I made everything myself, mostly because I had to. George was a milkman and didn't earn much and neither did I.'

Tassie's old hands defied their age when she cast on the

cotton yarn she had instructed Clara to buy and soon she was knitting away.

'The moss pattern is good for scrubbing and the one you're doing, with the plain and purl is good for glasses and china.'

So Clara sat in the armchair opposite Tassie and knitted slowly. Sometimes she dropped a stitch but Tassie showed her how to loop it back on and keep going.

'It feels like a nice metaphor for life.' Clara laughed. 'Fall down once, get up again.'

Clara watched Tassie knit. Her fingers flew and the wool formed into a pretty pattern called moss stitch according to Tassie.

'Who taught you to knit?' asked Clara, as she tried to wrangle her own needles.

'My mum,' said Tassie looking up. 'She could knit a boat if I had asked, and there wouldn't be a leak. Could have sailed it to Australia and back again.'

'Tell me about your mum,' said Clara.

She doubted she could have been more at peace than she was at this moment.

This was why she moved to the country, she thought. And Tassie was the best part. She looked forward to seeing her friend and would do little things to help her when she could or when she saw she needed help.

Rachel was bringing her meals now instead of meals on wheels, so Clara knew she was getting proper nutrition. Henry had helped in the garden and put in smoke alarms in the house, after a horrified Clara had learned there were none.

'You could die in a fire,' she admonished Tassie.

'I could also die being run over by one of those tour

buses that come for Rachel's cream puffs and rabbit pies,' Tassie had answered back but she seemed very intrigued when Henry came on his ladder and put them on the ceiling. 'Sometimes accidents happen. I once read about a man who was hit by a falling turtle that an eagle high above him was carrying home for supper. A tragic accident.'

There were many arguments Clara could have given to dispute Tassie's reasoning and story but then she heard her own mum's voice in her head.

'Sometimes it is better to be kind than right.' So she said nothing; besides, who was she to say why things worked out the way they did?

'There are no accidents,' Mum used to say, which didn't make what happened any easier. She should have never said what happened to her father was an accident – no one would have believed it, certainly not a jury.

Clara pushed the thoughts of her father away as she tried to focus on her knitting but she had lost her place.

'In through the front door
Around the back
Out through the window
And off jumps Jack.'

She heard Tassie remind her and she reworked the line until she had the rhythm again.

'It's harder than it looks,' she said.

'What is?'

'The knitting,' said Clara, trying not to put her tongue out the side of her mouth as she worked.

'Everything is hard to start with but eventually you find your own way,' Tassie said as she pulled more yarn from the ball and kept going.

'Can you sew?' asked Clara as she worked slowly, stopping after every row to check her work.

'Naturally, all women my age and from my background can sew but don't ask me to show you because I couldn't even thread a needle now.'

Tassie had whizzed through her first dishcloth and cast it off and patted it flat on her knee. 'There you go, first one down.'

Clara looked at the neat stiches compared to hers, with a few missing ones, and sighed.

'Don't compare,' said Tassie, putting down her knitting needles and pushing herself to standing. 'Now I will put the kettle on. Rachel has left us some lovely Monte Carlo biscuits with blackberry jam from Joe's garden.'

'I can do that,' said Clara. Tassie seemed so frail at times, Clara worried she would fall and break a hip or worse. If it could happen to Moira, it could easily happen to Tassie. Then at other times she seemed fitter and faster than Clara, especially when Pansy was around. When Clara had commented on it, Tassie had laughed. 'I am taking some of her energy, because she has yards and yards of it to spare.'

It was true, Clara thought, Pansy's energy was contagious and most nights she and Henry were in fits of laughter at Pansy's antics.

Clara made to turn on the kettle but Tassie was up before her, waving her hand at her.

'No, dear, stay there – it's good for me to move about. Before you came and before I was friendly with Rachel, I would never move about. Never felt better since I have some reason to potter about.'

Clara finished off the row and then followed Tassie into

the kitchen, where she was carefully putting the Monte Carlos onto a pretty plate decorated with violets.

'Do you think Joe and Rachel might become an item?' Clara asked, as she pulled out Tassie's cups and saucers.

'Oh, I can't say yet,' said Tassie vaguely. 'Could be. I saw a little heart in my cup this morning.'

'Perhaps we should seek out a Wise Woman in Chippenham and see if we can't make a spell for them to fall in love,' said Clara with a cheeky smile at Tassie.

'Oh no, dear, you can never do a love spell for someone else, because it comes back to you.'

Clara wasn't sure if Tassie was serious. 'What do you mean?'

'If we do a love spell for Joe to fall in love with Rachel, then he might fall in love with us, and the last thing I need is a man hanging about my garden with a hangdog face. I have already had a litter of rescue dogs in my lifetime to care for.'

Clara laughed. 'I love that! Well, if he fell for you, it would be because you're amazing and you are the brightest, smartest woman I know, so he's only human if he does.'

Tassie reached over and patted Clara's hand.

'The best thing we can do is make the conditions right for Joe and Rachel to find their way to each other. Clear the path for them to see each other. Moira was the first obstacle and since there are no accidents, then we have to believe that they will find their way to each other.'

Clara looked out of Tassie's kitchen window at a group of crows on the fence, as Tassie came to her side to warm the teapot with hot water from the tap and also looked out at the birds.

'One for sorrow, two for joy, three for a girl, four for a boy, five for silver, six for gold, seven for a secret, never to be told, eight for a wish, nine for a kiss, ten for a time of joyous bliss.'

Clara counted the birds on the fence. Seven for a secret, never to be told.

She felt a shiver run up her back and a sound in her ears like fingernails on a blackboard and she wondered if she could ever talk about what happened to her that night and who would ever understand.

40

The cinema in Chippenham was busy when Joe and Rachel walked inside.

'I'll get the tickets,' he said and walked to the counter.

Rachel nodded, holding on to her large tote bag. She had bought her own snacks for them because she wanted what she wanted, and she had read about someone who saw a mouse inside the popcorn machine at a cinema and couldn't get the image from her mind.

Sweet and salty popcorn, drizzled with honey, vanilla and salt, and homemade orange cordial in glass bottles to wash it down. And a little freezer bag with two cones of chocolate ice cream that she had made, scooped into a handmade waffle cone, and dipped in milk chocolate that she had melted on the double boiler that morning.

Joe had asked her to the movies on a Sunday afternoon, and Clara and Alice said they would look after the shop, which was mostly tourists wanting Devonshire teas on a Sunday. Everything was going smoothly inside the bakery and tearooms when Joe picked up Rachel in his butcher's van.

He seemed nervous but he couldn't be as nervous as she felt. Her hands fumbled with the seatbelt and Joe had to help her pull it so it then clipped with a sharp snap to let her know it was in place.

Joe had leaned across her to pull the belt out and she noticed he had a dry scalp. Mother would have said something but she didn't because she couldn't understand why you would point out negative things about people other than to make them feel sad about themselves. He also had acne scars on his skin but he smelled nice. Like soap and black pepper. It reminded her of her dad and she wanted to kiss his neck.

He was the first man she had ever wanted to kiss who was in close proximity and not on the television or in a book.

Her romantic interests had been confined to Daniel Radcliffe, Michael Bublé, Ed Sheeran and Mr Rochester but Mother reminded her the first time she wore lipstick that she was as plain as a scone and no amount of jam would make her appetising to any man.

Rachel was trying to not call Moira Mother but she found it was hard to remember. Old habits die hard, as Tassie reminded her.

Joe came over to where she stood pretending to be interested in a poster for a horror movie.

'You like horror movies?' asked Joe.

'Not really,' said Rachel. 'You?'

'Oh, I hate them,' said Joe. 'I spend all my days cutting up carcasses so why would I want to watch that for entertainment. Give me a good action movie or a nice romantic comedy and I'm happy.'

Rachel felt relief at his words but she wasn't sure why.

Maybe it was all the pain and abuse she'd had from Moira? She wasn't sure but she knew she didn't want to see that on any screen or live it again. She wanted a quiet life with the tearooms and the bakery and to save enough money to do them up one day.

'Do you want snacks?' Joe asked.

'No, I brought us some things,' said Rachel, anxious he would think less of her, as though she was frugal in the wrong ways.

'Oooh, I'm excited now,' said Joe. 'I'm sure they will be better than anything you would buy. Now I think I'm more excited about the snacks than the movie.'

Rachel walked with him into the cinema and Joe checked the tickets.

'L twenty-two and twenty-three,' he said peering at the letters and numbers in the little brass plaques on the floor.

Soon they were in their seats, and as the lights went down, Rachel pulled the container of popcorn out and handed it to Joe to hold, while she opened them an orange drink each and handed him one.

The movie started and soon Rachel was swept away into the glamorous world of spies with impossibly beautiful women and exotic locations that seemed remote and unlikely for her to visit, doing things she could never dream of doing.

But as she handed Joe the ice cream in the middle of the movie, and he looked at her in the darkness of the film and whispered, 'You're amazing,' she felt a thrill as though she was as beautiful as the girls on the screen, and in the most exotic place in the world, instead of a tired cinema with soft-drink-stained carpet and God-knows-what-stained seats.

Their arms touched on the armrest and Joe took her hand. It felt like the most natural thing in the world and her hand felt right in his.

Joe the butcher. Now away from the barbs of Mother, Moira, she self-corrected, she could see him clearly away from the snide comments about his skin and his intelligence. Joe the butcher was an idiot, Moira used to say. But Joe wasn't an idiot.

He had finished school. Then he took over his dad's shop when he had a stroke. He raised Alice when his mum died and his dad had a final and devastating stroke. She understood responsibility and guilt and grief. He had no time for anything but work and Alice but now he had time for Rachel.

In fact, she realised he'd always had time for her. The timing of his deliveries were mostly when Moira wasn't there. He always brought her the best cuts of meat. One time he had brought her a bunch of daffodils because he said they made him sneeze but now she wondered why he had daffodils in the first place. Rachel had told Moira that a customer dropped them off for her, and Moira had put them proudly on the table upstairs and mentioned them whenever she passed, commenting on how many admirers she had.

Rachel had smiled at them when she passed because of the secret she held from Moira but now she wondered if she smiled because Joe gave them to her.

She squeezed his hand. It was impulsive but it felt right, thinking about the past and being here now.

Joe squeezed her hand back, and Rachel realised that there were parts of her past that were okay, maybe even nice. If only she could block out the other parts, she might just survive it with Joe holding her hand.

41

The mornings were still warm, with the roses on the fence demanding attention when Clara went out to try and tie them back. She had been clearing the undergrowth of weeds and volunteer plants that had popped up over the past decades, happy in their wild setting.

Tassie had loaned her a book of common garden plants and she was outside every morning trying to identify them, and work out which ones she wanted to keep, train, tame or do away with. Between gardening and knitting and looking after the chickens and finishing the painting of the inside of the house Clara was busy and tired at night. It was a different sort of tiredness than she had felt before. More bone-weary but happy with what she had achieved. She could see the work starting to emerge in the garden, with a sense of order among the wild plantings.

There was a peace in the garden in the mornings; even the chickens seemed to respect her time, as they pottered about in the coop. Pansy would always check for the eggs before Henry took her to Tassie's for reading lessons in the morning.

When he was back, Clara would have made them coffee and they would talk about what they wanted to do that morning around the cottage or the garden.

Sometimes plans went awry and they ended up in bed again, learning each other's bodies and desperate to be in constant physical contact.

Other times they pottered about. The roof was finished, the insulation was in, and the insurance company had taken the van away to be repaired.

It seemed odd to look out the window and not see the van with the oak tree branch on top, but it also felt safe. The van was a constant reminder that Henry and Pansy could go at any moment.

They hadn't talked about what next after the cottage was finished and the van was fixed.

Henry didn't discuss the future or make overtures about them being married or staying in the cottage or even what was happening next week.

They had a month before Pansy started school and there was a sense of avoidance around both issues.

But Clara didn't know how to bring it up. If she said, *Stay with me and keep your dead wife's ashes in the cupboard in the cottage pie container, and let's get married and I will love Pansy as my own*, she thought he would run.

She wondered if she was actually his rebound relationship.

But there were moments when it was so perfect she thought she would die from happiness.

'Take a mental snapshot,' her mother used to say when something nice happened.

Clara's mind was filled with them now: Henry handing her tea in the garden and admiring her digging work in the vegetable patch.

Pansy on her lap as she read her the stories about the chair with wings and a naughty pixie.

Pansy calling out excitedly when she found an egg in the chicken coop, as though it was extraordinary and she hadn't collected three the day before.

Henry's face when he was above her. His face when he was below her. The look in his eyes when she knew he was going to lead her to bed.

Henry was taking Pansy to Tassie's, so she walked to the oak tree and stood quietly underneath its beautiful canopy.

'Listen to the whispers,' Tassie had said.

She stood in the silent morning, waiting.

'What do I need to know?' she whispered to the tree. A slight breeze drifted past, and she closed her eyes and tried to hear.

She could hear the occasional chat of the chickens. Leaves rustling. But nothing else was coming into range.

She tried to block out all the sounds and focus on the trees but still couldn't hear anything.

She laughed at herself as she heard her car pull up outside and walked around to see Henry, holding something in his arms.

'What have you got?' She smiled at him. He was being very careful and tender as he moved towards her.

'I bought you something, although Pansy will fight you for it.'

Clara peered into his arms and saw a blanket and a little black nose.

'What is that?' she asked.

'It's a puppy.' He held it out for her to take.

'A puppy?' Clara was genuinely confused. 'You were taking Pansy to lessons. How did you come across a puppy?'

She moved the blanket and saw the little face and was instantly in love.

'Oh my God. What's its name?' asked Clara, as she held the tiny thing to her face.

A little pink tongue licked her cheek.

'Whatever you want to call him,' said Henry, beaming at her and the puppy.

'What sort of dog is it?' She held it up to look at him. He was brown with black markings and he was squat with tiny legs and a funny-shaped long body and a larger head. He was completely out of proportion and Clara was madly in love with the dog and Henry.

'Joe the butcher had him in his van. I saw him when I was leaving Tassie's. He was going to see Rachel and showed me him in the car. Rachel said she couldn't have him in the bakery. Joe thinks he is part-dachshund, part-labrador. His neighbour found him in a gumboot. They thought it was a rat. Perhaps another farmer put them out to die and this one escaped. They're not sure.'

'Oh, darling,' said Clara, holding the pup close to her. 'In a gumboot – that is the saddest thing I have ever heard.' She looked up at Henry.

'We will need to go to Chippenham and get puppy things,' she said and handed the dog to Henry. 'Put him in the garden and encourage him to do a wee and let me get my bag.'

'Okay,' said Henry and she leaned up and kissed his cheek. 'You are a sweet, sweet man. I didn't even know I wanted a dog until I met Gumboot.'

'Gumboot?' He laughed as they walked through the gate and Henry put the dog onto the grass.

'He is shaped like a gumboot and was found in one. I think it's fitting. If the gumboot fits, as they say.'

'Okay, Gumboot it is then,' said Henry.

Clara rushed inside and picked up her handbag and her phone. She saw she had three missed calls from an unknown number but no messages were left, so she ignored them and found a box and blanket for Gumboot and went out and put it on the back seat.

'He can sit in the back,' she said, as Henry carried him over and carefully placed him in the box on the soft blanket.

'You drive,' she said. 'In case he needs me.'

Henry laughed as they got into the car.

'We should get him looked at by a vet,' said Clara.

'Joe already did. He's fine but small. Needs proper food and care and he will bounce back.'

By the time they drove back to Merryknowe, Gumboot had a new bed, special puppy food, toys, a little hot water bottle for night-time and a little jacket to grow into for cold days.

He also had a navy-blue collar with a silver tag engraved with his name and Clara's phone number.

'We'll pick up Pansy and then head home,' Henry said as they drove into the village.

Lunchtime was busy at the bakery, with people spilling around the front eating sausage rolls out of brown paper bags and the tables inside were filled. A large tourist bus was parked further down near the church. Gumboot was asleep in the box, exhausted from the time in the pet store and the car, where he'd cried until Clara held him.

Clara walked into the shop and went behind the counter.

'So busy,' she said to Rachel who passed with three plates of Devonshire teas.

'We were named on some website as being the best tearooms in the area and this is the second bus to come and they said there will be another one later. I can't keep up.' Rachel rushed out to the tables, frazzled.

Clara saw Alice was helping and another girl she presumed was a friend of Alice's.

'I would stay and help but I have a new dog,' she said as Rachel whizzed by again, as though on roller skates. She looked down at Rachel's feet and saw she was wearing new fashionable sneakers.

'Nice shoes,' she commented.

'Thanks. Alice recommended them, so Joe took me to Salisbury to buy them,' said Rachel and Clara saw her blush.

'Lovely,' she said. Rachel looked her age now, not like a retired nun, and whatever was happening with her and Joe was giving her a spring in her sneakered step.

'I will need to talk to you later about what we can do about Moira. Do you want to catch up at the pub tonight?'

Rachel nodded. 'Seven?' she suggested.

Clara agreed and left them to the rush.

Her phone rang as she was leaving the tearooms. The same number as before and she answered it, hoping it wasn't Judas or Piles.

'Clara Maxwell?' asked the voice.

'Yes?'

It's James Lang from Commercial Property in Salisbury. I am trying to get onto Rachel Brown but she isn't answering, so her mother gave me your number.'

'How can I help?' asked Clara carefully. What was Moira

up to now? she wondered. Moira Brown was a piece of work and Clara's instincts told her this call wasn't good news.

'Mrs Brown has decided to sell the bakery and tearooms and I am to come and take measurements, and she wanted you to ensure Rachel would be there.'

Clara stood in the middle of the road, as Pansy and Henry stepped out of Tassie's house and waved at them.

She paused and then she spoke clearly and firmly.

'Moira Brown doesn't own that property. Her step-daughter Rachel Brown does, so tell her she can go and stick it up her jumper, because we are about to take her to court for everything and more. So tell her to get ready because I'm about to make her life as unpleasant as she has made Rachel's for the last twenty-five years.'

42

Convincing Rachel to see Moira at the rehabilitation centre took some serious negotiating and swift talking from Clara but in the end, losing the bakery and tearooms was a bigger fear than the venom that Moira spat out. Clara had driven her to the hospital and was waiting in the car park in case she needed her. Rachel just had to call, using the new phone that she had bought with Joe when they went shopping. She held the phone in the pocket of her jacket as she walked towards the centre.

The automatic doors of the hospital opened and Rachel saw Moira sitting inside the reception area. She was without makeup and her hair was flat and without colour. She looked much older, thought Rachel but not unkindly. It was the truth but she wouldn't say it aloud to Moira. She had worn a new denim jacket and a sundress with tiny green and pink flowers on it that Clara had given her, stating it didn't suit her. Everything suited Clara, so Rachel knew it was because she thought Rachel dressed like an old woman, which she did because Moira had always chosen her clothes.

But Clara wanted to take her shopping for clothes and for ideas for the tearooms. Her world was so exciting now, but the sight of Moira made her feel sick. She took a deep breath as Tassie had told her to – she said it helped settle the nerves and blow the bad spirits out, and then the truth will be said.

'I'm here to get you to sign some papers,' she said as Clara had instructed.

Moira waved her hand at her. 'Go away, I'm not signing anything for you.'

'You took the money Dad left me and spent it and now you want to sell the bakery and tearooms and keep the money? And you lied to me about you being my mother.' Rachel shook her head. 'I don't understand how you could do that.'

'What have you done to your hair? It looks awful,' said Moira but Rachel knew it did not look awful, so she ignored the insult. For so long she had thought everything Moira said was true. But she was coming to realise she was nothing of what Moira said and so much more of what Joe and Tassie and Clara saw in her.

'Clara says I could sue you,' stated Rachel, trying to remember everything Clara had coached her on, and in what order.

The real estate agent had told Moira what Clara said and in three days Moira had called the shop relentlessly until Rachel agreed to go and see her.

Clara had offered to but Rachel knew Moira only wanted her, so they discussed the approach.

'You owe her nothing,' said Clara. 'Do not respond to insults or her manipulation. She's only saying it to try and get you to get upset and cave to her demands.'

But Rachel was worried. No one was as good at

manipulation as Moira Brown, and no one could survive one of her emotional attacks. Rachel prayed for neither but wasn't holding out hope.

'Sit down and tell me about the shop,' said Moira, changing tack.

Rachel sat on one of the visitors' chairs and remembered Clara's words. 'Tell her nothing. Everything is the same as usual.'

Rachel cleared her throat. 'It's fine. Same as always.'

Moira looked at her closely. 'But that's not true surely?'

Rachel tried to think what Clara had advised if Moira doubted her but she realised they hadn't covered this part.

'It's true,' said Rachel but her voice sounded uncertain to her.

'Have you put the prices up?' asked Moira. Rachel could feel her eyes searching her face.

'No,' she said, happy to have told the truth.

'So nothing has changed but you're making four times as much? How is that possible?' asked Moira.

Rachel was silent, trying to think, wishing she had brought Clara, who was outside in the car waiting.

Moira leaned forward and dug her long nails into Rachel's bare leg. 'Why are you lying to me? I see the bank deposits. You didn't think about that, did you? What have you done to my shop?'

'It's my shop,' said Rachel in a small voice.

Moira's nails went deeper. 'No, it's my shop. I bought it. I raised you. I fed you and clothed you. I gave you a job because you couldn't do anything else. You owe me everything. I could have given you to the orphanage. You're a sad, retarded girl whose own father didn't want to be around her so he hanged himself for me to find.'

Her words pierced Rachel's heart like Moira's thumbnail was piercing the skin on her thigh but she thought of Joe and Clara and Alice and the shop. She thought of Tassie and Pansy and the lady who wrote to her saying she wanted to write a story about Rachel's baking skills, and she thought about her father.

'Get your hand off me,' she hissed so fiercely that Moira did. Then she leaned forward. 'You are a sad, ugly woman who my father hated so much he would rather die than spend another day with you. I read his will. Did you know he left a copy at the probate office?'

Moira's face went even paler than it already was.

'He left the money to me and his sister and somehow, you managed to not let my aunt know and you took me and the money and turned me into your slave.'

Rachel paused, trying to gather the right words. She had never been one to give speeches. Since her father had died, she had been told to be quiet, that she was stupid, that she was useless and hopeless.

Clara and Tassie showed her this wasn't true. Her own skills in the kitchen proved Moira wrong but there was something else and she grasped the tiny acorn in her pocket that Tassie had told her to carry for strength and luck.

'I don't know how you have been able to live with yourself this entire time, Moira, so how you move forward in life is your decision, but my decision is I do not want you anywhere near me and my shop. I will pay you half of what the building is worth, so you can have some money to get started and that's my final offer.'

'I won't accept,' said Moira haughtily.

Rachel leaned forward and whispered in Moira's ear. 'You don't have a choice, Moira. Otherwise I will go from here to the police and have you charged with abuse and fraud, so can you tell me if you will accept the deal now?'

She stared at Moira, waiting for the reply even though she knew the answer. Eventually Moira nodded and turned her face away from Rachel.

Rachel walked out of the building into the bright sunshine and to Clara's car.

Gumboot jumped up at the window when she came to the side and Clara grabbed him so Rachel could open the door.

'How did it go?' asked Clara as Rachel sat in the seat and stared ahead.

'She didn't sign the papers to hand over the deed of the building.'

'What a bitch, give them to me, I'll get her to sign.' Clara went to pull them from Rachel's hands.

'No,' she snapped and held on to them.

'Rachel, you can't let her win. We talked about this at the pub. You agreed she needs to do the right thing.'

But Rachel shook her head. 'I am not letting her win. I'm letting her go. I don't want to spend the rest of my life hating her. I don't hate her; I feel nothing towards her. I will sell the tearooms and give her the money, and keep the bakery. It will be enough to live on.'

'But your dream for the tearoom,' cried Clara.

Rachel thought about spending the future fighting Moira over her fraudulent claim to her money and having to relive the pain and loss of her parents, and the lies Moira had told her.

Moira was a sad and lonely woman who had once been a beauty and who was now bitter from her decisions in life.

Tassie had once said there was nothing sadder than a faded beauty, and she realised that was true. Moira was truly lost and part of Rachel felt compassion but she couldn't forgive her.

She turned to Clara. 'I can't let this guide my life. I hated her for so long and would dream of one hundred ways to kill her. What does that make me? I don't want to live with that anymore. I just want her out of my life and for my life to move forward. If that means I have to have a smaller life to be free of her, then that's okay with me, so it should be okay with you.'

Clara was silent, clutching the steering wheel and Rachel noticed her knuckles were white.

'I don't expect you to understand about those things I spoke about, Clara. The pain, the violence, the guilt, and the sadness, but this is what works for me now. I just want her gone from my life.'

Clara drove them back to Merryknowe, and when Rachel got out of the car, she went to say thank you to Clara but she drove away before she could speak.

She watched the red car disappear into the distance, then saw Tassie's curtain flicker in the window across the road.

Tassie would understand. She walked to the old woman's front door and as she was about to knock, it opened.

'Cup of tea, love?' Tassie asked and Rachel burst into tears.

'Come in and let it out, love. Nahla came and cleaned and made a nice butter chicken for me, not too spicy, and some of her fancy thin bread. Come and share, and we can talk. I will read your future and show you that everything has a funny way of working out.'

So Rachel did.

43

Tassie folded a tea towel over the handrail next to her sink, as Pansy ran outside in the neatly trimmed garden at Tassie's house.

'I just don't understand why she let Moira get away with it all,' Clara said.

'But she's not getting away with anything. She's left with nothing, not a friend in the world and not enough money to live the way she thinks she ought to live,' said Tassie. 'That's not much of a life. She'll have to get a job, as she's not the age for the pension yet.'

'Still…' said Clara, now tapping her nails on the table.

'Still nothing,' said Tassie firmly. 'Just because you want a type of justice doesn't mean you get it. She got the justice that Rachel feels comfortable with. You wouldn't want her to have to live with guilt forever, would you? That's not good for anyone. Secrets and guilt get very heavy to carry after a while.'

Clara was quiet; all her previous fight had gone with Tassie's words.

Tassie sat opposite her with a bowl of peas and started to shell them.

'Did you grow these?' asked Clara, as she picked up some pea pods and started copying Tassie.

'I did indeed,' said Tassie.

'I'd like to grow peas,' Clara said, as she ate one.

'You can grow anything in that soil out there,' said Tassie.

They shelled peas in silence, Tassie occasionally looking at Clara and then out through the open back door to check on Pansy who was doing a dance routine and singing to the apricot tree.

'You all right, pet?' Tassie asked Clara.

'Of course, why?' Clara's voice was tight but Tassie could sense the emotion beneath the tone.

'You seem frustrated,' Tassie stated.

Clara shelled some more peas and then looked at Tassie.

'I don't know where I am, or what I'm doing, and I don't know what Henry wants. We never talk about the future. It's only about what needs to be done in the cottage, but what happens when it's finished? What then?'

Tassie kept shelling the peas. 'Why don't you ask him?'

Clara said nothing.

'Because you don't know what you want?' Tassie encouraged.

'I thought I wanted the country life, but I think I'm going to be bored… but I don't want to go and work in a bank in Salisbury. That defeats the purpose of the move.'

'Life in a small village isn't for everyone, no,' agreed Tassie.

'And once the cottage is done and the garden is sorted and planted and besides maintaining it, and collecting the eggs, what else can I do?'

Tassie shrugged. 'You could start a business.'

'Doing what?' Clara scoffed.

'But it's not just about the cottage is it?' Tassie said being careful. Clara was in a mood and everything in her way risked being pummelled.

'I don't know,' said Clara but Tassie did know and she understood.

'Pansy is a fast learner,' she said. 'Whipping through the letters easily. I think she will be right as rain for school soon.'

'And that's the other thing – Henry still hasn't got her uniform. He said he would go into Chippenham and get her sorted but he hasn't and I don't want to be in the nagging wife role, reminding him, but he hasn't done it yet and it's annoying me. She needs shoes and hair ribbons and new pencils and a bag and lunch box and, well, everything.'

'That she does,' said Tassie, nodding in agreement.

'My mum always had my things ready for me when school started,' Clara said. 'But I can't say anything, because what am I to him and Pansy? And meanwhile his dead wife is in my cupboard in the cottage pie container and I swear to God I can hear her sometimes.'

'What does she say?' Tassie asked, looking up at Clara.

'I don't know but it feels like judgement,' said Clara, making a face at the peas in the bowls between them.

'You look like a child when you make that face,' said Tassie.

Clara sighed. 'I know what I sound like. I'm feeling like I'm in between two worlds right now and I don't know where I'm heading.'

'None of us know where any of us of are heading,' said Tassie. 'But you can draw a map of things that make your heart sing. What would be on your map if you could choose?'

Clara sat in thought.

'Henry. Pansy. You. My grandmother. My mum. The cottage.' She paused.

'What else makes you happy?' Tassie encouraged.

'Seeing Rachel safe. Her plans for the bakery. The tearooms. But I don't think she can do that without money and no bank will lend her the money with her history and age.'

'That seems unfair,' said Tassie shaking her head. 'Her ideas are lovely and would be the makings of this village. Hopefully one day she can make enough money to make that dream come true. What she needs is some business help. Or a partner.'

Tassie felt Clara's eyes on her and then she heard Clara laugh.

'Oh wow, you are good,' said Clara shaking her head.

'Good at what, dear?' asked Tassie as she swept the pea pods into her apron and carried them to the bin.

'Whatever you did just then,' said Clara.

Pansy walked into the kitchen and climbed into Clara's lap.

'I can read letters,' she said to Clara.

'I know, Tassie told me. She said you were the brightest one in her class.'

Pansy beamed at Clara and then nestled into her. 'I'm tired. It's hot outside.'

'Yes, we will go home and see Gumboot and Daddy.'

Clara looked at Tassie who was washing the peas in the sink.

'Do you think Rachel might want to talk to me about it?' she asked tentatively. 'I don't want to push in where I'm not wanted. Like with Henry. He might not want me once the cottage is finished.'

Tassie turned to Clara.

'Clara Maxwell, you are not only wanted in Merryknowe, you are also needed. Now go and take that child home and talk to Henry about what you want and the ribbons and shoes and everything else on your mind and then have a swim down at the creek and cool down. You Taurus girls get so het up when you don't have the bullseye in your sight.'

44

The walls of the cottage were rough and worn as Henry patched and sanded them, preparing them for the pink paint.

He hummed a song. He couldn't remember where he first learned the tune or even what it was but the song was company as he worked.

The roof was fixed; the inside walls were painted. The living room was becoming more habitable, and Clara had ordered a sofa online to be delivered soon. They had chosen it together while lying in bed one night, their feet rubbing as they scrolled through the iPad. Henry had bought her a rug she had admired but said she couldn't afford just yet, and he was excited to see her face when it arrived.

Now they had the internet and the washing machine was busy spinning in the kitchen.

The chickens were laying and chatting as they moved about their coop, and Gumboots was lying on the path in the sunshine, being patient as Pansy drew around him in chalk.

'We have to get your uniform tomorrow, Pansy,' he said, 'and then head in to get some school shoes and a bag.'

Pansy didn't seem to hear or wasn't interested. Perhaps

he was speaking aloud so as to remind himself, he thought.

He had thought about asking Clara to come but he didn't want to burden her with being in the stepmother role. This was his responsibility and he needed to do it.

Pansy's work with Tassie was helping her not only learn her sounds and letters and some words, but also to be less impetuous and inappropriate. He realised she got away with more than she should have because he didn't want her to be sad, but sadness was a part of life, and him telling Pansy off for being rude or using swear words wasn't being mean, it was being a parent.

He checked the time and wondered when Clara would be back. He missed her when they weren't together. She had brought Pansy back from Tassie's, dropped her off and said she had something important to do. She seemed to be grumpy and he wondered what was going on.

'Pans,' he called out.

'Yeah?'

'Yes, Daddy, not yeah,' he said.

'Yeah, Daddy?'

Close enough, he reasoned.

'What did Clara say at Tassie's house before you left?'

Pansy thought for a moment. 'She said that you won't want her when you have finished the cottage.'

Henry felt his mouth drop open.

Why on earth would she feel that?

He put down his tools and walked into the cottage and sat at the kitchen table. Fresh eggs sat in a little pink bowl that they had found at the second-hand shop in Chippenham. The last of the roses were in a glass on the windowsill. Pansy's special cup that she drank her milk from was drying on the dish rack. His shoes were next to Clara's by the back door.

And Naomi was in the cupboard.

He knew what he needed to do but he didn't know if Clara wanted it also.

God, love was complicated. Old love, new love, all love.

And Naomi.

He left his chair and went to the cupboard and opened it and took the container of her ashes out and put them on the table across from where he was sitting.

'Hi, babe,' he said to her.

Hi, babe, he heard her say.

'I'm in love with Clara.'

I know.

He smiled.

'It doesn't mean I love you any less.'

I know.

He paused.

'What am I saying yes to?' he asked and he closed his eyes and listened.

All of it, came her voice and he felt his eyes hurt with tears and he swallowed his pain.

'Can I love you and love her?'

Yes, Naomi said and he reached across the table and pulled the container to him, holding it.

'I have to let you go,' he said.

I need to go, she said. *It's time.*

'I know,' he wept, holding her close.

Will you let me go now, Henry? Will you promise to love our daughter and love your girl and be fully engaged in this life, not our old life?

He nodded, struggling to speak.

Say yes, Henry, say yes.

He opened his eyes. 'Yes,' he said to the empty room.

And he knew she was gone.

45

The bakery was busy so Clara washed her hands, put on an apron and stepped in to help Alice and Rachel. People were waiting to be served and to sit at the tables in the tearooms, as Rachel rushed out of the kitchen with plates of sandwiches, the chicken and leek pie that was so popular and the vegetable Cornish pasty with a chilli tomato relish that Joe had made.

Clara rushed from serving to taking orders to refilling the sandwich trays and making pots of tea for customers but no one was cross or impatient in the shop. Perhaps the smell of the delicious food, or the flushed red faces of the staff, or the genuine sense of good food and good intentions was enough to keep the crowd from uprising.

Since Moira had gone, it was as though a type of fog around the shop and tearooms had lifted and the sun was shining down on the little store.

Clara served butterfly cakes to a happy family visiting from China and then saw to some American retirees who wanted to try the chicken and leek pies. She later waved them goodbye as she met Rachel over the register.

'Thank you,' said Rachel, 'I would be lost without you.'

Clara smiled, nervous about what she was going to ask

after the shop was closed. As a response, she found herself working extra hard for Rachel, perhaps showing Rachel her worth and what she could bring to the store. She could see what Rachel wanted to achieve was possible but only with money and reliable tradespeople.

Clara had often wondered about her relationship with money. While she had never been a big spender like Giles, or Judy, she was also aware of the importance of quality – but since she had been in Merryknowe, she had also understood the value of reusing items. Reusing plastic bags to line the bins, and the compost bin she had started, with Henry and Pansy happily contributing scraps from the kitchen to the mix.

Glass jars and containers were washed out and reused. Clara was cooking more and Henry would bake bread every few days. It was easier than driving into the village or to Chippenham for basics. 'Make do,' she used to hear her mum saying when Clara was a child. Only now did Clara realise how lazy she had been with everything so close as a child and as an adult. How many times did she order takeaway when she couldn't be bothered cooking?

The crowd in the bakery eventually thinned and then Alice went home and Clara helped Rachel clean and close the store.

'Everything sold again,' said Rachel proudly. 'Moira wouldn't believe it if she saw it.'

Clara wondered how Rachel was processing Moira's betrayal but Rachel wasn't very complicated. There was no doubt Moira's terrible abuse impacted her but Rachel lived in the moment in a way that Clara had never been able to achieve.

'Can I talk to you?' she finally asked Rachel as the last chair was put in place.

Rachel paused before she spoke. 'If you want to ask why I'm not doing anything about Moth... Moira, it's because I don't know what to do.'

'No, it wasn't about that. I think I have some ideas for that but we can talk about that later,' said Clara. 'This is about you.'

They went upstairs and sat on the sofa. Clara felt like she was at a job interview.

'I was thinking about something, and I spoke to Tassie about it, and she said I should talk to you so that's what I'm doing.'

Rachel looked worried. 'Is it bad? This thing you're thinking about?'

'I don't think so,' said Clara. But now she wasn't sure. Maybe Rachel wanted to be alone and do the tearooms and bakery her way. Maybe she would see Clara's offer as condescending or controlling like Moira was. She regretted coming and now finding herself in this position.

What had seemed like a great idea with Tassie now felt rude and presumptuous.

'I had an idea but now I think about it, it's not the right idea, I'm sorry,' she heard herself say.

Rachel was silent.

'I think I have to sell the tearooms,' she said suddenly and then started to cry. 'It feels like I am being punished again, just as I am starting to enjoy everything. I used to wake up when Mother... Moira was here and wish I didn't wake up. I used to wish either I was dead or she was, and now she's gone away and I want to wake up. I wake up so excited wondering what I will make today. Sometimes I wake up and I hear what I should make in my head. Things I never thought of making before; it's like I have a magic baking fairy inside my head.'

Rachel's head was in her hands and she rocked on the sofa, her cries cutting through Clara's heart. Grief and shame will ruin her, she thought, remembering the sound and the feeling.

Rubbing Rachel's back, she let her cry until the sobs slowed down and then she spoke gently to the girl. 'You don't have a magic baking fairy in your head, it's just that you're not stressed by Moira anymore, that's why. You can focus on your work and your gift, which is really creative. You're not using your stress thoughts; you're using your artistic talents.'

'Baking isn't artistic. It's just baking. Artistic people do art, not pastry,' said Rachel, as she wiped her eyes with the back of her hand.

Clara went to the bathroom and came back with a box of tissues.

'It is absolutely artistic. Anything that makes a person feel something is art. I don't care if it's a poem or a book or a song or a slice of cake so perfect that it makes you close your eyes and think: I could die right now and I would be happy. If it makes you feel good to be alive or reminds you why you're alive, then it's art.'

Rachel said nothing as she wiped her eyes and then loudly blew her nose.

'Now tell me why you need to sell the tearooms?' asked Clara. She felt like she was back in the bank, helping her clients see reason or sense and not to panic. Panic about money made people do silly things and she did not want Rachel to panic, because Moira would find her way back into the cracks.

As though Moira could hear Clara's thoughts, Rachel spoke.

'I have to sell because Moira needs money and I don't like her but she has nothing. I don't want to ruin her, but if I decide to do something about it, then I would have to sell it all anyway and start again. I thought if I sold the tearooms part of the business and that building, I could put a wall up and just keep the bakery.'

Clara gasped. 'No, the tearooms are where the potential is. That's the cream on top, so to speak.'

'But the kitchen is connected to the bakery,' Rachel reminded her.

'So maybe my idea isn't so stupid now,' said Clara.

'What idea?' asked Rachel.

'I had an idea that I thought was probably too forward and pushy but now I think it might be the answer.'

She paused, feeling strange at being on the other side of the desk, so to speak, pitching her idea like her customers at the bank used to have to pitch to her. She took a deep breath and spoke.

'Let me buy the tearooms and give the money to Moira, and I can be a partner. You will have a bigger cut since I can't really bake, but I'm good with business and we can do the renovation. Henry could do it, and I can help with marketing and so on. I mean, I think we could make the tearooms the best in the country. Really inject some life into the village again.'

Rachel's eyes widened as Clara was speaking. 'How can you afford that?'

Clara swallowed. 'I have money.'

'But that's such a lot of money,' said Rachel. 'Are you rich?'

'Not rich, but I got some money after my dad died. Well, Mum got some, and so did I, and Mum saved it. I invested it when I learned banking at uni, and it grew. Was supposed to be for my retirement but why not start living now?'

The money from Victims of Crime for the death of her grandmother and father had been a weight since she had become aware of it after the court case. It was blood money, she had told her mother who had disagreed. 'Money is money, Clara. Don't tie emotion to it; it will help you one day.' Clara had never wanted to spend it until now. It could help Rachel and it would help her create a life in Merryknowe.

'Please let me do this,' she said. 'It's only money and I want to do this. It will help me also – I'll have an actual job in the village and can stay here. I would have a purpose, a source of income, a reason to get up every day.'

'You could do that?' Rachel asked, still looking confused.

'Which part?' asked Clara.

'All of it.'

Clara heard her mind click into gear and she nodded. 'Pen and paper?'

Rachel jumped up and found both. Clara started to write on the pad and scratched out some figures.

'Okay, we can do it. Moira doesn't deserve anything from you, except maybe criminal charges, but I understand you not wanting to create any more drama in your life. In fact, I respect it.'

She showed Rachel the numbers she had in her head to buy the tearooms and invest in the shop for the renovations.

'That's too much money. It's not worth it,' said Rachel shaking her head.

'It is worth it, your talents are worth it, and I can afford it,' Clara said firmly.

Rachel looked at the figures again and then handed the notepad back to Clara. 'I'm not great with numbers or the accounts.'

'I am.'

'And Henry would help us?'

Clara liked that Rachel used 'us'.

'I think he will.' Would he say yes? She still had to talk to him about them, their 'us'. Why was it all so complicated or was she making it complicated? She was trying to have a simple life in Merryknowe and now she was offering to buy half a business and was in love with a man who was still in love with his dead wife.

'Okay, let's do it.' Rachel's voice interrupted her train of thought.

Clara was surprised. 'Don't you want to think about it? Speak to a lawyer? Get some advice?'

Rachel frowned at Clara. 'Why? I trust you. You saved me.'

'I don't think I did. I mean, life just worked out a funny way for you.'

But Rachel shook her head. 'No, I know what you did

for me and I know what I could have done if Moira came back here.'

Clara was silent for a moment as she played with the pen. 'That's finished now. You don't have to think about it again,' she said though she wondered if she was really saying it to herself. So why did she always think about what happened?

She hadn't told a soul throughout her life. She had gone to school and university and dated boys and had friends and lived with Giles and had a career and no one knew what she did.

Did it matter? Did she need to tell anyone anyway?

But deep down she knew, she had to tell Henry. She had to be honest and tell him and if he left then that was that. At least she would know.

She had imagined telling Giles when they were together. She even tried once but Giles had been so scathing of the story on the news about the woman who killed her husband, she'd said nothing. He wouldn't understand, he couldn't understand, she justified. Giles's mother and father were seemingly perfect like him, balanced and equal and educated. She wondered how they were going with Judy although if she gave them a much-wanted grandchild then she would be fine.

'Let me go home and talk to Henry,' she said to Rachel.

'About the tearooms?' Rachel asked excitedly.

'Among other things,' said Clara as she got up and felt Rachel hug her awkwardly.

'You are amazing, Clara, thank you.'

Clara hugged Rachel back. 'So are you. We are going to turn the tearooms into something everyone will want to come to and it's going to be amazing, I promise.'

And Clara felt truly excited for the future, if she could just bring herself to talk to Henry about her past.

46

Clara – aged 15

Clara walked up the path and silence greeted her. She stopped and listened closely and then ran to the chicken coop.

Screaming, she ran inside and then she saw him. Gran was on the floor. Blood was everywhere and his hands were around Mum's neck and she was turning blue, so Clara grabbed the knife Gran had been using to cut up the potatoes.

She stabbed him until he fell and then he cried her name.

It was a plaintive sound that rang through her bones and ended in her matching his cry. She used a tea towel on him to try and stop the bleeding from his back but the tea towel was soaked through.

Mum had gasped for breath and Clara wasn't sure who to help but Dad grabbed her hand and held on, looking at her, trying to speak but he couldn't get the words out.

'I'm sorry, Dad, I'm sorry,' she had said and he had whispered something to her but when she leaned down to try and hear him, he had died.

Mum had looked at her and at Gran and started to cry

and then she picked up the knife and stabbed him again in the front, four times in the heart.

'Call the police, Clara,' she had said. 'Tell them I've killed your dad.'

So Clara did.

And later, when the police told her that Mum had been arrested and Gran was dead, Clara realised she was all alone in the world and that she had murdered her own father.

47

Henry was holding Naomi's ashes when Clara walked through the door. He saw her look at him and then the ashes, and then she turned and ran upstairs, where the bedroom door slammed.

He put down the container and went and knocked on her door.

'What?' came the reply.

'Can we talk?' he asked.

'Why?' she said.

'Because you're in a bad mood and I want to help.'

'Go and be with Naomi,' he heard her say.

'That's unfair.' He opened the door and saw her lying on the bed, facing away from him.

'Clara, what is going on? Why are you so angry with me?'

'I'm not angry with you, I'm angry with myself.'

She still didn't look at him.

'Why are you angry with yourself?'

She said nothing. Henry had forgotten how to be in an argument with an adult, so he stood helplessly at her side.

'Clara, you're being...'

She rolled over and sat up. 'I'm being what? I come home to tell you exciting news. I want to talk about us and what is happening and you're sitting at the kitchen table hugging your dead wife's ashes. I mean, it's not exactly reassuring that you want to be here with me. You sleep in this bed every night. We make love, you kiss me, but are you imagining it's her? Am I merely a substitute for Naomi?'

Henry felt his body tighten with anger and he walked to the window.

'That's incredibly unfair, and you are making assumptions that are so wrong it's insulting.'

'Am I?' Clara had raised her voice now. 'You don't talk about us, the future, what happens after the cottage is finished. You haven't even got Pansy's things for school.'

Henry went to speak but Clara was roaring now.

'And the fact she is going to school, well that's something else. I mean if it weren't for me, she would be stuck in the van with you, colouring in for the rest of her life.'

That was too far for Henry.

'How dare you say that. You're insinuating I'm a bad parent because I held her back a year.'

Clara laughed and it sounded mean.

'A year, two years, who knows? You are stopping her from having friends and sleepovers and parties and everything else that little children deserve and need but most of all, if it wasn't for me and Tassie, you would be stopping her from learning to read, the most important skill of all.'

'You are out of line,' he said.

'And you're deluded.'

Henry walked out, went downstairs and drank some water to calm down.

How could he have been so wrong about Clara? Why was she being so angry and nasty?

He heard her walk down the stairs and storm into the kitchen.

'You don't want to be here with me, you want to be with her, but she's dead.' Clara tapped the container on the table.

'Stop it,' he warned.

'Stop what? Being honest with you?' she said.

Henry heard himself scoff at her words. 'Honest? That's rich coming from you.'

'What do you mean? I've told you everything.'

'No, you haven't. You said there was something you needed to tell me when we met and since then it's hung like a bloody guillotine over us and every day I wonder if you will tell me what it is. Every day I see it in your face when you are lost in thought. When you're so passionate about helping Rachel. What happened, Clara? What happened?'

She shook her head at him.

'Nothing happened.'

'I don't believe you.'

'You don't have to believe me. I don't know what you're talking about.'

She crossed her arms and stared at him. He sat down at the table.

'I'll wait for you to tell me.'

'There's nothing to tell.'

Henry could hear Pansy talking to Gumboot in the garden. Everything Clara had said, he had worried about himself. He felt like a bad father who had held Pansy back to keep himself happy. He worried about her not having friends or normal childhood experiences. He knew he was doing the right thing by sending her to school and getting her prepared with Tassie but sometimes it was all so hard and he didn't have all the knowledge he should. But Clara? He looked up at her.

He had been wrong about her. She was cruel and knew where to place her cuts so they hurt the most.

'When the van is repaired, Pansy and I will be on our way,' he said quietly.

'I think that's best,' she said.

He could hear a fly angrily buzzing somewhere.

'And I'll get a new box to put Naomi in.' He tapped the lid of the container.

'Oh keep it. I'm sure she won't mind being carted around in your substitute wife's cottage pie container.'

Henry had had enough and he stood up so quickly, his chair fell over with a loud bang. He saw Clara jump and step backwards.

'You are so out of line, I can't believe it. You know nothing about what is in my head, because you don't ask. You're not any more interested in a future with me than you think I am with you. You haven't asked about Pansy starting school, or even invited us to live with you. We have no idea what you want and we are essentially homeless while fixing you this lovely home, which you don't spend any time on. You say you want this simple life but you're filling your life with other people's problems. Rachel and Tassie and the bakery. What are you running away from, Clara?' His voice was raised now, which was rare for him but he was furious at her assumptions and unreasonable attitude.

'Nothing – mind your business. I'm not paying you for your advice,' she screamed in return.

'So what are you paying me for? To fix the cottage or to

sleep with you?' As soon as he said that he regretted it and her face was shattered.

'Oh God, I'm so sorry.' He rushed to her side but she pushed him away.

'No, no, no.' She ran upstairs and he heard the door slam and then just the angry buzzing of a fly somewhere.

48

Tassie had watched Clara leave with a wave and knew the plan had worked. She would get the tearooms up and running and put Merryknowe back on the map again. The little village had so much to offer and now Rachel and Joe were swinging hands and Henry and Clara were an item, soon there would be more little ones in the village and those empty shops and houses would fill up again.

For years she had watched the village contract until it was barely even a place to stop for passers-by. It wasn't as pretty as some of the other villages around with their window boxes and watermills in the town square or Roman ruins and tour guides. But Merryknowe now had Clara and Rachel. They were the real love affair, she realised as she closed the curtains.

A gentle friendship that gave them both what they needed. Support and a purpose.

But there was still the issue of Clara's secret.

Tassie didn't know what it was but she felt it heavy and always around Clara, following her, watching her like a ghost.

And that's when Tassie knew the secret was Clara's father. He was the ghost of regret and guilt and anger.

And if Clara didn't finally admit the secret, let the truth out where it couldn't grow in the darkness of shame, it would eat her alive and she would end up like Sheila Batt: alone, and dead in her bed.

Tassie rushed across the road, not even bothering to close her front door, and banged her small fist on the glass door of the bakery, calling out Rachel's name.

Please come, Rachel, she said to herself, as she heard a car behind her.

'You all right, Mrs McIver?' she heard Joe's voice say.

'Oh, Joe, can you take me to Clara's cottage? It's urgent.'

Joe frowned and called out to Rachel and rang the bell above her head, which she was too short to reach.

Rachel came downstairs with a grin on her face, seemingly happy to see them both.

'Hello there,' she said, opening the door.

'Mrs McIver needs to go to Clara's; says it's urgent,' said Joe. 'Shall I take her?'

He looked to Rachel for approval.

'Is everything all right?' Rachel asked Tassie. 'Did she tell you about our plans?'

'What plans?' asked Joe.

But Tassie shook her hands at them both. 'That can all wait. Joe, take me to Acorn Cottage now, and then come back to see Rachel and she can share it all with you then.'

Tassie spoke in her best schoolteacher voice and Joe and Rachel both immediately responded.

'Righto then. Let's go to my van and I'll give you a quick hoick up.'

'No one will be hoicking me up or down. I can get in myself,' said Tassie as she marched down to the van.

She did need a small hoick from Joe but neither of them mentioned it and they were soon on their way to the cottage.

Tassie played over the strategy in her head as they rounded the corner and she saw Clara's red car outside the cottage.

'Thank you, Joe, I can take it from here. You head back to see your Rachel.'

'My Rachel, I like that,' he said as he opened the door for her and helped her down.

'Oh and, Joe?' She turned to him as he walked to the driver's side of the van.

'Yes, Mrs McIver?'

'Can you shut my front door for me?'

Joe smiled, waved and drove away while Tassie stood outside the gate of the cottage.

She could see the patches where Henry had been preparing the walls for new paint. The roof was on and looking very proud. The garden was somewhat more tamed but Clara needed to spend more time in it. But the gate was fixed and the sign reading *Acorn Cottage* was strong and sturdy.

She pushed open the gate and heard a little bell ring and Pansy came running around the side of the house with the small dog.

'Tassie,' the little girl cried. She ran to the front door and opened it calling inside. 'Clara, Daddy, Tassie is here.'

She saw Clara look out from the upstairs bedroom and she was wiping her eyes. She hoped she wasn't too late, as she could feel the energy in the air of an earlier storm.

Clara came downstairs, speaking in a bright, cheery voice that Tassie recognised as a cloak to cover her pain. 'Oh my goodness, how did you get here? I swear you are a witch. Where's your broom?' she joked.

Pansy held her hand, so soft and new against her old skin.

'Don't be ridiculous, Joe dropped me off.' Tassie wasn't in any mood to play. 'Pansy, go and play, dear. Clara and I need to talk.'

Henry came out behind Clara. 'Cup of tea, Tassie?' he asked. She could see strain on his face and through the open door she could spy Naomi's ashes on the table.

Oh dear, yes, something had happened and it wasn't good.

'No tea,' said Tassie, almost rudely, but she had no time for pleasantries now. 'But Clara and I will have a gin and tonic. I suggest, if you don't have any in the house, you drive to the shop and get us some. Lemon required also. You must plant a lemon tree, dear – they are so useful.'

Clara nodded and Henry, as though under a spell, picked up the keys to Clara's car and left the house. Pansy was outside again, playing on the swing that Henry had tied onto the sturdiest of the oak tree branches, singing under the leaves a song that Tassie couldn't quite place but it sounded familiar.

'We need to talk,' said Tassie, and she walked into the kitchen and sat down.

'You're making me worried. What's happened? Is it Rachel?' asked Clara.

'No, it's not Rachel, it's you.'

Clara sat down opposite her.

'What do you mean?'

'You've had a terrible row with Henry, haven't you?'

'Henry and Pansy are leaving when the van is fixed,' Clara said. Her voice sounded tight and pained.

'Well, that's a big mess isn't it? I know it wasn't her.' Tassie tapped the lid of Naomi's container.

'Of course it was her; it's always her,' snapped Clara. 'He won't let her go.'

Tassie shook her head. 'I don't think it's him that won't let her go, love; I think it's you. I think you hang on to the dead because it's safer than being with the living.'

'That's the stupidest thing I ever heard,' said Clara, but Tassie noticed she couldn't look at Naomi's ashes.

'Why are you competing with a dead woman? You won, Clara, you're alive. You get to kiss Henry and love Pansy.'

But Clara shook her head. 'Not anymore, he doesn't want me.'

'Oh, Clara, you don't want to be happy.' Tassie sighed and thought for a moment.

'Tell me about your father.' Tassie stared at Clara, looking for something in her face but she wasn't sure what it was exactly.

'My dad? Why?' Clara sat back in the chair and crossed her arms.

Tassie noticed but said nothing. She'd learned from her years as a teacher that the less she said, the sooner the students would say what they knew. She would never cajole or push; instead she led them down the path and then let them find their way out by using the truth.

Clara glared at her but Tassie remained unmoved.

'What has my father got to do with anything? He's dead,' said Clara.

'Tell me about his death,' she prompted.

'No,' snapped Clara. 'Why are you here? Why do you want to talk about him? I never think about him.'

Tassie shook her head. 'But you do, love, all the time, and he feeds off it, doesn't he?'

Clara gasped. 'You need to leave.'

'No, pet, you need to say that to him, not to me,' said Tassie.

'What do you mean?' Clara asked.

Tassie could hear Pansy singing the song but she still couldn't place it.

'Clara, we haven't got much time, but you need to tell the truth. You need to tell Henry what happened with your father. It will ruin you if you don't. He's with you every moment, every day. You carry him with you wherever you go. That's why things don't turn out right for you. They start out well but then they end badly. And I know you and Henry need to be together. Naomi told me but your father will ruin your life if you let him.'

Clara stood up, her chair making a loud clatter on the wooden floor. 'Leave. You're out of your mind,' she said loudly.

'No, dear, I've never been more sane and besides, I'm eighty-nine years old. I can't walk home, can I? Now sit down and talk to me and I will tell you what I know.'

Clara sat, albeit reluctantly, and looked at Tassie, but with less hostility.

'My father died when I was twelve,' she said. 'He was an abusive, awful person, who killed my grandmother, and tried to kill my mother, so my mum killed him in self-defence.'

Tassie stared at her for a long time but Clara didn't flinch.

She realised that this lie had been told for so long it almost felt real to Clara.

'Were you there when your mum killed him?'

'Yes,' said Clara. Clara started to cry. All her former anger and bravado had dissolved, and she put her head on the table and sobbed.

'Tell him, tell him.' Tassie touched Clara's hair.

'I can't; he won't want to be with me,' she said, her voice strangled.

'He will,' said Tassie.

'You don't know that,' Clara said. 'You are telling me this old wives' tale stuff to scare me or something. I don't know why you're doing it but it's awful. I thought you were my friend.'

'I am your friend but I know what I know and your father is still with you and will be until you let him go.'

They were quiet for a moment. A fly and the sound of Pansy's song came through with the breeze.

Clara looked up and Tassie saw her eyes widen.

'That song. Where did Pansy learn that? Pansy?' she called out.

Pansy and Gumboots ran inside. 'Yeah?' she asked.

'That song you're singing, where did you learn that?' Clara asked her.

'This song?' Pansy sang it and Clara put her hands to her ears. Tassie saw her turn white.

'Daddy was singing it and now I'm singing it. I can teach you if you like.'

Clara shook her head.

'Thanks, pet,' said Tassie to Pansy who ran outside again.

'What is the song, Clara?' she asked gently.

'It was on the radio in the kitchen the night he died,' she said. 'My gran loved it. It was an old Elvis song called "Don't Cry Daddy", fitting really.'

The sound of Clara's car made Clara wipe her eyes quickly and move to the sink to have a drink of water as Henry walked in the door, humming the song 'Don't Cry Daddy'.

Clara looked at Tassie who stood up.

'I am going to talk to the trees with Pansy. Come and see me when you're done,' she said to them both.

'I bought you gin and tonics,' Henry said looking confused.

'Pour one for each of you and sit and listen for a bit, pet,' she said before patting his arm and walking into the garden to listen to the old oak tree.

49

Clara waited for Henry to make them the drinks and then he sat opposite her.

'You've been crying,' he said but not unkindly.

She ignored his comment because she knew there were more tears to come and deep down, she knew Tassie was right. Ghosts, spirits, God knows what it was but yes, she held her father with her closely and every day he was with her, every day that final moment was with her.

If telling the truth to someone helped lift that weight, then she would do it. She couldn't live with all of it anymore.

She'd never told Giles, God knew he wouldn't have understood, nor had she told her friends through high school or university or work. She never even divulged it to the therapist she saw briefly when she found out her mum was sick.

She took a sip of her drink and then another. 'You asked if I murdered someone.'

Henry nodded and frowned.

Clara sipped more of her drink. A large gulp – the gin burned but it was bracing.

'I did. I murdered someone.'

Henry started to laugh and then he saw her face. He was silent and she didn't speak so he could process what she told him.

'Who?' he asked. His drink was leaving condensation marks and they ran down onto the table. Clara paused then spoke slowly as though reaching for every word to ensure it was the right one.

'My mum and dad had a difficult relationship. They were both disappointed in how their lives unfurled and they drank. They were each disappointed in choosing the other, and not wanting more in life. They were nearly going to divorce and then Mum got pregnant with me.'

She sipped her gin and then kept speaking.

'Mum left three times that I can remember. Each time the beatings were worse than the ones before that had made her leave. He had taken everything from her by then. She didn't have a job, or friends, and she hadn't seen her own mum since I was a baby.'

She breathed out again and she noticed it sounded a little jagged, as though she had been running. She twisted the glass around on the table and dabbed at the ring marks.

Henry seemed to sit very still, as though he didn't want to scare her into not speaking but she couldn't stop now. It was as though Tassie had undone her.

'Then I told my teacher about what Dad used to do to her, which was both good and bad, because you know, teachers have to tell the police and then it's out of your hands.'

She paused, thinking about the next part.

'It set off a chain of events that I don't think I could have stopped, even if I tried.'

Henry nodded. 'That was very brave of you,' he said but she didn't respond. She didn't need platitudes. She needed to be free.

'The social workers and the police visited Mum at home

and Dad wasn't there, thank God. And she told them she had nowhere to go. But they found her mum and they spoke on the phone then and the next day, which was good.'

She took a deep breath and kept speaking. 'I was taken out of school at lunchtime by a policewoman and someone from social services and Mum met us at the library, and they drove us to my gran's house in Luton. It was like a holiday. My gran was a truly wonderful granny, you know? She would draw faces on boiled eggs before she cooked them for me, to have with toast soldiers.'

Henry smiled at her but she didn't let him speak. Her voice was an out-of-control train now and it would keep going until it crashed at the inevitable ending.

'And she would make me cocoa and serve it in a cup and saucer in bed, and Mum stopped crying. And we were happy, the three of us all together for the first time. My granny had chickens. I used to love to go and collect the eggs every morning. It became my job. I had names for them all and I would pat them and sing them songs. That's why the chickens you bought me meant so much to me.'

Henry nodded as Clara went on.

'Mum got a job at the grocer's and she told me she would save enough money to buy us a cottage with chickens. It was all we talked about and Granny said she would come and visit us and we would have vegetables and I would preserve things. I read *Little House on the Prairie* more than three times. I wanted to be a pioneer.'

Henry smiled at her.

'So this was the dream, where I am now, except it was supposed to be with Mum and then with Giles but it's you, and I love that it's you and Pansy but I know that what I will tell you will ruin everything, which is why I didn't want to tell you but Tassie says I have to or else I will be ruined.'

She felt the tears forming and took a deep breath to try and keep them at bay.

'Anyway, I digress. So the chickens, which symbolised new beginnings and everything wonderful in my life, were also the signal that Dad was back.'

'What do you mean?' he asked.

Clara looked at his handsome face, his beautiful smile. No man would keep a woman like her around his child.

She spoke slowly.

'I came home from school and went to see the chickens and they were all dead.'

Henry gasped. 'What?'

'Dad had cut their heads off, one by one, and lined them all up. I started to scream and ran inside. I remember the radio was on. There was newspaper on the bench with potato peelings on it. Gran had been preparing dinner.'

She closed her eyes. She was back there now. 'He had Mum in a headlock from behind, and there was Granny on the floor. She was bleeding. The blood was everywhere.'

She could hear her mother's gasps for breath and see her face turning blue, and she felt hot tears falling down her cheeks.

'I picked up the knife that Gran had been using and I plunged it into my dad's back. It went in easily and came out easily. I did it five times, until he fell down and Mum grabbed me and the knife from my hand.'

She opened her eyes and Henry was sitting very still.

'Mum took the knife and stabbed him four more times in the heart and then told me to ring 999.'

Clara was looking over his head as she spoke.

'Gran was dead. He had choked her. And Mum had come home from work and saw him. Then he started on her when I walked in. I think he would have killed me too.'

She felt like she was in court again.

'The police said it was manslaughter but her lawyers said it was self-defence. She served three years.'

'Oh, Clara,' said Henry. 'Who looked after you?'

'No one. Myself. I lived with a cousin of Mum's who worked at a meat works. She was never home and when she was she was getting ready to go to bingo or the pub. She left me alone and I visited Mum in prison and went to school and became an adult. Worked hard at school. When Mum came out of prison, I started university. We never spoke about it, not even when she was dying. It was the big secret in our tiny two-person family and yet it was so big.'

Clara saw tears in his eyes.

They both sipped their drinks, steadying themselves, she thought.

'So I understand why you won't want me around Pansy – I do. But I needed to tell you.'

They were silent again then she spoke. 'But you know? What was the saddest part?'

Henry shook his head. 'No?'

'I didn't stab him because of what he had done to Gran or what he was going to do to Mum, God knows what that would have been, but I stabbed him because he killed the chickens. All I wanted were the chickens and he killed them, and I guess, in some way, he killed my dream.'

Henry nodded. 'The chickens were a symbol though. And they were like you. Defenceless.'

She nodded and looked him in the eye. 'So yes, that is the first time I have told my whole story to anyone.'

Henry stood up and she lowered her head. He would go now, she was as sure of it as she was that the sun would come up tomorrow.

But he walked to her side of the table and lifted her head to him and leaned down and kissed her gently on the mouth.

'I love you, Clara Maxwell, and if you think for a minute that I wouldn't want you in my life when you are one of the bravest, smartest women I know, then you are wrong, so very wrong.'

Clara smiled at him and he searched her eyes.

'I want you to stay with me. I want to marry you and care for Pansy together and have a baby and have this be our dream.'

She'd said it. She'd finally said everything that had happened and everything she had wanted and he was still standing before her.

He pulled her to her feet.

'All I have done since I arrived is make this a home for us, even if I didn't realise it. I want it all as much as you do. I think I have from the moment you burst into tears at the hole in the roof.'

'I am so, so sorry for everything I said,' she cried, holding his face. 'I was wrong and rude and awful, and all I can say is, I was afraid. I hope you can find it in yourself to forgive me.'

But Henry shook his head and kissed her forehead. 'You said some truthful things to me and I needed to hear some of them. Some of them were a bit harsh but I don't hang on to grudges.'

Clara hugged him. She loved the way her face buried into his shoulder and she kissed his neck.

'You're lovely,' she said.

'You're lovelier,' he replied and then he kissed her so well her knees buckled and she thought she might have died and gone to heaven.

50

Secrets can be so heavy that they can drown a person, Tassie used to say to children who wouldn't tell her what was on their mind. Sometimes she knew when there was trouble at home, or things happening that shouldn't to small children. She could tell when she looked in their eyes, by the way they fought for others instead of fighting for themselves. They raged against everything in the world except what troubled them, fighting the fight for everyone else. Tassie had seen it in Clara when she first noticed Rachel in the tearooms. Clara was a wounded fighter who hid her scar beneath practicality and reliability. She had worked to become everything her father wasn't and stronger than her mother could ever be. When Clara arrived in Merryknowe she was drowning but the cottage was her buoy and slowly she made it to the surface.

Now Tassie sat on one of the plastic garden chairs that Henry had bought for the garden, watching Pansy play on the swing in the tree.

Clara walked up beside her, sat on the grass and handed Tassie a gin and tonic.

'I told him,' she said.

Tassie nodded and took the drink.

'I guess I should tell you now,' said Clara but Tassie shook her head.

'I don't need to know, love. I know enough that something happened and changed you. It pushed you down for so long that you chose the wrong boys and the wrong friends and the wrong job because you wanted to make people happy. You thought if you made people happy then that would absolve you.'

Clara was silent next to her.

'But you had nothing to forgive yourself for. You did what you did to survive and you did survive but now...' Tassie looked around at the cottage and Pansy on the swing and Henry coming out with the other chairs for him and Clara. 'Now, you are living.'

Clara wiped a tear away and Tassie patted her on the head.

'The secret needed to come out eventually. It was too big to keep between you and Henry,' she said.

Clara nodded and allowed Henry to pull her up from the grass so she could sit on the chair.

'Can you text Joe and ask him to come and get me?' asked Tassie to Clara.

'I can drive you,' offered Henry.

'Oh no, you've been drinking.' Tassie sipped her own drink. 'I haven't had a sip of one of those for years. It is most refreshing.'

She watched as Clara texted on her phone, marvelling at the ease of communication between humans and yet how much was still hidden and unsaid between friends and lovers.

They sat peacefully under the tree for a while, the last of

the summer bees lazily swimming through the heat waves, looking for crumbs of pollen.

Tassie turned to Henry. 'And what about you, love?'

Henry looked at Tassie in mock horror. 'Please don't tell me it's my turn to be in your spotlight.'

'What are we going to do about Naomi? She's ready to go, you know?'

Henry nodded. 'I know – she told me.'

He looked at Pansy swinging with the puppy jumping up trying to reach her on his short little legs.

'She wanted to be in a vegetable garden but I don't like the idea of digging up carrots with her bones in it.'

Tassie listened to the trees for a while and then heard the sound of Joe's voice coming from around the side of the house.

'Righto, I must be off. I have a lovely chicken schnitzel dinner from Rachel coming. Did I tell you I've cancelled meals on wheels now? Rachel brings me whatever she is having for dinner. Last night it was an egg and bacon pie with your eggs from Clara's Cluckers. Very good it was too.'

Tassie waved them goodbye.

It was nearly all falling into place, she thought, and then it would be time.

But first dinner and a little television and then off to bed. She had another busy day tomorrow.

51

The bakery closed and Rachel took the cash takings to the little safe and locked them away. She had changed the code since Moira had gone, at Joe's suggestion.

'You can't trust her,' he had said.

'Do you think she will come back?' Rachel had been terrorised by the thought. Some nights she lay in bed and wondered if Moira could come back, if she was outside. She had changed the locks at Clara's suggestion, but Moira was able to find a way into anything.

Clara had helped her pack up Moira's things into boxes and had them shipped to an address in Suffolk. She didn't know whose address and she didn't want to know. Moira was a survivor, Tassie said, but she took a lot of people down in her desire to live. She knew she was lucky that she had survived Moira. She wouldn't have if it wasn't for Clara.

She wondered what would have happened that night if she hadn't called Clara. She wondered if she would have left Moira on the floor or if she would have put her hand over her mouth and nose and let her fight her until she died.

She couldn't admit to anyone she had those thoughts until Clara told her what happened with her own father.

Clara was worried Rachel might judge her but she said she needed to know what her business partner was capable of.

Rachel had said nothing but held her friend's hand and afterwards gave her some lemon cake, because lemons were good to break through sadness.

But weeks later she'd told Clara what she had thought about the night Moira fell.

'I'm glad you called me. Guilt isn't a good thing to live with,' Clara had said. 'It eats you up and you spend so much time trying to remember the secrets and lies you told people. It's exhausting.'

Rachel held Clara's secret close, not even telling Joe, but she did tell Tassie because it was Tassie and she needed to talk about it to someone.

Tassie had nodded. 'I thought it was something like that. Poor poppet. What a thing to grow up with.'

They had sat in Tassie's living room, with the heater on and the music on the radio, and Rachel thought about Joe coming over that night and she couldn't have been happier.

'When are you turning ninety, Tassie?' she'd asked.

'Oh, I am not turning ninety. Ninety is an obscene number and even worse when it's someone's age,' Tassie had said with distaste.

Rachel had laughed. 'I would like to give you a little party.'

But Tassie had waved her hand. 'No parties, no more birthdays for me.'

'Even if you don't want to celebrate them, we can still celebrate you,' Rachel told her old friend.

Tassie had said nothing but Rachel wondered when her birthday was. It had to be in winter, she thought, wondering if she could find Tassie's purse and look at her pension card or something.

Rachel headed upstairs where Joe was waiting. They were going to play a board game and get fish and chips, with an extra serving for Tassie, and Joe would stay because Alice was at a friend's house.

Joe had been patient with her as she explored her new feelings and experiences – but as he said, he wasn't very knowing either, so they might as well learn together.

Clara had taken her to the doctor to put her on the pill and now she felt very grown up when she took one every morning.

Rachel opened the door to the upstairs and saw Joe had decorated the room.

White balloons covered the ceiling with silver ribbons coming off them, and red paper hearts were strung across the room from corner to corner.

'What's this?' she asked, as Joe stepped out from the bedroom in a dinner suit and Michael Bublé music started playing from somewhere.

'What is going on?' she asked, bewildered as she looked around. 'It's not Valentine's Day.'

Joe moved to her and held her as though to dance a waltz.

'I don't know how to dance the old-fashioned way,' she admitted, trying to be heard over the loud tones of Michael Bublé singing about coming home or something.

'Neither do I,' said Joe and she saw he was very red in the face.

'Come into the room,' he said.

She looked up at the ceiling. 'I don't want to.' She felt sick.

'Why?' Joe's face crumpled.

Rachel felt stupid and childish but she had to be honest with him.

'I'm afraid of balloons. I have been since I was a child and Moira used to blow them up and pop them to make herself laugh.'

Joe gasped and quickly ran into the bedroom and turned off the music and ran out to Rachel. He closed the door to the room, and stood at the top of the stairs with her.

'I am so sorry – I should have known,' he said.

'Why should you have known? It's not something people talk about is it? Hello. I'm Rachel, how do you feel about balloons?'

Joe shook his head at her. 'But I should know what Moira did to you and I don't.'

Rachel sat on the top stair and Joe sat next to her.

'The thing is, Moira did a lot to me. Some of it I have forgotten but then sometimes I will see something and it will jolt an old memory and it's not nice but it goes away. I can't tell you everything she did because I can't remember it all off the top of my head but when it comes I will tell you if I want to, but sometimes I might not want to open that all up again.'

Joe nodded and took her hand.

'So what was that about?' She nudged him with her elbow.

'It was my badly thought-out attempt at a marriage proposal,' he said and she looked at him and saw he was serious.

'Oh, Joe, you don't need all that to ask me to marry you; you just had to ask.'

But Joe looked downcast. 'I did a lot of reading about it, and people said I needed a grand gesture.'

Rachel laughed but not unkindly. 'I don't need grand gestures. I would just like you, so if you want to ask me...' she encouraged.

Joe stood up and pulled her to her feet. He then got onto one knee and pulled a black ring box from his pocket and opened it. Inside was a beautiful ruby ring with tiny seed pearls around it. It was exactly what Rachel would have chosen if asked.

'Rachel Brown, will you do me the honour of being my wife?'

'Yes, Joe, I will,' she said firmly, and then he stood up and pulled a ring out of the box and slipped it onto her finger.

'Mum had fat fingers,' he said, as the ring was a little large on Rachel's thin hands. 'But we can get it resized.'

'This was your mum's?' she asked, feeling overwhelmed.

'Oh yes, and she would have loved you. Always loved a baker and a woman who had her own mind and business. She was clever like you, Rach, and I am sorry you never met her.'

Rachel felt her throat constrict with tears and she kissed Joe for a long time.

'Now get rid of those balloons please,' she asked, 'or I will have nightmares for the rest of our married life.'

52

Clara and Pansy stood in the clearing between the oak trees as Henry dug a hole in the ground. Pansy had one hand closed tightly, and the other hand was holding Clara's.

She watched her father dig the hole with his spade. He was wearing a suit, something she hadn't seen him in before, and it looked strange when he came out of the van wearing it.

The van was back but Pansy didn't really want to be in it anymore. They had a sofa with a long bit that Pansy could lie on like she was a queen and Clara had given her a blanket shaped like a mermaid tail, which she loved playing with.

Daddy had said she could play in the van whenever she wanted but she hadn't wanted to yet.

Pansy felt Clara squeeze her hand and she looked up at her. Clara looked sad but Pansy didn't really know why – maybe she was sad for her and Daddy.

She squeezed Clara's hand back as she saw her father put down the spade and wipe his brow.

Daddy had told her to wear her best dress, which she did, so she was wearing her new school dress. She loved it so much she couldn't stop looking at herself in the mirror.

It was yellow checked with a white collar and buttons down the front. It had a zipped pocket for special things and right now it was holding a piece of chalk, a silver button that Clara had found in a button jar in the spare cupboard from the lady who used to live here and a cowrie shell that Tassie had given her from the bowl of shells at her house.

Clara had on a red dress and a black shawl and red lipstick. Pansy thought she looked like the beautiful doll from Spain that her grandmother had sent her in the post.

Her father cleared his throat and held a wooden box, which had been sitting on a table that he had carried outside before he dug the hole.

'Naomi Roberts Garnett. Today is the day we place you at rest. I know you wanted to be in a veggie patch but it's not possible, so this is the next best thing. We will place you among the oaks, and let you be with the beautiful trees you loved so much.'

Pansy watched as he kissed the top of the wooden box and then he stopped for a moment and then put the box into the hole in the ground.

Her dad looked down at the ground where the box was.

'I am grateful to have loved you, darling, and for our beautiful girl.' Pansy saw him glance at her and she smiled at him. Poor Daddy. He cried a lot lately, she had told Tassie, but Tassie said it was good to cry because if you didn't cry you got blockages in your heart and then you would burst and explode, or something like that.

'And I am grateful for you bringing me to Clara's cottage and for us finding a home here.'

Pansy swung on Clara's hand. She was happy to have the pink house as her own also. And she was happy to have her own room, which Daddy had painted for her and she had white furniture and a desk and a whole bookshelf and a doll cradle that Daddy had made for her and her toys.

Clara had put down a rug that was red with white dots that looked like a toadstool and she had fairy stickers on the roof that only showed when the lights were out.

Daddy was still talking to the ground, as Pansy looked around the trees and she saw the owl again.

She saw a baby owl next to it and she smiled.

Mummy and baby, she thought. She used to see her mum all the time. She used to sit with her on her bed at night and sometimes she told her stories about when she was a baby. But that hadn't happened for a while now.

Part of Pansy missed her mother's visits but part of her was also forgetting her. Clara talked about Mummy but Clara didn't know that Pansy thought that she was very good at being a mummy to her. She knew how she liked her toast cut – triangles, thank you. And she helped her make a fairy garden under the big oak trees where her swing was. And she practised reading the books with her that Tassie gave her.

Last night a bird had come into the cottage and Clara and Daddy had tried to catch it but it flew upstairs and sat on top of the stairs. They had laughed a lot but Pansy was scared of the bird. It looked at her with its dead beady eyes and she felt like something bad was going to happen. She had stayed hidden under her covers with the doors shut while Daddy opened every window and he and Clara eventually got the bird to leave.

Now Daddy was crying again and he threw some dirt onto the box in the ground.

'Your turn,' said Clara to Pansy who looked away from the owl and to Clara.

'What do I do?' she whispered.

'Just put some dirt on the box and if you want to say something you can – or not, it's up to you,' Clara whispered back.

Pansy dropped Clara's hand and walked to the hole in the ground. She picked up some dirt in her hand and placed her hidden object into the dirt. She dropped it into the hole and then went back to Clara and wiped her hand on Clara's dress as she didn't want to put dirt on her school dress.

Clara put some dirt into the hole and then Daddy filled it in with the spade and they were all quiet for a moment.

'Amen,' said Pansy very firmly, just like she had seen on a television show about a lady who was a priest or something.

Henry and Clara laughed but she didn't know why. It felt right to say. She looked up to see the owl and baby but they were gone.

'Bye, Mummy,' she whispered and she felt her eyes hurt like she was going to cry. She remembered what Tassie said about crying and so she let it out and she hugged Clara for a long time, while she let all the tears out.

Later on, Rachel and Joe and Tassie came for afternoon tea, and Rachel had made a jam and cream sponge cake, and there was lemonade and everyone hugged a lot and Pansy had fallen asleep on the sofa.

And when she woke up, it was morning and someone had put her into bed, and she was still wearing her school dress and she jumped out of bed to run down and check for eggs, because today was Pansy's favourite day.

53

The end was close. Tassie felt it down into the marrow of her bones. She wasn't pretending when she said to Rachel she wouldn't have another birthday. She had decided she'd had enough of living. The last few months had been more exciting than anything she had experienced before, even when George was alive.

The tea leaves couldn't hold the truth back any longer and Tassie knew that, even if it hurt her soul to know, it was coming to an end.

Clara and Rachel were filled with life and filled with lives yet to come. So many generations to create. She might have missed having biological children but she had been a teacher and a mother and more to hundreds of children through her life, and Pansy Garnett was her last and most important student.

That girl was meant for something bigger than all of them; she was sure of it and she knew Naomi would keep her safe as she grew up.

She moved about her little house, straightening up the cushions on the sofa, and pulling the curtains closed.

Joe and Rachel would pop over soon with the news about the engagement. She had seen the balloons taken from his van when Rachel was in the shop. She could have told him they weren't necessary but he hadn't asked – however, she was sure it would be fine. Joe and Rachel were just fine.

She turned on the television and sat down to watch the news. More sadness and anger and pain. So many people losing their homes and countries. What was the world coming to, she wondered. No wonder people wanted a simple life when the world was so complicated.

As though they had heard her thoughts, a knock at the door told her Joe and Rachel were there and she turned off the television and opened the door to their joy.

This was the only sort of news she wanted, she thought as she looked at their shiny, happy faces.

They didn't stay long, as they wanted to see Clara and Henry so she smiled at them and sent them on their way.

It wasn't far away now, she thought as she sat down again. She didn't turn on the television, she just sat in the quiet, listening.

The clock on the mantel stopped ticking as though trying to be quiet and she counted the seconds before it started again. Clocks couldn't bear not to tick. Not ticking was like holding their breath, and she looked around the room.

George was here. That's why the clock stopped. Time stops when the dead come back.

'Give me some more time, pet. I have some things to see off first,' she said aloud.

The clock stopped again. She counted the seconds, one, two, three, four, then the clock started back again.

Four more days she counted, and then she was going to die, and for the first time since old age had captured her in its grasp, Tassie McIver felt sad she couldn't see it all happen.

She wanted to see the tearooms finished and she wanted to see Joe and Rachel get married, and she wanted to see Henry and Clara's faces when they realised Rachel was pregnant with a little boy. Why else would she have told Pansy to put acorns under Clara's mattress? And she wanted to see the oak tree grow from the acorn that she had told Pansy to put on top of Naomi's ashes. There was always something to look forward to in life, if you looked hard enough and blocked out all the bad news that you couldn't change.

She had time left but not as much as she would have liked and that night she slept fitfully, her mind drifting to everything she had to do before she died.

In the morning, she drank tea and wrote a list in her little pocketbook.

The first thing she needed to do was see a man in Salisbury. She rang the taxi company in Chippenham to arrange one to take her and bring her back.

'You sure, love? That will be expensive,' the man at the taxi company had said on the phone.

But Tassie didn't mind. It was only money after all, and as George used to say, there are no pockets in shrouds.

Tassie dressed carefully, putting on her good coat and hat and changing over her handbag to the patent leather one that she had bought when she was first married.

She had polished it through the years so the leather was still supple and she could see her reflection in the side.

After closing the door behind her, she waited for the taxi to arrive. The bakery wasn't open yet so she knew Rachel wouldn't see her leaving. The less people knew right now, the better, she thought, as she saw the cab come down the road and turn to pick her up.

She chatted to the taxi driver who was a very nice man and who was happy for the large fare to and from Salisbury. Tassie felt pleased she could help him, especially when she found out he had twins at home.

'I taught several sets of twins when I was a teacher. Are yours identical?' she asked.

'Yes, twin boys.'

'Then be careful, as they have their own language,' she warned. 'They will get into trouble in ways you never dreamed they would and you can't do anything about it, because their language is all in their minds. They're very clever – twins. They are essentially one person.'

The taxi driver had laughed and said he had already seen evidence of this and Tassie listened to his stories.

When they arrived in Salisbury, the taxi driver waited for her while she went to her appointment at the office with the brass doors. They were so heavy, she had to wait for someone else to open them so she could slip in behind them and she went up the elevator and to the floor marked on the downstairs board.

When she was finished, and she managed to leave the office, she went home again in the taxi. The bakery was busy and she slipped inside without Rachel seeing her.

Soon she saw Clara arrive with Henry and she saw them head into the tearooms, which were closed for renovations.

Everything was happening, Tassie thought, and she felt tears in her eyes. It had been wonderful, all of it, every single second and she would do it all again, exactly as she already had.

Tassie turned on the kettle and looked out the window and saw the bird on the clothesline. One for sorrow – she nodded her respects to the bird. People didn't give birds enough respect, she had often said to George when he was alive. They were the carriers of the messages of those who had passed and they knew what was coming on the winds of change.

Tassie made her tea and sat at the table and sipped it slowly, enjoying it with a piece of the lavender shortbread that Rachel had made with the last of the summer lavender. When she finished the tea, she swirled it three times and spun the cup and placed it upside down and waited a few minutes.

She took a moment and then turned over the cup and saw the raven. It was time. She couldn't run from it anymore and a sense of peace came over her tired body.

She went to the front room and found her good onion-skin paper and her favourite pen. Then she went back to the kitchen to write her letter and sealed it in an envelope. She carefully wrote Clara's name on the front and then propped it up against the cup, turned down on the saucer.

Clara would be the one to find her and while she wished she could have made it easier for Clara, she was selfish in her last moments. She wanted to be with a friend and Clara was that and more.

You have done what you said you would do – teach people, help them, show them they are worth loving, she heard a voice in her head say as she closed her eyes, while sitting at the table.

54

The tearoom renovation was underway. The bakery had stayed open but Henry had hired two men from Chippenham to help gut the rooms and now he and Clara stood in the open space.

'I have a fireplace coming from a yard in Salisbury,' said Henry. 'Lovely Victorian one with a mantel. We can put a gas fire in it; they are very realistic nowadays.'

Clara walked around the space.

'What about these floors – can we polish them?'

'We can,' said Henry, 'but they need some TLC.'

'I'm going to pop over and see Tassie,' said Clara. 'I've haven't seen her since she came over after Naomi's ceremony.'

Henry nodded and pulled out his measuring tape and started using it on the walls, so Clara went out into the bakery, which was in between rushes of customers.

'All okay?' she asked the new girl who had taken over from Alice who was back at school.

'All fine, Rachel is in the kitchen,' she said to Clara.

'Tell her I am seeing Tassie if she asks,' she called and went outside. The air was colder, with a crispness to it that signalled autumn was on its way. She was looking forward to some cooler weather in the cottage. The sofa had arrived and they had rugs and even a television, which Pansy was thrilled about and Henry less so.

The oak trees seemed to be quieter now, less rustle of the leaves and some were turning yellow at the tops and the garden was slowing down also. The cottage was painted pink and the garden beds were dug up and edged.

Tassie had given Clara boxes of cockleshells that she had in her little shed. George used to collect them, she said, but didn't say why he collected them, and Henry had attached them to the garden bed edging.

And they finally had the vegetable patch where she had planted broccoli and carrots and rhubarb. Henry had made little wooden labels and painted the names of them onto the front and Pansy had carefully read the letters out to him as he worked.

Tassie had done wonderfully with her lessons, she thought, as she knocked on Tassie's door.

She waited for a bit but didn't hear the sound of Tassie coming to open it. She knocked again but nothing. A gnawing worry grew in her chest and she knocked louder and called Tassie's name.

Running back across the road, she grabbed Henry.

'Tassie's not answering.'

'She might have gone out,' said Henry, writing measurements down on a small pad.

'She doesn't go anywhere,' said Clara, glancing back at Tassie's house, hoping the door would suddenly open and put all her worries to rest.

'That's not true, she went to Salisbury yesterday,' he said.

'How do you know? Why didn't you tell me?' Clara demanded to know.

'She asked Joe to ask me to come and get some boxes out of her roof cavity and she told me then. She made it sound like it was perfectly in order.' Henry stopped writing and looked at her. 'Is she supposed to tell you when she comes and goes?'

Clara stamped her foot in frustration. 'No, of course not but I don't like this. She's old, and alone, and she might have fallen. I think you should break in and check on her.'

'Or you could use the key that Rachel has,' said Henry.

'Rachel has a key? God, why doesn't anyone tell me anything?' she said crossly.

'I'll come with you,' said Henry, and Clara got the key from Rachel, and they crossed the road together. A magpie stood on Tassie's fence, his head tilted in interest.

'Tassie will know what magpies mean when they sit on your fence,' said Clara as she slipped the key into the lock.

'It means they're tired of flying?' Henry joked as Clara opened the door.

But Clara wasn't listening. The house was still, not even the loud, old clock on her mantel was ticking. She closed her eyes.

'She's gone,' she said.

'To Salisbury?' asked Henry.

Clara shook her head. 'She's died. I can't look. You look.'

Henry called out Tassie's name and waited and then went to the bedroom. 'The bed is unslept in,' he called out to Clara but Clara had gone to the kitchen to wait and that was where Tassie was sitting. Still upright. In her purple cardigan with the little brooch of flowers on the lapel and her pretty blue dress. Her hair was neatly combed and her eyebrows drawn on perfectly but Clara knew she was gone.

'She's here,' she called out, hearing her own voice catch.

'I told you she was…' Henry walked into the kitchen and saw Tassie.

'Oh, love,' he said and Clara wasn't sure if she meant Tassie or her. It didn't matter now.

Oh, love, she thought. Love was everything. It was the meaning of life, it was the way to live life, it was everything and more. Without love we are nothing, thought Clara as she sat next to Tassie at the table and held her cold hand, which had started to stiffen.

'Can you call the ambulance?' she said quietly. 'And then tell Rachel.'

Henry kissed the top of her head, and then Tassie's and then left her alone in the house with Tassie.

She held her old friend's hand in hers and stroked the paper-thin skin.

'I love you, Tassie – you understood me, you saw me and you saved me from my father,' she said, feeling the deep grief welling inside her.

'What will I do now you're gone? Who will tell me about what ladybugs mean and magpies on fences and what to do when you see a three-legged dog?'

Clara held Tassie's hand tight. She noticed the letter addressed to her against the upturned cup and slipped it into her pocket. That was for later, she thought. She turned over the cup and looked inside. There was something; she peered closer. A blackbird, no, too big for that; she narrowed her eyes and then she saw it. The raven.

'One for sorrow, two for joy, three for a girl, four for a boy, five for silver, six for gold, seven for a secret, never to be told, eight for a wish, nine for a kiss, ten for a time of joyous bliss.' She whispered in her friend's ear and started to cry.

'You brought me here and Henry, and you knew there was something special. I don't know how but you saved us from ourselves and being lost in the past, and helped Pansy and Rachel – oh, Tassie, how I love you.'

And Clara kept crying. She cried like she should have cried for her father and her mother. She cried for her heartbreak and she cried for her losses. And then she cried because she was simply so grateful to Tassie for her love and friendship.

Rachel came bursting into the kitchen and fell sobbing into Henry's arms who was behind her.

Clara sat, her thumb stroking the back of Tassie's old hand.

'The ambulance is on its way,' said Henry.

'I will sit with you until they come,' said Clara to Tassie. Her face was peaceful; maybe she could see a hint of lipstick. She knew then that Tassie had been preparing to die. Tassie might not have been able to summon life and have children of her own but she could summon death the way she could speak to them.

She glanced around the kitchen and saw everything was spick and span and put away. There was a fresh tea towel on the rail next to the sink and the dishcloth was carefully folded and on the rack.

Tassie was house-proud, even in the afterlife, she thought, and she wished she had remembered to ask her what a bird in the house meant after Naomi's ceremony. Tassie would have known; she knew everything.

She held Tassie's hand until the medics came and said she was dead, because that's what they are supposed to do, and they called the doctor, who came and declared her dead, because that's what doctors are supposed to do, and then Henry called the undertaker in Chippenham to come and get her, because that's what undertakers do. Clara held her hand the entire time until they put Tassie into the back of the van, and drove her away, because that's what friends do – they stay till the very bitter, as Tassie used to say.

55

The morning of the third Thursday in August, Tassie McIver's earthly body faced the flames and her ashes were thrown out into the oak tree clearing by Clara and Rachel, as she had expressed in the letter she had left on the kitchen table.

There was to be no funeral, she had instructed, as she didn't have time for that and nor did anyone else. People's lives are busy, she had written in her perfect, if a little spidery at times, handwriting.

Instead, the village opened up the church hall and they had a memorial service, which the tearooms catered with mini egg and bacon pies, butterfly cakes and eclairs, and little shortbreads shaped like oak leaves. They served China tea and lemonade, and the hall was filled with former students that Tassie had taught over the years in Merryknowe.

'We used to think she was a witch but a good witch,' said one with a nose piercing.

'She would bring us dinners when Mam was sick,' said another who now wore a suit and a silk tie.

She heard stories of Tassie's enormous impact on the students from gaining a love of reading to pushing themselves to want and expect more from their inner lives.

Every time another person spoke, Clara felt humbled by her short friendship with Tassie.

After the service and all was cleaned up, Henry and Clara sat at home in silence.

'I thought I was special you know, but seeing all those people speak today, I realised she was the one who was special,' Clara said, her head on Henry's shoulder.

'We are all special; she just saw it when we or others couldn't,' said Henry.

Clara sighed. 'I don't feel well. Too much stress I think since this all happened. It's been relentless.'

'Do you want to have a lie-down?' asked Henry. 'I have to go and get Pansy – can you believe it's been five weeks since she started school?'

She thought for a moment and then sat up. 'Five weeks?'

Henry nodded. 'Yep, coming up for six.'

She stood up. 'I'll come with you. I need to go to the shops in Chippenham.'

They drove in Clara's car and she tried to remember when she had her last period.

So much had happened in the last five weeks, she couldn't remember anything in a straight line. Joe and Rachel's engagement, Naomi's ceremony, the renovations on the tearooms, Pansy starting school, Tassie's death.

'What's wrong?' asked Henry as they drove.

'Nothing – I don't know, I just feel weird,' she said, being evasive. There was no point saying anything until she knew for certain, but what would Henry say if she was pregnant?

They drove into Chippenham.

'Drop me off here, get Pansy and come back for me?'

she said, pointing to a park on the side of the road. Henry stopped the car and she jumped out.

'See you soon,' she said and before he had time to answer, she had walked into the shopping centre.

She went to the chemist and looked at the tests. She wondered if Judy had used one of these. She picked up an early pregnancy test. Their baby would be due soon, and she thought about everything that had changed since she had learned of their affair.

The odd thing was she barely thought about them now and when she did, she felt nothing. Not anger or indifference, it felt like a different person and a different life. She chose a test and paid for it then went hunting for the bathroom. Sitting on the toilet, she read the instructions and then did as it asked.

Not exactly a glamorous task, she thought as she waited in the noisy cubicles, with the bright light overhead creating a mood more suited to an interrogation than an insemination.

And there it was. The double line. *Oh, Tassie.* She shook her head. *I think you planned this all along.*

Henry was waiting for her when she went outside and Pansy was filled with news about school and the artwork she had to show Clara.

'Can you show me when we get home? I'm not feeling well,' said Clara, ignoring Henry's worried looks.

Pansy sat back quietly, mumbling to herself in the back seat but Clara didn't have the energy to respond.

She always indulged Pansy and her needs but right now, she needed to be alone and gather her thoughts.

Henry tried to make conversation as they drove home

but neither Clara nor Pansy engaged, both staring out the window. The trees were turning orange now, noticed Clara and she felt bad for snapping at Pansy.

She turned in the seat to Pansy.

'I'm sorry, darling, I felt a bit sick. I want to see your art. Can you show me?'

Pansy picked up her painting and handed it to Clara. It was actually very good. Far more sophisticated than anything Clara had thought Pansy was capable of doing.

'Wow, is that our house?' she asked.

Pansy nodded.

Clara looked at the pink house with the brown roof. There was the gate and the chicken coop with little chickens running around.

Pansy was on the swing and Henry was on the roof. Clara smiled as she peered closely. She saw herself next to the vegetable garden.

'Is that me?' she asked pointing at the figure in the big hat that she often wore.

Pansy nodded.

'And what else is there?'

'There is Mummy,' she said and Clara looked closely but she couldn't see another person in the artwork.

'I can't see her? Point to her?' asked Clara, handing the picture back to Pansy. Pansy put her finger on a thin tree next to what she presumed was the large oak out the back.

'That's Mummy,' she said.

'Mummy is a tree?' Clara said, smiling at Henry who raised an eyebrow.

'Yes, because Tassie told me to put an acorn in and I did

and I never told you and soon she will be a big tree,' said Pansy proudly.

Clara gasped and looked to Henry who was laughing and smiling. 'Oh, you and Tassie were always up to something.'

'Yes, Tassie used to tell me things to do all the time that I didn't tell you,' boasted Pansy.

'Oh yes? Like what?' asked Henry as they turned down the road towards the cottage.

'Like when we put the shells in the garden. She said you needed them and I had to tell you I wanted them, and then she made me put acorns under your bed.' Pansy laughed and laughed to herself in the back of the car.

56

The packages were on the front doorstep when they arrived home.

'What are these?' asked Henry.

Pansy spied her own name and picked up the box and shook it. 'I can hear something rattling,' she cried.

'It's probably broken with that shake,' Henry said to Clara as he picked up a small box with his name printed on the front.

He opened the front door, and Clara picked up the large envelope and walked inside and went to the table.

'Cup of tea?' he asked and she nodded.

Pansy was in the living room, the television was on but neither Clara nor Henry had the energy to tell her to turn it off.

She opened the drawer and pulled out a knife and slit open the padded envelope. She pulled out a letter and a notebook, which she put down, because she recognised Tassie's old-fashioned script.

Dearest Clara,

What a blessing you are to me and to Merryknowe and to Rachel and Henry and Pansy and your chickens.

*I think everyone who has ever met you benefitted in
some way...*

Clara gasped and started to cry and handed it to Henry.
'She wrote me a letter. I can't read it. Can you?'

Henry sat down and cleared his throat.

'Dearest Clara,

'What a blessing you are to me and to Merryknowe and
to Rachel and Henry and Pansy and your chickens. I think
everyone who has ever met you benefitted in some way
from your giving nature and true nurturing soul.

'But when you give all the time, you become empty inside
and you try and please everyone else and eventually you
become just a husk of yourself. I used to worry about
you but that won't happen now because you have learned
to ask for help. To ask to be loved and to have received it
so joyously.

'I was not a wealthy woman but I was comfortable as
I lived a quiet life, which suited George and I. Perhaps we
might have travelled more. I would have liked to have seen
Paris but maybe you and Henry can go now.

'I am leaving you my pension fund, which George
invested very well, and with your clever money skills, I have
no doubt you will triple this in no time. I am leaving Pansy
some money also, which you can manage for her until she
is twenty-five. That is a smarter age than twenty-one, I am
sure you will agree.'

Henry looked up from the letter and smiled. Clara waved
at him to continue.

'I have left you my Welsh dresser and china, as I know
you loved it so and there is a spot for it in your lovely little

kitchen. Perhaps you can paint it pink like I did in mine. Pink is such a happy colour. And finally, there is a notebook for you. You always wanted to know what I knew, all those little superstitions I shared, and old wives' tales and the tea leaf symbols. I have been writing these down since I was a girl. Some of them are from my own mother, and grandmother and probably her grandmother before that. You can add to it now, as I bequeath it to you. It is one of my most treasured possessions; the other one I have given to Henry.

'I didn't have children in my life and I taught and cared for many other people's children, but of all of them, you, Clara, were the one I thought I most would have liked to have been my own.

'You were more a daughter to me than anyone else and you cared for me, and for that, I thank you.

God Bless,

Tassiana McIver.'

Clara wiped away tears as Henry turned the paper over.

'PS,' Henry read, 'your son is named James.'

Henry looked confused.

'What son?'

Clara started to laugh and cry simultaneously.

'I'm pregnant,' she said, pulling the test from her bag and handing it to him.

He held it up and looked at it and then at her and then at the test again.

'Nooo,' he said but he was smiling broadly.

'Yes!' He came around and picked her up and kissed her over and over and then on her stomach.

'Oh, Clara, I love you so much,' he said and she saw tears in his eyes.

'Will you marry me? Can I live in your pink cottage with your cockleshell borders and chicken coop and magical oak trees, be a part of your crazy, complicated, simply perfect life? Please say yes?' He kissed her again, and looked at her. 'Say yes,' he whispered.

'Yes,' she whispered back.

'I don't have a ring,' he said after he kissed her again.

'Open your gift from Tassie,' she said, feeling like the world was spinning but she didn't want it to stop.

Henry opened the box and lifted a smaller box from it. Across the top was a sticker reading: *For Henry, for Clara.*

He opened it and it was his turn to laugh and cry.

'Maybe I do have a ring,' he said. He fell to one knee and, taking Clara's hand, put the ring on her finger.

It was a beautiful cluster of diamonds with tiny oak leaves making up the band.

'It's perfect,' they both said in unison and Pansy walked into the room.

'Tassie sent me her shells,' she said showing them the box. 'Why are you on the floor, Daddy?' She looked at Clara. 'Why are you crying again?' She shook her head. 'Grown-ups are so weird.'

Later that night, when Henry was dozing on the sofa and Pansy was tucked up in bed with her shells nearby, Clara went out into the garden.

It was nearly cold she thought, as she pulled her cardigan

close around her. Rachel had been teaching her to knit and her cardigan was the first thing she had finished. It wasn't perfect but it was warm and Rachel had taught her to sew it up properly.

She stood under the oak tree and looked back at the cottage. The lights inside gave it a warm glow. She could hear the chickens chatting quietly as they settled down for the night. The scent of the roses tickled her nose and the crisp air felt like the first bite of an autumn season apple.

I wish you were here, Mum and Gran, she thought to herself but then she felt them with her in all she did; when she collected the eggs, when she read stories to Pansy, when she watched Rachel twist pastry into plaits.

This was it, she realised. This was what she had been waiting for and searching for when she was young. How long do we go through life looking for something, a feeling inside us about what we think we want, not realising we were actually living it all along? And only after do we realise we missed it, after it's all gone.

Clara walked back inside the cottage and locked the back door, then switched off the lights in the kitchen. She locked the front door, went into the living room and turned off the lamps, then leaned over and kissed Henry on the mouth.

'Hello,' he said sleepily.

'Time for bed,' she whispered and she took his hand and led him to their bedroom.

'I love you, Henry,' she said as he pulled her to him.

'I love you too, Clara Maxwell.'

'I'm happy,' she whispered as his hands began to explore her.

'Let's see if I can't make you ecstatic,' he murmured in her ear and she smiled in the darkness, knowing this was as good as life could get but with the intense feeling that life was about to get even better.

Early Winter

57

The pink ribbon was strung across the door of the bakery, tied with a large bow, and Clara slipped under it as she opened the door, the bell singing happily, as Rachel came out from the kitchen in her crisp white apron with the name of the tearooms beautifully embroidered in pink silk cotton across the front.

TASSIE'S TEAROOMS

Henry had done a wonderful job on the renovation, with floor-to-ceiling bookshelves on one wall and a fireplace with an elegant Persian rug in blue and green lying in front of it, bought for a song in Chippenham at an auction.

Two cosy armchairs sat either side of the fireplace with a little table next to them, for tea or to rest a book on.

Another wall showed off some art from a local woman who was very skilled at watercolours and who was thrilled to have her first mini exhibition.

Henry had already bought the one of Acorn Cottage as a surprise for Clara, so she was very sad when she saw it had a red sticker next to the frame. But Henry couldn't wait to give it to her tonight so he would hand it to her after she opened the tearooms.

'How are things in the kitchen?' asked Clara, as she touched her stomach. She was five months gone and the sickness had vanished and now she was so hungry she might have eaten the crusts from the chicken sandwiches if allowed.

'Great, Nahla is a wonderful cook. Who knew all this time she was cleaning for Tassie she had such nimble fingers for pastry?'

'I guess we don't know as much about people as we should because we put them into little compartments and it's only by talking that we find out what else is inside them.'

Nahla and Rachel had chatted at Tassie's funeral where the women talked about Tassie and the way they had been helped by their old friend.

'For years she told me to come and tell you about my cooking but I was afraid to,' said Nahla.

'Why?' Rachel asked.

'Because your mother said to me when I came into the shop once that she doesn't sell curry pies, so I left.'

Rachel had been so embarrassed by her racist stepmother.

'I am so sorry, and I do sell curry pies and many other pies. I make French-style pies and Thai chicken pies and even an Irish stew pie. The bakery is very multicultural.'

Nahla had laughed. 'I know, I never thought it was you but it wouldn't have worked back then when she was still in the shop.'

Nahla was given a job and soon she had the kitchen humming. Rachel was Executive Creative Director of

Tassie's Tearooms and Nahla was Head Chef, and Clara was taking care of the business side of things.

Clara had made a website, and had invited journalists from local papers and influential social media users to the opening along with the entire village of Merryknowe.

Mrs Crawford from the post office was front and centre, ready to come in, and Mr Toby the bus driver had stopped the bus down the road and had come to line up for the new curry pies he could smell when he got out of the bus.

The staff were all lined up against the counter in their white aprons and comfortable sneakers. Rachel had insisted on these for the staff because she wanted them to never have the pain of the blisters on her feet from the shoes Moira had forced her to wear.

'Are the tea trays ready?' Rachel asked Nahla, who stood at the front of the line.

'Yes, all ready to go.' Nahla smiled.

Rachel and Clara had gone to so many tearooms over the last few weeks, Rachel wondered if she could ever face a scone with jam and cream again. Clara's nausea hadn't made the trip entirely enjoyable but they found some wonderful ideas to add to their own dreams for Tassie's Tearooms.

They had Russian Caravan tea in honour of Tassie and Henry, and Assam and Darjeeling from Roasted Oolong and herbal teas including a chocolate tea that Pansy was obsessed with.

With triangle point sandwiches with Scottish smoked salmon, poached chicken in Nahla's lemon and dill tangy mayonnaise recipe and the classic cucumber sandwich, there was something for everyone.

The cakes were a triumph, with lemon teacake and

chocolate and orange profiteroles; red velvet cake and mini-Victoria sponge with lemon curd and cream. Vanilla cupcakes with edible pansies on top looked so sweet and tasted just as sweet, and Rachel's exquisite eclairs finished off the afternoon tea menu.

Clara had bought the tearooms a fancy Italian coffee machine and all the staff had done a barista course from a clever Australian girl who was bringing Melbourne coffee to the cafes of England, one espresso shot at a time.

And now they were ready for the opening.

Henry came through the front door, slipping under the ribbon like Clara had.

'The flowers are up,' he said. They had festooned the archway of the door with flowers and ribbons in different shades of pink, creating a magical entrance for the people lining up.

'Everything is ready,' he said to Rachel and Clara.

Clara leaned up to kiss him. 'You're clever and I love you.'

'You're beautiful and I adore you,' he said in her ear.

Pansy walked out from the kitchen wearing her own small apron and chef hat.

'Can we hurry up? I want to eat cakes,' she said. Clara noticed pink icing on the corner of her mouth and used her thumb to wipe it away.

'I think you've had a head start already, sweetie,' said Clara.

Pansy went to the window of the shop and looked down the street.

'People are hungry; we need to get ready.' She turned to everyone in the tearooms.

'Okay, Marco Pierre White,' said Henry. 'Let's go to the back and let Clara and Rachel get ready.'

Clara buzzed about the tearooms, straightening the mismatched chairs, all painted by Henry in varying colours set around the tables of differing sizes, all painted white with a book cover copied on top. There was *Jane Eyre*, *Mrs Dalloway*, *Emma*, *Clarissa*, *Rebecca*, *Tess of the D'Urbervilles*, *Cousin Kate* and *Arabella*.

Little touches around the tearooms reminded Clara and Rachel of the path they had walked to this moment.

Tassie's book collection was on the shelves and bowls of acorns and pinecones from behind Clara and Henry's cottage were on the mantelpiece. Photos of Clara and her mum and grandmother, and Rachel as a baby with her parents, and Naomi and Pansy, all in silver frames, were grouped together with fresh flowers in a small silver vase from Tassie's house. Today, the last of the pink roses from Clara's garden tumbled over the edges of the vase, the scent catching Clara's attention as she passed.

She stopped to drink in their scent and remembered Henry's little teacup of flowers next to her bed. She hadn't realised love was like this. So warm, so real, a meeting of mutual needs and balance. She never felt that she was doing all the work in the relationship, as Henry loved her with his energy and creative abandon and with a tenderness she had not seen in a man before.

When he suggested she start to see a counsellor to work through her pain and guilt about her father, he never made her feel that she had failed or was broken. He told her she needed to forgive herself and that only came with real professional help and understanding.

Creating that boundary in their relationship had been the making of them, and when she suggested he do the same to work through Naomi's death, he did and when he came home with his eyes red-rimmed and needed time to sit in the oak tree clearing, she let him be.

Because she knew they were as strong as a pair of oak trees and their little acorn was growing inside her.

Clara went to the door and looked at Rachel who nodded at her.

Joe was outside directing the lines and he turned and waved at them both.

They were ready.

Clara and Rachel stepped forward and Rachel pulled scissors from her apron pocket. They were Tassie's gold sewing scissors, shaped like a heron, and she handed them to Clara and held the ribbon.

Clara cut the ribbon and then spoke loudly for all to hear.

'Welcome to Tassie's Tearooms. Purveyors of fine baked goods and tea leaf reading and anything else that brings magic into your lives.'

About the Author

KATE FORSTER lives in Melbourne, Australia with her husband, two children and dogs, and can be found nursing a laptop, surrounded by magazines and talking on the phone, usually all at once. She is an avid follower of fashion, fame and all things pop culture and is also an excellent dinner party guest who always brings gossip and champagne.

Acknowledgements

I wish to thank my beautiful and patient editor, Rhea Kurien, who really helped me shape this book into something I am so proud of. Thank you to Tara Wynne, my agent and friend. Thank you to David for holding the space while I wrote for my life. Thank you to my Ladybirds Writing Group who are 1800 members strong and are the best online cheerleading group I could have. Women supporting women is always a good thing.

Hello from Aria

We hope you enjoyed this book! If you did let us know, we'd love to hear from you.

We are Aria, a dynamic digital-first fiction imprint from award-winning independent publishers Head of Zeus. At heart, we're committed to publishing fantastic commercial fiction – from romance and sagas to crime, thrillers and historical fiction. Visit us online and discover a community of like-minded fiction fans!

We're also on the look out for tomorrow's superstar authors. So, if you're a budding writer looking for a publisher, we'd love to hear from you. You can submit your book online at ariafiction.com/we-want-read-your-book

You can find us at:
Email: aria@headofzeus.com
Website: www.ariafiction.com
Submissions: www.ariafiction.com/we-want-read-your-book

Ⓕ @ariafiction
Ⓨ @Aria_Fiction
Ⓘ @ariafiction